THE
MYSTERY
OF THE
MOVING IMAGE

SNOW & WINTER: BOOK THREE

C.S. POE

The Mystery of the Moving Image
Copyright © 2018, 2020 by C.S. Poe

Published by Emporium Press
https://www.cspoe.com
contact@cspoe.com

Cover Art by Reese Dante
Cover content is for illustrative purposes only and any person depicted on the cover is a model.

Published 2020.
First Edition published 2018. Second Edition 2020.
Printed in the United States of America

Trade Paperback ISBN: 978-1-952133-05-3
Digital eBook ISBN: 978-1-952133-04-6

For Rhys and Bru.
This One will always pick up the coffee for you.

CHAPTER ONE

If there was one thing I'd taken away from the last six months of murder and mystery, it was to expect the unexpected.

Max Ridley and I stared at a four-foot-tall wooden crate that had been delivered to the Emporium that morning. Neither of us had spoken for a good minute.

"Five bucks says there's a dead body inside," he finally said.

I shook my head. "We'd smell decomp."

"A normal person wouldn't say that," he replied, not looking away from the box.

"Normal is relative."

"Let's not get into a philosophical debate before 10:00 a.m."

I took a step forward and snatched the shipping label from the plastic envelope slapped on the front of the crate. I unfolded it and held my magnifying glass up to the small print.

"Who's it from?" Max asked.

"I'm not sure."

"Should I call 911?"

I glanced up. "The last time we did that, they sent a vigilante who tried to kill me."

"That's true." Max held up his cell. "But I know three cops and an FBI agent by proxy, so we have options."

"Calm down."

"I don't trust mystery packages, Seb. Not anymore."

I looked at the label again. "It came from a shipping company on the Upper East Side."

"But no name?"

"No."

"Is it addressed to you?"

"Owner," I clarified.

"I'm calling the cops."

I looked at Max, reached out, and put my hand over his cell. "Calvin probably just ordered something for the apartment."

Ah yes, that had been one bit of good to come out of losing my home to an explosion back in February. It'd taken just over two months of searching and Realtor harassing, but as of yesterday, Snow and Winter were the new tenants of 4B—a loft apartment in the East Village above a coffee shop and hippy-dippy clothing store. And despite the insurmountable odds, I was able to tick off every single one of my neurotic must-haves and still keep to a rent that wouldn't bleed me and Calvin dry.

I mean, it was by far more expensive than my old, cozy, rent-controlled place, but seeing as how I was putting my name on the bills with a guy I liked *a lot*— yeah. Seemed worth the extra cash.

"Call him and ask," Max replied.

"He's busy with manly stuff," I answered.

"What?"

"Unpacking, lifting heavy things, inserting tabs into slots…."

"I'll quit."

"Jesus, Max—"

"Just call him."

I let out an annoyed huff, took my phone from my back pocket, pulled Calvin up in the recent contacts, and called.

"Hey, baby," Calvin answered.

"Hey," I said. "Got a second?"

"For you? Several."

"Aren't you cute."

Calvin laughed. "Everything okay?"

"Yeah. I just had a package delivered here at the Emporium and was wondering if you'd ordered something big—like, a chandelier—for the apartment?"

"And had it shipped there?" he asked, sounding unsure.

"Uh-huh."

"No."

I frowned and glanced sideways at Max. "I've got a four-foot-tall mystery box in the middle of my showroom."

"Since when has that ever stopped you, Hercule?"

I smiled a little. "*Ohhh*…."

"Like that?" Calvin asked.

"I do."

"I knew you would."

I laughed, much to Max's displeasure. "Figured I'd check in with you before cracking it open. I tend to get a lot of junk this way. People cleaning out grandma's attic ship me garbage and say 'keep it until it sells,' like I'm a warehouse."

"No return address, then?" Calvin asked, and in the background, I could hear tape being torn off a cardboard box. I'd offered to close the Emporium to help him finish unpacking the apartment, but he'd politely kissed my forehead and shoved me out the front door that morning.

"Some shipping and supply office way the hell uptown."

"Huh."

"Were you expecting a housewarming gift?" I tried.

Not that anyone in Calvin's family even knew we'd moved in together. They'd completely stopped talking to him at Christmastime when he'd come out—the exception being Calvin's Uncle Nelson. Nelson was a sweet old guy. I'd said hello on the phone a few times. He was nothing like the impression I had of Calvin's father, a retired military man who hated me on principle alone.

"No," Calvin answered.

"I'm going to tear into this crate."

"Don't let me stop you."

"I'll see you tonight," I said.

"I'll be the big sweaty guy in the house," Calvin replied.

"I love when you're sweaty."

"*Boss,*" Max interrupted, and I swear I could hear his eye-roll.

Calvin chuckled. "Bye, sweetheart."

"Bye." I stuffed my phone into my pocket.

"When's the honeymoon?"

"Stop it," I muttered.

"It's not Calvin's, then?" Max asked.

I shook my head. "Nope. Would you grab a hammer from the office?"

"All right," he answered a bit reluctantly. Max left my side, hiked up the stairs, went past the register, and disappeared into my closet-sized office. "But if there's anything inside that's dead, dying, or threatening to kill either of us, I'm burning this place to the ground because it's totally cursed."

"I'm not sure whether you're trying to save me or screw me over," I said, mostly to myself, but Max heard me.

"Saving you, believe me," he replied. He jumped off the stairs and approached with the hammer. "Move aside."

"You want to open it?"

"Maybe if I'm the one to do it, it'll negate any potential chaos that would otherwise befall you."

"You're so sweet." I took a step back and crossed my arms.

"Is that guy from the Javits Center's Antique Fair still coming by today?" Max asked as he stuck the back of the hammer under the wooden lid and pushed down on the handle. The nails squeaked loudly as they were pulled free.

"He's supposed to."

"He was supposed to on Saturday."

"*And* Sunday," I clarified. "Then I canceled yesterday so I could move. If he doesn't come today to pick up my items for the show, they can kiss my ass next year when they're looking for sponsorship money."

"Seriously." Max moved the hammer and hoisted the lid once more. "So how's the new place?" He glanced over his shoulder at me.

I winced as more nails screeched free from the wood. "Good. I'm hoping our bed will be delivered today. Spent last night on the living room floor."

"At least you had a hunky ginger to keep you

company."

"Very true."

There'd been a lot of change in my life as of late. Mostly for the good, of course.

Business was going great, despite the seemingly bad luck the Emporium had in terms of being a target in the Nevermore and Curiosities cases—but we'd all escaped those with our heads still attached. And after a long line of bad-for-me boyfriends, I'd just moved in with a guy who was my soul mate. Friends and family were healthy, happy—I was even a pet owner now.

So yeah, a lot of things were good.

But I guess that's why I'd also been sidelined by anxieties lately. I wasn't expecting old self-doubts when I was on top of the world. Like, one too many of Calvin's compliments had gone to my head, and when my clothes had been torched in the fire, I'd purchased a *new* wardrobe for the first time in… at least a decade. No more secondhand crap. I now owned formfitting, colored clothes. I thought they'd finally give a boost of confidence to my appearance, an insecurity I usually hid with self-deprecating humor, except it'd turned out to be nothing but dread since day one.

And I knew how… *stupid* it must have sounded. But until someone has been intensely uncomfortable in their clothes, I didn't think people realized just how much a wardrobe could make or break them. Yeah, the secondhand shit didn't fit, was old and worn-out, but it was safe. I didn't need to check a color wheel before putting something on. I disappeared into a crowd. Now every morning was approached with a certain level of trepidation. Were people staring because I clashed and was an eyesore? Were they staring because I wasn't the best-looking guy and these clothes made me stand out when I used to blend in? They must wonder what Calvin was doing slumming with a guy like me.

Of course I hadn't said any of this out loud.

Hell would sooner freeze over.

Max lifted the top from the crate, set it on the floor, then peered inside. "Lots of padding. Looks like a piece of furniture."

I took a few steps forward to see for myself. Wedged between the object and the crate wall was a smaller wrapped item. I tugged it free. "Pull the front of the crate off, will you? We can't lift that out."

"Sure thing." Max took the hammer and went at more of the nails.

I set the smaller item down on a nearby display table and carefully removed the bubble wrap. Nestled within was a round metal canister. I carefully picked it up. There was weight to it.

"You know," Max said, around the tearing of wooden planks. "If we go through all this and it's some fugly television from the 1950s...."

I stared at the canister for another moment. "Not a television," I murmured.

"What?" Max tore off another piece of wood.

"It's not a TV," I said again, turning to look at him.

He glanced at the crate and motioned to the item within. "It's hard to see through the wrapping, but it looks like one of those with the built-in cabinet."

I walked back to the crate, reached inside, and yanked away the padding. "This is—" I caught myself from finishing, almost like I didn't want to jinx it. I tore out layer after layer of careful packaging, revealing a spectacularly well-preserved cabinet. "*Jesus Christ,*" I swore.

"What is it?"

"A Kinetoscope."

"A what-o-scope?"

"Kinetoscope. A one-person movie viewer, patented by Thomas Edison," I said, looking at Max. "This was before they'd figured out how to project a moving image to a large audience." I leaned into the crate and pointed. "See here, you look through the peephole on top. There's a bulb inside that backlights the frames, and the film is spooled through the cabinet."

"It's original?" Max asked.

I rubbed my bristly chin and stared hard. "I think so. Help me pull it out. And for the love of God—"

"*Be careful*," Max finished for me.

"The Kinetoscope wasn't around very long," I said as we walked the cabinet out of the crate. "As the film industry grew, inventions became obsolete fairly quickly."

"How did these work, though?" Max asked. "I mean, people didn't have them in homes, right?"

"Oh no. You'd go to a Kinetoscope parlor. There used to be one here in New York, you know. Taking inflation into account, Edison was charging the parlors somewhere around six hundred dollars for the reel of film."

"Hell of a businessman." Max began picking up the mess once we'd gotten the Kinetoscope situated in an empty space of showroom floor. "What was in the little package?"

"A film reel," I said, hands on my hips as I made a slow circuit around the case.

"Really?" he asked excitedly.

"Niche market makes this difficult to price. It'd be the historical value—"

"Seb. Home movie. Focus."

I glanced up. "What about it?"

Max made exaggerated gestures at where I'd left the canister. "Let's see what's on it."

I dropped my hands from my hips and went to the table. "I doubt it's in any sort of salvageable condition."

"Why do you say that?" he asked, going to the register counter and retrieving a pair of cloth gloves.

"Films simply weren't well preserved back then. Acid ate away at the celluloid. Sometimes there were studio fires, or old reels were just destroyed. They had no intrinsic value at the time," I explained.

Max offered the gloves as he joined me.

I put them on. "This would have also been before silent film stars like Charlie Chaplin or Harold Lloyd began protecting their work." I picked up the canister again and held it close, studying the front and back side.

Max leaned against the table and crossed his arms lightly. "I remember watching *Fred Ott's Sneeze* in my Film History class. That was Edison's, wasn't it?"

"Yeah, first copyrighted film in the United States," I murmured.

Fred Ott had been a gentleman who worked for Edison, who by all accounts had a particularly memorable sneeze. It was one of the test reels shot by W. K. L. Dickson, Edison's assistant, who was the brilliant inventor of the Kinetograph camera and Scope viewer. "But even that film didn't survive," I continued. "It was submitted to the Library of Congress as a series of still images, later reanimated into a movie."

"*How* do you know this?"

"I took notes in college." I carefully removed the canister lid.

"You're the guy at the cocktail party everyone regrets striking up a conversation with."

"Yeah, probably." I set the lid aside and stared at the spool of film. It looked... okay. Better than okay. Intact. *Playable*, even. "This is incredible. Look here—it has the perforations along the side of the frames."

Max leaned close, reached out, and hovered his finger above the strip of film I held. "So, what, those holes feed in the Kinetoscope, right?"

"Right. Edison patented that concept as well, but it was Dickson who came up with the idea to slice 70mm film in half and make perforations. Afterward, the company was able to submit custom orders for film stock with these exact specifications for their machines."

"Hundred-twenty-year-old movie," Max said with an astonished tone. "It's going to be either porn or cats."

I took the film canister with me to the Kinetoscope, stooped, opened the cabinet, and studied the mechanical setup.

"Are you going to try to play the film?"

"Sure." I looked back at Max. "You want to see what it is, right?"

"Duh."

We sat in front of the Kinetoscope, studying old patent schematics I brought up on my phone, and tried to duplicate the arrangement with our mystery film stock. After about twenty minutes of "Be careful," "No, the other way," "The other, *other* way," and the classic, "Oh shit," we got it fed through the long system of spools.

Max was tearing through the crate's packaging once again.

"What're you doing?" I called, carefully shutting the cabinet.

"Looking for a note."

"Is there one?"

"No." More shuffling followed, and then Max peered down over the top of the cabinet at me. "This has to be from someone you know, don't you think?"

"Why do you say that?"

"Trusting you with such a rare artifact."

"I do love a good ego stroke," I muttered before getting to my feet.

"Not to mention that shipping a crate is expensive, even if it's just from one end of the city to the other," Max concluded.

The shop phone rang and he left my side to answer it.

"I'll call the shipping company today," I said, mostly to myself once Max started talking on the phone. "See if they can provide me with the client's contact information...."

"Boss," Max said. He wove in between displays, reaching the phone out. "It's Pete-Ain't-Never-Gonna-Show from the fair."

My shoulders dropped a bit. I took the phone. "Pete?"

"Hey! Snow. I got your message about the pickup."

I pursed my lips. "I left that message on Sunday. It's Tuesday."

"Well, yeah, but you weren't open yesterday."

"You were supposed to be here on Saturday, Pete. I've had my stock for the fair boxed and waiting since last Friday."

"Look, I'm sorry about missing the pickup window, but it's been a busy week of prepping for the event. We welcome our sponsors to drop items off at the Javits Center themselves."

"I don't drive," I replied. "And I shouldn't have to trek to the ass-end of Hell's Kitchen myself when I'm paying a sponsorship level that includes the pickup and delivery of all inventory on display for the fair."

Max winced, I think on Pete's behalf.

The antiquing community didn't have a lot of thirty-three-year-olds in it. And there were some members who didn't enjoy taking a young'un like me seriously. Most had no idea how hard I'd worked to get where I was in the business.

I'd gone into debt to obtain an MFA and put in several years as a sort-of apprentice under one of the biggest assholes in the industry, my late boss Mike Rodriguez. I took pride in my shop and had labored for three years to cultivate and bring attention to obscure relics of our past. Now, my clients returned time and again because they knew the knowledge, inventory, and attention to detail they'd receive from me was top-notch. Snow's Antique Emporium has since become the sort of business that the Javits Antique Fair reaches out to, requesting I sponsor their event.

So I might have been one of the younger members of the community, but God save the poor bastard who took my hard-earned money and didn't meet my expectations in return.

"I'm coming by today," Pete answered, sounding rather unfazed by my agitation.

"The fair opens tomorrow."

"And that's why I'm coming today," he reiterated, like *I* was the dense one.

The bell above the Emporium's door chimed. Max and I both turned to see Beth Harrison standing in the open doorway. She was my business neighbor and the owner of Good Books, was about Pop's age, and had long ago lost her last fuck to give.

"Good morning!" she declared, walking toward us with something in her hands.

"When will you be here?" I asked Pete as Max left me in favor of Beth.

"Oh… should be between eleven and… threeish?"

"Traffic across town must be a real bitch," I answered, deadpan.

"You'll be there when I stop in, right?"

"Unfortunately."

"Good. I'll need you to sign a few forms."

"Fine."

"Will you be at the fair tomorrow?" Pete asked next.

I looked up. Beth was giving me a curious expression. Max was staring at his phone. "Let's just focus on today first, shall we?" I muttered a goodbye and ended the call.

Beth walked forward. "Someone's got his grumpy pants on this morning."

"I'm actually in a good mood," I corrected. "That was Pete White from the fair. He was supposed to be here four days ago to pick up my collection for the show."

"How professional," she said sarcastically.

Max raised his head and turned his phone to show me the screen, even though I was too far away to make out the image. "Marshall's Oddities is a sponsor, and he's already set up at the Center."

Marshall's Oddities, owned and operated by copycat Greg Thompson, was my only real competition in the city. I said "competition" because he'd basically stolen my shop's image of "curious and bizarre" and still tried to pilfer my customers whenever possible. I was more than happy to supply the names of fellow dealers to my clients if there's something they want outside my wheelhouse, because in turn those businesses sent customers to me. But not Greg. He'd never once scratched my back.

Frankly, I didn't *want* him to. Or trust him to.

We did not get along, and I was okay with that being the entirety of our relationship. Although… it might also be partly due to the fact that last December I suspected Greg was the nutjob behind the Nevermore murders. But hey. Honest mistake.

"How'd you find that out?" I asked.

"Facebook."

I grunted.

Max put his phone away.

Beth held up the plate in her hands. "*So*... how're you boys on this fine May morning?"

"Why are you so chipper?" Max asked. "You're talking like a fairy godmother."

Beth snorted. "I am not. You've just spent too much time around your boss, whose good moods resemble most people's bad moods."

"They do not," I grumbled.

"Be nice," she responded. "I've got cookies."

"Were you going to share?" I asked. "Or were you just taking them for a walk?"

"I don't know why the hell I put up with you sometimes, Sebby." Beth handed me the plate. "I come bearing gifts and you give me sass."

"It's my default setting," I replied. I picked up a cookie and took a bite.

"Well, you'd better watch it," Beth continued, "or that's the last cookie I share with you."

I held the plate out of reach. "No take backs," I said around a full mouth.

Beth was always complaining that customers were stealing her pens. I noted she had three or four stuffed into her bun that morning but decided to let her find those on her own. She was wearing a feline-inspired top, although subtle today—just a cat nose and whiskers—but she also wore leggings with creatures on them that looked half-taco, half-cat, so... a typical wardrobe day for Beth.

"Are you dating a mechanic?" I asked, pointing at

her clunky boots.

Beth looked down briefly. "My cat barfed in my Birkenstocks this morning."

"Charming," I answered.

Beth put her hands on her hips and walked toward the Kinetoscope. "What have you got here?"

"This is a whatchamacallit," Max said, pointing at the cabinet.

"A what?" Beth asked.

"Kinetoscope," I said around the final bite of cookie.

"What does it do?"

"It's a one-person movie viewer," Max answered, parroting my explanations back to Beth. "It even came with a 120-year-old film."

"You don't say?"

"My money is on porn or cats," he continued.

"I like those odds," she agreed.

I set the plate on a nearby table and wiped crumbs from the front of my sweater-vest.

"Sebby."

I looked up. "Seb, Beth. *Seb.*"

She ignored me. "You look so handsome in green."

"I thought this was blue."

She and Max shook their heads.

"Christ," I muttered to myself, looking back down.

"Seb was about to turn the Kinetoscope on," Max said, almost like he'd caught my it's-not-blue anxiety and changed the subject. "Want to stay for the big unveiling?"

Beth clapped her hands together. "Oh yes! Let's see what you have." I stepped back to the cabinet and gave the Kinetoscope a final once-over before daring to power it on for what might have been the first time in over a hundred years. But against all odds, the machine came to life, the wheels inside making sound as the film was set into a continuous loop. I moved around to the front and glanced in the peephole. The bulb illuminating the projected stills was bright, and I had to squint as I watched.

It turned out the mystery footage wasn't Victorian porn or cats, but instead, a boxing match. And one I recognized, at that. The Leonard-Cushing fight of 1894. It was sold by Edison as an authentic fight, but the truth was, it was staged and filmed at his studio, Black Maria, in Jersey. Regardless, it was the first boxing match to be recorded, and of the six reels that were once for sale to the Kinetoscope parlors, less than a full round still existed today. The knockout footage—naturally the most popular round with customers—hadn't survived.

At least, it hadn't thirty seconds ago.

Because I was watching it now.

Leonard won. I knew he would, but no one in modern times had ever *seen* it.

I opened my mouth to say… *something*, but there was a weird blip in the film, some distortion, and then the scene was different. It was outdoors, the image dark and grainy. Some odd lighting, just above two figures in the scene, illuminated a street that otherwise would have been engulfed in nighttime. The figures appeared to be men—neither from the prior boxing scene. One had very distinctive muttonchops and a bit of a gut. The second man was pretty nondescript. They seemed to be arguing, but the frame rate the movie had been shot at was different from what was used today, making their motions quick and dramatic-looking, so it was hard to tell.

Without warning, Muttonchops pulled something from inside his coat, and the motion blurred as he lunged. Nondescript Man held his neck and then crumpled to the ground. Muttonchops stared down at him for a few seconds, dropped whatever he had been holding, and ran.

The scene looped and brought me back to the fight.

"So?" Max asked excitedly.

I raised my head, looking at him and Beth. "I think I just witnessed a murder."

CHAPTER TWO

"The infant feeding bottle was all the rage in the late Victorian era," I told my customer as she crouched in front of a display case to inspect an item. "It was often a glass bottle that came with a rubber tube and nipple, allowing a child to feed themselves."

"I imagine that was beneficial when women wore corsets," she replied, looking up at me.

"Yes, exactly," I said. "That was the major selling point for mothers at the time. Unfortunately, by the turn of the century, it had earned the moniker 'murder bottle.'"

She made a face and looked at the bottle, situated beside its original packaging. "*Murder*?"

Was it just me, or were the murders of bygone days making themselves a bit too known today?

I'd called Calvin after watching the boxing match turned death show. I didn't know what else to do. It wasn't like the perpetrator could be arrested, what with being unbelievably dead by now, but there was no statute of limitations on murder. And *that* had been a real killing. So I called the cops, like any good citizen would. It was just convenient that *my* cop was fairly accustomed to the outrageous at this point.

The customer—shit, what had she said her name was? Nancy? Nancy.—Nancy was staring up at me expectantly.

"Er—yeah, sorry. The rubber tubing was very difficult to clean," I hastily said, tapping the glass case. "Which made it an ideal breeding ground for bacteria. Coupled with the famous Martha Stewart of the time—Isabella Beeton—advising it wasn't necessary to clean the nipple for several weeks…." I waved my hand. "It became the murder bottle."

"That's awful," Nancy said. "And the infant mortality rate was already so high then."

"Oh yes. The feeding bottle exacerbated the problem."

Nancy stood, still eyeing the item.

"Not too sure this will be a suitable birthday present for your coworker, though," I stated.

"We all have that one friend who's super interested in weird and morbid things," Nancy said with a laugh.

Don't judge me, Nancy.

I moved around the backside of the case, opened the sliding glass door, and removed the bottle and packaging. "Would you like this gift wrapped?"

"That'd be wonderful," Nancy answered.

When I looked up, I noticed a customer who must have slipped into the shop as quiet as a mouse, carefully eyeing the Kinetoscope. I waved to Max and asked when he joined me, "Would you ring Nancy up for this feeding bottle and wrap it for her?"

"Sure thing," he said.

"Thank you for your business," I said to Nancy.

"Thank you for all of your help!"

Once the two left my side, I moved away from the display case and approached the new customer. "Hello. Ah, sorry, this isn't for sale." I patted the top of the Kinetoscope briefly.

I realized he was considerably younger than I'd pegged him to be at a distance. I usually had an uptick of college-aged customers come autumn, with students new to New York exploring the neighborhoods, some looking for odds and ends to spice up their dorm rooms, though a few came in for legitimate school research. I didn't have anyone his age shop at the Emporium who wasn't usually a student somewhere nearby. Although, it was May, and most terms had just ended... but I supposed he could have been enrolled in an early summer program at NYU or SVA.

He gave me an annoyed look. "I don't *want* to buy it."

"Was there anything I could help you with, then?"

"*No.*"

Snotty shit.

I sighed and rubbed the spot above my left eye where a headache was starting. "Okay."

The kid looked around briefly. "Why do you have so much weird crap in here?"

"What constitutes as weird for you? Because some may think it mundane."

He pointed at a framed photo hanging on a nearby wall. "Are those dancing skeletons?"

"The Arsenic Waltz," I corrected. "It mocked the usage of arsenic in dyes for clothing during the nineteenth century."

"*What?*" He looked confused. Or disgusted. I wasn't sure.

"Arsenic is a poison."

I glanced over my shoulder when I heard the bell ring at the shop door. Calvin stepped inside, with Dillon on a leash. The pup was probably thrilled to be out of the house and on a walk with his dad. Calvin pulled off a pair of sunglasses and hung them from his AC/DC shirt, which had to be nearly as old as me. He was wearing those ass-hugging jeans I loved and an old, beat-up pair of Vans sneakers. Calvin made home decorating look damn good.

"This place is like a basement full of useless shit."

I turned back to my charming new friend. "Why're you here?" I countered.

"I'm not—I'm leaving," he said, as if between the two of us, *I* was the bigger asshole.

"By all means, the front door is right there." I stepped sideways and motioned with both arms outstretched.

He took a brief look around the shop again but appeared increasingly frustrated as he did so. Like he had sincerely come hunting for something, didn't want to admit to it, and was angry I didn't have it—*whatever* that might have been. The kid finally shoved by me and made his way through the aisles toward the door. Calvin saw the push and looked at me, but I shook my head and waved my hand in a shooing motion.

Calvin moved aside, watched the brat storm out, and then joined me. "Who was that?" he asked, leaning down briefly to remove Dillon's leash.

"The Future."

He gave me an amused smile. "I see the inclination toward enjoying the company of our country's youth skips a generation in your family." He kissed me. "Why'd you call me here?"

"I like you."

"Nice try."

"You know how there's no statute of limitation on murder?"

Calvin reached up to massage his temple. "It was my day off."

"Look at this." I tapped the Kinetoscope. "This is an Edison Kinetoscope."

"Are we talking Thomas Edison?" Calvin crossed his arms, and his biceps flexed and bulged and... *distracted.*

"Uh—huh. Yeah. That's the guy." I looked at the cabinet. "But there was no contact information from the owner inside the crate. No documentation, letter—not even a postcard."

"I've yet to see the correlation between a piece of furniture and murder."

"It's a movie viewer," I corrected. "And—you're absolutely certain it's not for you?"

He gave me a critical look.

"Maybe someone sent you a really morbid birthday present?" I suggested. Not that I sincerely thought it was a gift, but Calvin *did* work homicide and he *was* going to be forty-three this Friday. And it had been established how susceptible the Emporium seemed to be to death and mayhem since the two of us met.

"No one would send me an Edison Kinetoscope. What is this about?"

I let out a heavy breath. "It came with a reel of film. It still works, Max and I watched it. It's the final round of the Leonard-Cushing fight of 1894. It's not supposed to exist, by all accounts."

"And did Leonard kill Cushing?" Calvin asked dryly.

"*No.*" I paused for a beat. "Someone else died, though."

"It's a movie."

"Not—no, the murder isn't part of the film, Cal.

Someone spliced two scenes together. It's not staged or fake. A man actually *died* and someone recorded it." I turned the Kinetoscope on and tugged Calvin close. "Watch it."

With a sigh, he relaxed his arms and leaned over the peephole to watch the scene.

I waited, anxiously studying Calvin's body posture as the seconds ticked by. Louis Armstrong projected from the shop speakers, Max was chatting up customers, and Dillon wove around this and that across the showroom. When enough time had passed that Calvin would surely have reached the outdoor scene, I noticed his jaw tense. And *that* was the only reaction I needed to authenticate what I too had seen.

"So?" I asked, for the sake of nicety.

Calvin straightened and looked at me.

"It's real, isn't it?"

"Seb—"

"I *told* you."

"Don't get carried away," Calvin chastised. "We don't know anything—when or where or—"

"Mid-1890s. It was filmed relatively close to the same period as the boxing match."

"How can you tell?"

"The frame rates match, they were both shot with a Kinetograph camera, the film itself was precut—"

"All right," Calvin interrupted, holding up a hand. "We still don't even know where this occurred. It could be any city in America that had a camera in the 1800s."

I looked at the Kinetoscope briefly. "It's New York—the Flatiron site."

Calvin narrowed his eyes.

"Before the Flatiron Building actually existed."

He was quiet, scrubbing his face with one hand. "Sweetheart… how the *hell* do you know that?" Calvin asked in such a calm, polite tone, it was nearly comical.

"You can sort of see the triangle shape of Fifth Avenue and Broadway in the background," I explained. "The illumination just out of frame—a man named Amos Eno owned the property until his death in 1899, and he used to project images from a magic lantern onto a canvas screen hung from a shorter building. It was used for advertisements, news bulletins, and even election results."

Calvin didn't say anything.

I smiled.

He put an arm around my shoulders, drew me close, and asked, "Anything else I should know?"

"The phrase 'twenty-three skidoo' likely originated from the Flatiron's Twenty-Third Street location."

"Why's that?"

"It's a windy corner. It was suggested that men would stick around the Flatiron to watch women's skirts get blown up so they could catch some hot ankle action."

"Of course."

"Police would have to chase them away."

"Perverts."

"Hence, twenty-three skidoo," I concluded.

Calvin smiled and lowered his arm.

"What're we going to do about the—" I paused when a customer walked by us. "M-u-r-d-e-r?" I spelled out.

"Nothing."

"No, not nothing," I answered.

"That's about all that can be done, Seb."

"I know a thing or two about handling evidence in a homicide," I pointed out.

Not that I was a detective or had a degree in forensics, but my ex-partner, Neil Millett, worked for the Crime Scene Unit of the NYPD. Four years of "tell me about your day" had taught me some. Like for example, there were records kept on homicides, even in the 1800s. And if it was an unsolved crime, that evidence was to remain in police possession until the cold case was a closed case.

"You know a thing or two about most everything," Calvin replied simply. "Which is why it makes it next to impossible to argue that you're wrong."

"This is one of those moments I'm not sure if you're complimenting me or not."

"Who's to say this wasn't solved a long time ago?"

I stared at the Kinetoscope. Call it one of my *hunches*, but I suspected that wasn't the case. Surely the evidence on film would have been used, even then, to catch the murderer. And after the crime was solved, it would have likely been destroyed by the police. Instead, over 120 years later, the footage was shipped to a moonlighting sleuth.

No explanation.

No reason.

No nothing.

"But what if it *wasn't* solved?" I countered.

Calvin crossed his arms again. "The oldest evidence I've heard of being held by homicide detectives only went back to 1909. And that was in the '20s, before complaints of sanitary conditions and limited space were taken into consideration."

"How do you know that?"

"Hi, I'm Calvin Winter," he stated, reaching a hand out to shake mine. "I've been an officer of the NYPD for ten years."

"I'm ignoring the sarcasm only because I'm

incredibly turned on by you spouting random facts at me," I answered.

Calvin smirked. "I'll remember that."

I looked around the Emporium, did a quick headcount of customers, and made sure Max wasn't inundated at the counter, before saying to Calvin, "So there wouldn't be a forgotten box somewhere in the Property Clerk's Office?" I tried.

Calvin shook his head. "There's very little, in terms of cold cases, prior to the 1990s."

"Why?"

He shrugged. "A lot of reasons. Fires, auctions, improper storage and disposal... take your pick."

"It feels wrong to not do something about it," I said.

And thankfully Calvin agreed. "I know."

"Maybe I'll call the shipping company."

"Seb—"

"Hey, as far as I am concerned, I'm being held responsible for the condition of the Kinetoscope," I said quickly. "I need to find the owner."

"But that's all," Calvin answered with a touch of reluctance. "Okay?"

"Okay," I echoed.

"If I get a call from an irate clerk at the property office this afternoon, we're going to have words."

I did not exasperate a property clerk.

Mostly because I had been too busy running a business that afternoon to dedicate any time to the task.

Oh, and I'd sworn off sleuthing. Of course.

"Boss."

"What."

"It's quarter to six."

I looked up from sorting mail at the counter.

Max was standing in front of the register. "Pete," he reminded me.

"For fuck's sake." I set the stack of envelopes down and reached for the shop phone. "Remind me next year to tell the fair to go suck an egg."

Max tapped his chin thoughtfully. "I'll update the lingo."

I dialed Pete's number and waited as the line rang. "I should have backed out of this event," I told Max. "It's been nothing but a headache for the past month."

"Pete stopped answering calls from my cell once he figured out I worked for you." Max put his arms on the counter. "What did you do to him?"

"Nothing."

"You had to have done something, because Greg is a bronze-level sponsor and he seems to be getting the princess treatment. You're gold, and the fair isn't touching you with a ten-foot pole." He leaned close. "Did you spurn Pete's advances?"

"He hasn't been around to *make* an advance." I hung up when I got said man's voicemail. I dialed the number again and put the phone to my ear.

"Maybe Greg slept with him," Max muttered. He grabbed the mail and sifted through it. "He's way too hairy for me."

"Insight into the inner workings of Max Ridley."

"Dude, he's got more hair on his feet than a hobbit."

"Why are you looking at Pete's feet?" I asked, staring hard at Max.

He shrugged. "It's hard not to. He's always got those neon pink flip-flops on. It's like a moth to the flame—I can't look away."

I frowned when Pete's voicemail message started once more. "Pete," I said firmly after the beep. "It's Sebastian Snow. From the Emporium—that place you promised to be at between eleven and three*ish*. It's quarter to six and I'm going home." I ended the call without saying anything else.

"Ish is a measurement of time found between 'I don't give a fuck' and 'this is who I am as a person,'" Max stated.

"Pete's dead to me."

"I can't decide if your dad giving you the middle name Andrew contributed to your award-winning personality, or if he had a premonition as to the sort of man you'd become."

Sebastian Andrew Snow.

SAS.

Those who knew my middle name eventually pointed that out.

Everyone was a comedian.

"Go sweep the floor."

Max smirked and left the counter.

I began tidying up for the evening, but paused when I picked up the plastic sleeve with the shipping label for the Kinetoscope. I brought it close, retrieved the phone once again, and dialed the office number printed on the form.

"Barnes Brothers Shipping. We do the heavy lifting so you don't have to. Save up to 15 percent on all packages shipped between now and May twelfth. Offer only valid with domestic ground service, maximum weight twenty pounds. Offer cannot be combined with other coupons. My name is Cindy, how can I help you?"

I held my breath.

"Hello?" she asked in the same bored, monotone voice as the monologue she'd just performed.

"Oh, is it my turn?"

Cindy popped her gum loudly.

"My name is Sebastian Snow, I run an antique shop in the East Village. This morning I received a large crate that originated from your office."

Pop, pop.

My left eye twitched. "There was no sender information."

"And so what did you need?" she asked.

"Sender information." Was there an echo in here?

"I'm afraid I can't provide that."

"Why? I was the recipient."

"Our customer's contact information is confidential."

Pop.

"Cindy, was it?"

"Yeah," she answered, unenthused.

"How about I just talk to your manager about this."

"No can do, sorry."

"Why's that?"

"She's out."

"And when will she return?"

"In like two weeks. She's having a baby." Cindy popped her gum again.

Sweet, merciful—

"Cindy," I said firmly. "The package I received is a very rare and expensive artifact. This isn't something I want to be responsible for. So may I please just read the tracking number to you and get some help finding out who the owner is?"

"What's the tracking number, Mr. Sneeze?"

"*Snow*. My last name is Snow."

"Sure."

I pulled the phone away, gripped it in both hands, and strangled the life out of it. When I heard the plastic of the receiver crack, I eased up, cleared my throat, and put it to my ear before reciting the number.

Max glanced over at me a few times throughout the conversation as he made passes across the floor with the broom. I was listening to the *click*, *click*, *click* of long nails on a keyboard when Max stepped around me to collect the trash from underneath the counter.

"You've already accepted the package," Cindy said after a minute.

"This morning," I agreed.

"So if you don't want it, you'll have to pay for shipping it back to us, sir."

"That's not—have you been listening to me at all?"

"An oversized crate with insurance, inside pickup, and expedited delivery... the total comes out to four hundred twenty-five dollars and ninety-three cents."

"Four hundred and twenty-five dollars?" I shouted.

"And ninety-three cents."

"I don't want to ship it back. I just want the sender's phone number so I can ask them why they sent it to *me* in the first place. Am I supposed to sell it? Auction it? Use it for a coffee table?"

"That information is—"

"*Confidential*, I know!"

"Is there anything else I can help you with?"

"Oh my God. Cindy... please let me talk to someone else."

"I'm the only one here."

"Of course you are."

"I can transfer you to the manager's voicemail," she offered before popping her gum. *Again.*

I took my glasses off and covered my face. "That she won't check for two weeks?"

"The baby might be early."

I laughed, in that weird way one did when they were losing their mind. "Sure. Transfer me."

"Thank you for calling Barnes Brothers Shipping. Have a good night."

Click.

Son of a bitch.

Max returned from tossing the garbage into the alley dumpster. He shut the back door and made his way toward the counter. "Get the owner's name?"

"No," I grumbled.

"So what do we do with the Kinetoscope?"

"Keep it until the owner contacts me themselves. Let's move it behind the counter tomorrow, okay?"

"Sure thing." Max glanced at the nearby wall clock and asked, "Do you need anything else?"

"No, you can get going. Thanks, Max."

"Have a good night," he called before exiting the front door.

I turned off the shop speakers, powered down my computer in the office, grabbed my shoulder bag, and shut the door. I left the bag on the counter, picked up a pair of gloves, walked to the Kinetoscope, and opened the cabinet. I crouched down and was weighing whether I wanted to unspool the hundred feet of film or keep it assembled, when the front door opened.

"We're closed!" I called.

"That you, Snow?"

I perked up a little and peered over the table blocking

me from view. "Pete?"

Short and stocky, middle-aged, with a thick, bushy beard, and polo shirt with the collar turned up like a frat boy, Pete White waved. "Hey." He walked down the aisle toward me.

"Did you get my message?" I asked, returning my attention to the film.

"Hmm… I don't think so. When did you leave it?"

"About three hours after you were supposed to be here," I replied flippantly.

"I've been having trouble with this phone. It's old."

"Get a new one," I muttered.

"Holy cow," Pete said from behind me. He gasped almost comically. "Is that a *Kinetoscope*?"

I looked over my shoulder again. He was gazing down at me from the other side of the table. "Yes," I answered.

"Is it a replica?"

"Original," I corrected.

"*And* with footage?"

"It's the knockout round of the Leonard-Cushing fight."

"Gol-*ly*," he whispered, his eyes wide.

"Golly?" I repeated, raising an eyebrow. "You auditioning for a reboot of *Leave It to Beaver*?"

Pete finally pried his gaze from the Kinetoscope and looked at me. "You shouldn't swear in the presence of someone you like, Snow," he answered.

Oh Jesus. This suddenly brought legitimacy to Max's claim that Greg might have slept with Pete to have gotten his shit organized at the fair before me.

"*Like*… as a person?"

"Aw, come on. I know you're into guys. I saw that

picture on your desk when I was here a few weeks back."

I got to my feet and turned to face him. "The one of the redhead with his arm around me?"

"That's it."

"*Yeah…*," I drew out. "That's my boyfriend."

"So what?"

I gave Pete what I felt was very clearly a are-you-fucking-kidding-me expression. "Wow. Really? You're four days and three hours late picking up my collection, and the only thing you care about is whether I'm the sort of guy who might be into side action?"

"Can't fault me for trying."

"It's extremely unprofessional of you," I replied.

"You haven't said no yet."

"No way in hell, Pete," I answered. "How's that?"

He shrugged. "Your loss. By the way, I can't pick up the collection," he said, without skipping a beat.

"*What*?"

"I don't have the van."

"Th-then why are you *here*?" I nearly hollered.

"To tell you." Pete smiled and rolled his eyes, like, *duh*.

I was ready to rip into Pete and smack that smug grin off his dopey face. I was frustrated and fed up, sick over the huge amount of money I'd shelled out, only to be treated like crap by the organizers. But at the same time, I didn't even want to bother wasting my energy on him when I knew it'd go through one ear and right out the other.

"You know what, Pete? Forget it."

"Don't you even—"

"Nope."

"—care—"

"No."

"—why I can't—"

"Do I need to say no in another fucking language?" I snapped. "I should have stayed home today." I got down in front of the Kinetoscope again.

There was a pregnant pause between us.

"So you want help getting the collection to the fair tomorrow?" Pete asked, his voice sounding loud in the silent shop.

I let out a breath. "I'll get it there myself."

"I thought you didn't drive?"

"I thought you didn't have a van?" I countered, sounding extremely bitchy.

"It'll be available tomorrow."

I knocked my forehead against the cabinet. "I'll ask my boyfriend to drive me."

"You know," Pete began, "you should bring this movie with you. That'd really draw a crowd. I wasn't even aware the knockout round of that match still existed."

I raised my head but didn't look at him. "It's manufactured for a Kinetoscope, Pete. It can't be viewed by a mass audience. Also, it's not even mine, so that's out of the question."

"I've got a guy."

I gradually turned around at that statement. "You've got a guy. A guy for *what*?"

"That's 35mm, yeah? A contact of mine in Midtown professionally digitizes old film footage. We could get a screen set up and project it at your table."

"You haven't been able to drive 2.9 miles to pick up some boxes since last weekend, but you've *got a guy* who will digitize 120-year-old footage *overnight*? Pete, get out so I can lock the door."

CHAPTER THREE

"I blame you for all this," I said on the phone as I hiked up the stairs to our fourth-floor apartment.

My antiquing buddy, Aubrey Grant, formerly of New York, who now ran a historical home in the Florida Keys, scoffed loudly over the line. "How's any of this dysfunctional mess my fault?"

"You convinced me that sponsoring the fair was a good idea."

"It was! I didn't know they had so many new team members this year who apparently can't find their own fucking asses with a flashlight."

"I dumped five grand into this event, and you aren't even coming up for it."

"Also not my fault."

"I beg to differ."

"Are you getting winded from stairs?" Aubrey asked.

"I'm mad at you—would you focus?" I took a breath

before starting up the final set.

"The nonprofit board decided not to fund my trip to the city. I have to save my vacation time for apartment hunting in August."

"You *do* remember that August in New York City is like slowly suffocating in a bag of hot garbage left in the subway, yeah?"

"Have you ever smelled low tide in ninety-degree weather with 90 percent humidity?" Aubrey countered.

"Why are we arguing?" I asked.

"You called me to complain about Polo Bro making a pass at you, and it just deteriorated from there."

"Part of me is kind of glad this whole van fiasco happened."

"*Why?*"

"Calvin will be with me tomorrow."

"Since when do you let your beau fight battles for you?"

"I don't. But Calvin's biceps are bigger than Pete's head. So."

"I guess that'd make a horndog think twice."

I stopped outside the door at the end of the hall, reached into my messenger bag, and retrieved a set of keys. "I just got home," I said as I unlocked the dead bolt and stepped inside. "I'll let you—God, what is that amazing smell?"

"Do I need an app update on my phone in order to smell this part of the conversation?" Aubrey asked.

"Bitch."

He laughed. "And you love it, cutie pie. Talk to you later."

I ended the call, slipped the phone into my pocket, and dug through my bag again for regular glasses. Once

I replaced my sunglasses, I set my bag beside the door and took a look around. Calvin had made decent headway on unboxing all of our belongings and turning the place into as much of a home as it could be with next to… no furniture. I thought that was all supposed to be delivered today?

The immediate area was mostly broken-down boxes and trash bags of packing material, but eventually it'd be a little eating nook. Down the hall to the right was an afterthought of a kitchen where the delicious aroma seemed to be originating from. Straight ahead was the living room, with big bay windows that overlooked the street below. Calvin had installed the blinds and hung curtains, which was sweet of him. The stairs on the left led to the loft bedroom and bath.

"Calvin?" I called, heading down the hall.

Dillon raised his head from where he lay on the floor. His tail thumped happily against the hardwood, but a few glances from me to what was happening in the kitchen told me he was very busy eyeing food that wasn't his.

I peeked around the corner. "Did you order lasagna?"

Calvin looked up and smiled. He shut the oven door. "I made it."

I stepped into the barely-big-enough-for-two kitchen and wrapped my arms around Calvin's neck. "You made lasagna?"

"I know you like vegetable, but I stopped at Rico's Corner on the way home from the Emporium, and their produce are shit on a good day, so it's chicken." Calvin put his hands on my hips and gave me a light kiss on the mouth. "I only bought enough for dinner—wanted to test the oven."

"I'm really into you making lasagna."

"I figured you would be."

"We'll have to invest in more kitchen supplies," I continued, letting go of him and taking a step back.

Calvin nodded. He moved to the counter and picked up his tablet. "I was searching for more dinner recipes and got a bit off track." He turned the screen to me and held it out. "Interested in donuts?"

I took the tablet but stared at Calvin. "Homemade donuts?"

"Yeah."

"Is this a trick question?"

He smiled and took the tablet back. "I'll look into getting some baking tools." Calvin leaned against the counter and crossed his arms. "It's a bit of a novelty to have a real kitchen again. Between college and the police academy, my service years, and that studio I had for half a decade...."

"I'm excited for you to start cooking," I said.

Calvin raised his eyebrows.

"Really," I insisted. "And more than because I like food."

He chuckled. "Why, then?"

"You said yourself that you find cooking relaxing. You deserve that. And you need a hobby."

"How sweet," he said dryly.

"That didn't sound rude in my head."

Calvin reached out and took my hand. "I know what you mean." He squeezed and let go. "My therapist will undoubtedly like hearing it too."

Calvin hardly ever talked about his therapist or their sessions together. Not that I expected him to. It was his journey. So long as he sought discussion with someone who would guide him to discovering self-forgiveness and healthy coping mechanisms, I didn't care if he never shared a word. But sometimes, hearing subtle assurances that he was comfortable with her and taking their conversations into serious consideration was a relief.

I went to the fridge and found a few bottles of beer had been picked up with the lasagna ingredients. "Drink?"

"I was waiting for you."

I popped the tops off two bottles and handed one to Calvin. "To our first homecooked meal in our new home."

Calvin tapped the neck of his bottle to mine. "Cheers." He took a sip and then moved to check the lasagna again. "Were you talking to Aubrey when you got in?"

"How'd you know?"

"The only other people you talk to on the phone are Max and your father—neither of whom you refer to as *bitch*."

"He was being a smart-ass."

"Calling the kettle black, honey." Calvin removed the tray and set it on the stovetop.

The smell of baked chicken and melted cheese filled the room, and Dillon whined from the doorway.

"Do you still have tomorrow off?" I asked.

"Yes."

"Can a bunch of old junk and I have a ride to the Javits Center?"

"Sure."

"You don't even want to ask why?"

Calvin glanced up from cutting dinner with a spatula. "Why?" he asked, more out of obligation than interest.

"Pete White and his sleazy little dick."

Calvin eased portions of lasagna onto two plates before handing one to me. He turned and looked through a few plastic bags on the floor before retrieving some utensils. "Go ahead and explain. I'm listening." He followed me out of the kitchen.

"He never picked up my collection!" I sat on the floor in the living room and put my food on an upturned box pretending to be a coffee table. Calvin sat beside me, set a fork and knife on my plate, and turned on the television that was propped on top of two more boxes.

"And why do we still have no furniture?" I asked offhandedly, looking around.

"The delivery company had a mix-up with the dates, so they'll be here tomorrow afternoon."

"Is it, like, a full moon for shipping companies? Cindy, Gum-Popper Extraordinaire, wouldn't give me the contact information of the person who sent me the Kinetoscope."

Calvin took a big bite of food as he flipped channels with the remote.

"Hairy Hobbit couldn't get across town to move my collection, but he sure as fuck made it to the Emporium in time to try to get into my pants," I continued.

"He what?" Calvin asked around a mouthful.

"And now we have to sleep on the floor for a second night in a row? This is why we can't have nice things, Cal."

Calvin stared at me, one hand still holding the television remote, the fork poised over his plate with the other. "But you didn't go sleuthing, right?"

A ringing phone is a lot louder at 4:00 a.m. when it's in a bare apartment with vaulted ceilings.

Calvin woke with a start beside me, jackknifing up from the pile of blankets and pillows on the living room floor.

I quickly sat up beside him and groped for his arm in

the dark. "Phone," I mumbled, half-awake.

Acknowledgment of what the sound was eased the tension in Calvin's body. Late-night calls were for him, and he'd become accustomed to them long ago. But I guess the ringtone sounding different in the new apartment, and the fact that he'd woken suddenly in unfamiliar surroundings, had been enough to throw him off.

Calvin felt around on the floor for where he'd left his phone.

I dropped back down on the pillows.

"Baby," he said, voice deep and scratchy with sleep. "Huh?"

"It's your phone." He rolled back, leaned over me, and grabbed my cell from the box coffee table. "It's not someone from your contact list."

"It's the middle of the night—fuck them."

But Calvin answered the call. "Hello?"

I was already falling asleep again.

"Calvin Winter speaking. I'm the secondary contact on the account."

I opened my eyes and looked over my shoulder at Calvin's blurry figure.

"And the police have been notified?"

I sat up.

"We'll meet them there. Thank you." Calvin lowered the phone and pressed a button. "Advice Line."

"My security company?"

"The alarm on the Emporium's back door is going off."

I wasn't wearing my contacts. I didn't have time to put them in before we'd left. The weird glow of streetlamps cast elongated streaks of light on the windshield as we drove by, like an artist experimenting in monochromatic watercolors.

"I forgot to lock the alley," I muttered, raking a hand through my unkempt hair. "*Fuck….*"

"It'll be all right," Calvin insisted.

It was hard not to believe him when he used that confident voice. Like he'd gotten a glimpse of the future and was confirming what he knew to be true.

I hoped he was right.

Calvin turned onto the Emporium's street and parked on the corner. He climbed out from behind the wheel, moved to the sidewalk to meet me, and held his hand out for mine. I took it and followed close behind, trying to mimic Calvin's long strides and sure footing. A few storefronts up from my shop, I saw two dark shapes exit the alley. I instinctively clutched Calvin's hand a bit tighter, but then I made out the hats and coats.

Cops.

Calvin eased his hand free from mine, reached into his pocket, and removed his badge. He made a brief flash of it, and both cops stopped where they were.

"Er—evening," I called. "I'm the owner. Sebastian Snow. My security company told me the back-door alarm was triggered."

One officer tilted his hat back and put his hands on his belt. "That's correct."

Calvin offered his ID to the officer's partner, who looked at it briefly and then shook his hand. "Was anything stolen?" Calvin asked, tucking the badge into his pocket once more.

"Nothing appeared amiss," the second cop replied. "We just finished securing the building."

"Can I take a look inside before you head out?" I

asked. "In case I need to file a report?"

Both officers nodded and led the way back through the alley.

"How was the property entered?" Calvin asked from behind the three of us.

"The alley door was open when we arrived," the first officer said over his shoulder. "The lock on the back door looks like it was probably picked, but it still works."

"May have been nothing more than a crime of opportunity," the second said as we stopped at the door. "And luckily your alarm system scared them off."

My gut twisted uncomfortably, even as I agreed with the cops and used my keys to open the back door once more. It *did* make perfect sense—I'd been distracted that night and completely spaced on securing the alley. It was my job, so Beth had no reason to check it herself before leaving the bookstore.

When I stepped into the Emporium and turned on the nearest bank lamp, my impression was the cops had been correct when saying that nothing appeared to have been so much as nudged out of place.

So why did I still feel like I was about to throw up?

"Mr. Snow?" the first cop asked.

"Ah, it looks okay," I answered. I made for the counter, walked up the steps, and checked my office door. Still locked. I opened it and glanced inside. Computer, fridge, coffeepot, shitty little microwave….

I shut the door again.

"Seb?" Calvin asked.

I turned on the bank lamp beside the register. "I guess everything is fine," I answered. I sat down on the stool as Calvin spoke with the police before they took their leave. He shut and locked the back door behind them. "What do you think?" I asked from across the shop.

"The alarm did its job and you're damn lucky." He walked the length of the showroom toward me.

"Something doesn't feel right."

"Your business has been violated. That's to be expected," Calvin answered. He hooked his thumbs through the belt loops of his jeans as he stopped before the counter. "I can install a dead bolt if you'd like."

I stood up again and walked down the steps. "I guess that's—" I paused and pointed. "What happened to the Kinetoscope?"

Calvin turned around to follow my line of sight. "What about it?"

"Why's the cabinet open?" I marched past him and went to the movie viewer. The side door of the machine was ajar. I bent down and noticed a bit of celluloid hanging from the opening. I yanked the door back the rest of the way and made a sound that was probably akin to a dying animal.

"Sebastian?" Calvin asked worriedly, quickly coming up behind me.

Only a portion of the film was still installed in the case, closer to the front end where it passed by the backlighting bulb. It was as if someone had reached inside, grabbed the film strip, and in their rush to get out, wrenched a portion of it free. It tore the footage in two, leaving what remained to slowly become unspooled and peek out from the opened door.

"Oh *fuck*." My heart hammered in my chest. "Oh my God. Oh my God."

"Baby—"

"Someone stole, like… twenty seconds, of my Leonard-Cushing fight," I was practically screaming.

"Sebastian," Calvin tried again.

"Maybe twenty-five seconds!" *Now* I was screaming.

Calvin grabbed my shoulders. "Calm down."

"The film isn't mine. Now it's destroyed. I'm so fucked!"

"This is why you have business insurance," Calvin said. "Sebastian. Take a breath."

I took one, but I wasn't happy about it.

"Let's take some photos and file a police report," Calvin continued. "So when you finally get in touch with the owner, you'll have proven this wasn't mishandling or negligence on your part. Okay?"

I gritted my teeth and nodded.

I really hoped this spectacularly shitty start to the day wasn't a sign of things to come.

CHAPTER FOUR

"Bacon or sausage?"

"Bacon," I muttered.

"Cappuccino or house brew?"

"House."

"Blowjob or handjob?"

"Blow—what?" I looked up from my phone.

Calvin smiled. "Just making sure you were in the same solar system as me." He set a take-out container and a cup on the register counter where I was sitting. "Scrambled eggs with a side of bacon. Large coffee with cream."

"What about the third one?"

"What about it?" Calvin stood on the opposite side, popped open the second container, and poked at his breakfast with a plastic fork.

"I think I deserve it. It's been a long night."

"Morning," he corrected.

I set my phone aside. "Whatever. It's been a day."

Calvin took a few bites. "Everything go okay with the police?"

"Yeah. Not that they'll ever catch who broke in."

After carefully packing up the remaining footage in its original tin and storing it inside my office for safekeeping, Calvin and I had combed through the shop's security footage, to no avail. The Kinetoscope was just a foot too far in the back to be seen by the register camera, and I had nothing angled at the back door. So with no footage of the break-in, no evidence to collect, and just a torn piece of celluloid that the cops cared very little about and I cared a whole fucking lot about—honestly, what could be done?

"Dillon okay?" I asked.

Calvin nodded. "Fed him and went for a walk. I stopped at the hardware store too." He pointed to my left.

I leaned over and saw he'd come back with not only breakfast and a plastic bag with a new door lock, but also my shoulder bag.

"I brought your contacts. They're in the front pocket of your bag."

"You're the sweetest man in this whole city," I stated.

Calvin smiled. "So what part of the film got torn off? The actual image, I mean."

"Most of the fight," I said. "From what I saw by examining the still images."

"Did that outdoor scene survive?"

"The murder? Yeah, it's still attached." I took a halfhearted bite of bacon.

"Who knew about the movie?"

"Me. But I have a freckled alibi."

Calvin sipped his coffee. "Who else?"

"Max, of course. Beth was here when we watched

it. You, and that's—oh, Pete knows about the film reel."

Calvin nodded and took another bite of the eggs.

"What?"

"I didn't say anything."

"I know. But you've got tells."

He let out a breath and wiped his mouth on a napkin. "How well do you know this Pete White guy?"

I shrugged. "I'm not inviting him over for eggnog come the holidays, if that's what you're asking." I finished the bacon and said, "Pete's new to the organization that runs the fair. Admittedly, when I've *managed* to speak with him, he's well versed in a number of subjects. He recognized the Kinetoscope and was familiar with the title of the movie when I mentioned it. But he's such a lazy, disorganized, lying shit that I'd have never supported the event if I knew about him in advance."

Calvin shoveled eggs into his mouth like they were going out of style.

"You think he had something to do with this?"

"No," he said around the last bite.

"Filthy liar."

"I'm just concerned," Calvin corrected. "This is an artifact you acquired suddenly and without notice. It's only been seen by a few trusted individuals—and him."

I considered what Pete had said last night, about showing the film at the antique fair and how it'd be a big pull for attracting more attendees. I looked down at the eggs. They suddenly weren't very appealing.

"You have a point," I replied. I leaned over the counter when I heard keys jingle and the front door unlock. "Hey," I called.

"Morning," Max said. He walked inside and shut the door behind him. "You're here early."

"You've no idea."

Max strolled toward the counter, gave Calvin their customary high five, then looked me over from head to toe. "Didn't you wear that shirt yesterday?"

"Probably."

"*Great*," he groaned. "What's happened now?"

Calvin nudged his takeout toward Max, distracting him with an offering of free sausage.

"There was a break-in," I answered.

Max stared at me, wide-eyed, with a link of meat sticking out of his mouth.

Too easy.

"They—whoever—came for the Kinetoscope movie."

Max bit the sausage in two, and I grimaced. "How'd they even know about it?"

Calvin cleared his throat and stepped around Max to grab the hardware store bag. He went into my office, took out a few tools, and walked to the back door.

"What'd I say?" Max asked before finishing off the rest of the sausage.

"Nothing. That was our concern too. But anyway, they ran off with only half of the footage. What's left is in the canister, on the shelf above my computer, okay? Don't mention it to anyone."

"I won't," he insisted. "But why did you say that like I'm working alone today?"

"Because you're working alone today."

Max groaned and dropped his head down on the counter. "I hate working Wednesdays alone! Every time you use Wednesday for any sort of errand or appointment, we always end up swamped with customers, the phone ringing off the hook, and the only time I have to eat lunch and take a piss is when I do them at the same time."

"Sanitary."

He looked back up at me.

"I won't be long."

"You always say that. But if someone flashes something shiny in front of you…."

I could hear Calvin laughing from the back.

"Pete didn't pick up the collection," I told Max. "Calvin's going to help me schlep it to the Javits Center."

"Promise you'll be back before noon."

"Sure."

"*Sure* isn't a promise," Max said firmly.

"I promise," I replied. "But out of curiosity, what happens if I'm not?"

"You buy me lunch."

"Done."

"For a week."

I pursed my lips.

"I'm a growing boy," Max warned.

"You are not. You're twenty-three."

"And I still make Mom fear my return home for Thanksgiving. Don't test my ability to eat you into a financial crisis."

"I'll be back before noon." I hopped down from my stool. "Come help me move shit to the car."

The longer I had to ruminate on the missing film and what Pete had said last night, the more uncomfortable I became. I mean, on one hand, he didn't strike me as a complete moron. And only someone with supreme stupidity would have broken into my shop to steal the very item they'd been waxing poetic about to my face. But that didn't change the fact that out of the handful of people who knew I'd obtained such old and rare footage, there was only one individual I didn't trust.

But what would Pete have done with the movie if he'd actually stolen it? Play it at the fair, as suggested? Like maybe I wouldn't notice that? Come on. It was absurd.

The lower-level exhibition hall of the Javits Center was enormous, brightly lit, and echoed with the voices of event planners, coordinators, security staff, and paying dealers making last-minute preparations before the event opened to the public in a few hours. Even with contacts and sunglasses, the huge spotlight lamps were washing out my sight, which was making the job of preparing my exhibit harder than it should have been.

I draped a runner over my assigned table, smoothed the top out, and then ducked under the ropes that separated our sponsor collections from the foot traffic of attendees. There was a provided stand with a box on top meant for business cards, which I started to fill up.

"I was beginning to wonder if the empty table was actually some sort of esoteric art installation."

I didn't bother turning around. I wouldn't have been able to identify the individual in this asinine lighting. So I relied on my ability to recognize him by voice alone. Gregory Thompson of Marshall's Oddities. "Hi, Greg," I said, finishing with the business cards.

I heard Greg's shoes *tap*, *tap*, *tap* across the robust exhibit hall floor. I finally looked up when I felt him stop at my side. Greg's hands were in his pockets, and he had that usual cocky expression. We hadn't seen each other since the Nevermore events, but little had changed. I was still crotchety. He was still arrogant.

"It's been a while, Sebastian."

"That it has. How're you?"

"Fine, fine." Greg looked at my table and nodded at

Calvin, who was helping set up. "I remember you."

Calvin paused his quick and efficient placing of small displays and artifacts on the tabletop. "Calvin Winter," he said politely.

"That's right. The detective." Greg looked down at me again. "So not a rumor, hmm?"

"Aw, Greg, did you miss the latest community newsletter where I took out a front-page ad proclaiming my relationship status?"

Greg smiled in that way one did when they didn't mean it. "*Love* the ensemble, Sebastian. Green shirt, maroon sweater, and what're those—plaid pants?"

I glanced down at myself. "It matches," I insisted.

"Oh, of course," he agreed.

I huffed. "Have you seen Pete?"

"Today? No, not yet."

"What do you think of him?"

"In what way?"

"As an organizer."

"He's all right. Personable. Why?"

"I don't know."

"What're you fishing for?" Greg questioned.

Do you think he's a thief? Better yet—has anything in your shop gone missing?

"Because the last time you and I played twenty questions, I was nearly shot," Greg continued.

"Hey, I warned you not to attend that damn book event," I countered, as if the whole Duncan Andrews fiasco had happened just last weekend and not nearly six months ago. "It's not my fault you've got cotton where your brain—"

"Seb," Calvin interrupted.

It physically hurt to swallow my ego in front of

Greg. "Forget it," I told him before slipping under the rope to help Calvin finish.

Greg would not forget it. "Whatever you're doing, you'd better stop."

I couldn't resist. "Whatever I'm *doing*?" I echoed, turning to face him.

"This fair is a huge deal for a lot of us. You might think you're a hotshot who doesn't need any sort of advertising to remain afloat, but don't underestimate how quickly success can vanish in this day and age."

"I paid several grand for this sponsorship table with the wobbly leg, didn't I?" I replied, shaking the table to make a point.

"If you ruin this event for me, I'll never forgive you," Greg said with an almost bullying tone.

"All right, Mr. Thompson," Calvin said, intervening for a second time. "You've made your point. I think you'd better get back to your own collection."

Greg looked at Calvin, and the malevolence that hung in the air between us slowly dissipated. "Of course, sir. Wouldn't want to get in trouble with the law over a minor, *private* disagreement."

Okay. That sonofabitch was implying that Calvin would abuse the power of his badge in order to help me. So now I had to kill him. I started back around the table, but Calvin took my arm and held me still.

"Have a good day, Mr. Thompson," Calvin said civilly.

"And you, Mr. Winter," Greg said with a polite gravity that would have caused a lesser man to piss his pants.

Calvin was unfazed.

I shot daggers into the back of Greg's head until he became too blurry to make out. "You should have let me beat him with my cane.''

Calvin let go of me. "And have to arrest you instead? He's an asshole, Sebastian. Don't let him bother you.''

"I *know* he's an asshole,'' I replied. I bent down to finish pulling the last items from the crates tucked under the table. "I swear he came out of the womb looking for a fight.''

"And you have a tendency to push people like that until they see red.''

"I….'' Okay, I couldn't really argue with that. I stood with a brochure stand, walked it to the ropes, and set it up beside the business cards. "Not because I like to.''

"Yes, you do.''

"Stop making me out to be an asshole too.''

"To a lesser degree, you are. But you're my asshole.''

"Thank you, I think.''

Calvin was smiling when I turned to face him. "How does everything look?''

I shielded my eyes with my hands to reduce the glare. "Fine. It's too bad we couldn't get the crate with the globe to fit in the car… would have been nice to have.'' I shrugged. "But everything looks good. Thank you for helping me.''

"It's no problem.'' Calvin cleaned up a few bits of packing debris and adjusted the table skirt.

I crouched down to pick up my messenger bag, paused, and plucked at a stray thread on the sleeve of my sweater.

Maroon.

Fuck. Did I really not match? Did I actually look ridiculous and neither my boyfriend nor assistant bothered to tell me? I know I got dressed in the dark this morning in our rush to the Emporium, but when I bought all these new clothes, Pop had helped to make sure interchanging them wouldn't be a faux pas so terrible that I'd cause society to collapse.

So much for that.

I yanked the sweater off, stuffed it into my bag, and then slung the bag over one shoulder.

Calvin moved around the table and joined me. He offered his hand—knowing I couldn't see well in the exhibit hall, and also because Calvin was aware that I really didn't like using my walking stick.

The simple gesture of assistance and affection made my heart beat a little faster.

Calvin had come so far. *Really*. In December, he was so deep in the closet that even holding a vision-impaired man's hand for aid likely wouldn't have happened. But when he decided to come out, an act of not only love for me, but self-acceptance for himself, Calvin never glanced back. That took an unprecedented amount of courage—to look decades of fear and self-loathing in the face and say *no more*. If he was able to overcome his anxiety about being an out gay cop, it really did convince me that Calvin would eventually cope with his PTSD in a positive and constructive manner.

I took his hand and we walked to the escalators together. We'd nearly reached the ground level when a sudden shout startled both of us.

On our left, riding the escalator down, was Pete. He waved excitedly, turned, and tried running up the steps. "Ah shit. Snow, hang on!" he called before disappearing out of view.

Calvin and I looked at each other when we stepped off the escalator.

I reached into my pocket with my free hand and removed a quarter. "Heads we wait, tails we leave him hanging out to dry."

"Behave."

"I'm in a pissy mood."

Calvin let go of my hand and reached up to stroke a bit of hair behind my ear.

"Sorry about that," Pete said as he appeared over the rise on the correct escalator. "So did you get set up?" he asked, walking toward us.

"Yeah," I answered. *No thanks to you.*

Pete looked at Calvin and held a hand out. "Pete White. I'm one of the organizers."

"Calvin Winter."

"Pleasure," Pete said before looking back to me. "You're not staying?"

"I've a business to run. I've left cards and brochures. There's extra stock of both under the table."

"Attendees would love to meet you," Pete insisted.

"I doubt that," I replied.

"You remind me of some of my old students from my teaching days. Bright young things getting interested in the past. You're the sort who makes it fun for everyone."

"I guess… I'll come by on the last day. Friday afternoon all right?"

"That'd be great. I know you don't think it, but you're a real attraction," Pete said, giving me that weird—I guess you'd say "charming"—smile. "You bring a youthful, hip vibe to history and antiquing. You make it cool for the next generation to want to take part in it."

I raised an eyebrow. "Er, what exactly is *hip* about me?"

"It's your whole persona, Snow."

I was wearing a dirty shirt and loafers, so I was calling bullshit on this.

Pete laughed at the expression I was likely making. "I love this guy," he said to Calvin. "Even our names go great together. Snow and White."

"I prefer Snow and Winter," Calvin replied simply.

Pete glanced at me and back at Calvin. "I suppose you would."

"You've got my number," I said, reining the conversation in hard and fast. "If anything comes up."

"Yup." Pete held out what looked like a perfectly decent mobile device. I didn't remind him that yesterday it was supposedly old and not working.

"I'll see you later, then."

"Bye, Snow."

I reached a hand out and Calvin accepted it.

We walked through the steel-and-glass concourse of the Center toward the main doors as someone else was entering. He had a dark-colored hoodie on, headphones, and some kind of convention badge around his neck—exhibitor, security, or attendee, I had no clue. But he was a bad person to play chicken with, because he never looked up from his phone, even after knocking into my shoulder. I stopped walking and turned to watch the kid step onto the escalator.

"Who was that?" Calvin asked.

I shook my head. "I don't know."

Calvin pulled his sunglasses down from atop his head as we made our way outside. At the end of the block, we crossed the street, heading to the nearby parking lot where we'd been charged the "special event" rate because of the fair, even though we were technically leaving before it opened. Nothing like flushing fifty bucks down the toilet.

"Can I ask you a question?"

"Of course," Calvin said.

I took a breath. "Maroon, like what?"

I felt him look at me, but I kept my eyes firmly planted on the sidewalk.

Left foot.

Right foot.

"Maroon is brownish red," Calvin answered.

"No, I know that. I mean... *like what?*"

Left.

Right.

Left.

Right.

He still hadn't answered.

I finally looked up.

Calvin was rubbing his chin with his free hand. "I guess a bit like autumn," he concluded after the thoughtful pause.

"Isn't autumn more red and orange?"

He nodded. "Yeah. But there are a few trees in Central Park that turn maroon." He let go of my hand and put his arm around my shoulders. "Maroon like Central Park in autumn."

Sounds pretty.

CHAPTER FIVE

I opened the Emporium door and immediately checked my watch: 11:47 a.m.

"Sweetheart," Calvin said from behind me. He was standing in the open door, brightly backlit by the midday sun.

"Come inside so you aren't glowing." I reached into my bag, pulled out my glasses case, and replaced the sunglasses with regular lenses.

"Do you need anything else?" Calvin asked as the door shut. "Otherwise I'm going to head home so I can catch the furniture delivery."

"Oh, no. I'm good. Thank you again."

"Seb," Max called from farther in the shop.

I turned and saw him standing near the Kinetoscope with a customer. "I'm back before noon," I answered. "Sorry to disappoint you."

Max didn't reply but instead gestured for the man at his side to follow as he walked toward me. "This is the owner, Sebastian Snow. He knows a hell of a lot more about the Kinetoscope than I do."

"Lee Straus," the stranger said with a big smile, offering a hand once he'd closed the distance. He was… very strapping. I suspected he was older than he looked, but what did I know? I was thirty-three going on eighty. Lee had an expensive-looking haircut, a light-colored suit—he was probably the sort of person who paid attention to the difference between summer and winter fashion—with a nice physique underneath.

"Hi," I said. "The Kinetoscope. It's not for sale—"

Lee glanced over my shoulder and let out a surprised sound. "I'll be goddamned. Calvin Winter, is that you?"

Say what now?

I turned away from Hottie Straus and looked at Calvin. He seemed just as surprised as I felt, so at least we were on the same playing field. "You know Calvin?" I asked, with all the grace of a drunk bull in a china shop.

"You can say that," Lee replied, still looking at Calvin.

"I *did* say that," I muttered.

Calvin took a few steps forward and stopped beside me. "Lee…," he said, like he wasn't sure what else to include in that statement.

Lee grinned and reached out to shake Calvin's hand. "Been a few years, hasn't it?"

"About eight," Calvin remarked.

"You look just the same as I remember. Hair's a bit longer, though," Lee continued, reaching out to touch Calvin's thick, fiery locks.

I opened my mouth to kindly let Lee know that this was a no-touching zone, thank you, but luckily Calvin moved away with a jerk of his head.

Lee recovered pretty quickly. "Sorry. So you came

back to New York after all. What have you been doing all this time?"

"I'm a detective with the NYPD," Calvin answered.

Eight years ago would have put Calvin where? Military, right? Or just leaving, actually. So these two probably served overseas together.

"What about you?" Calvin asked politely.

"Teaching. Adjunct professor. It's shit pay." Lee finally looked at me again. "I walk by this place and the Oddities shop all the time on my break and never actually stop inside. Last week I peeked into that place, and today I thought I'd check this one out. What incredible timing, huh?"

"Yeah," I managed to say. I might have been legally blind, but fucking *hello*.

Max looked grateful when the shop phone rang and he could back out of the conversation before it got even more uncomfortable.

"How'd you two end up becoming friends?" Lee asked. "An antique dealer and a cop. There's not much crossover."

"You'd be surprised," I said. "Antiquing is a dangerous business."

Lee laughed and put his hands in his trouser pockets. "You don't say?"

"Lots of murder," I continued.

Lee knitted his brows together.

"Seb," Calvin murmured. He said to Lee, "We're dating."

"Oh." Lee staggered a bit on the landing but made another decent recovery. "I remember a guy, back in the Army, who everyone called Heartless Winter. How'd he put it that one time? *I. Don't. Date*," Lee said in a deep voice obviously meant to be an imitation of Calvin.

"That was a long time ago," Calvin answered. "People change."

"Yes, they do," Lee said with a smile. But his tone, though pleasant, had at least a dozen different layers to it. I didn't even know where to start on deconstructing the meaning behind that statement.

Lee suddenly reached into his inner pocket, removed a business card, and offered it to Calvin. "I've got a class in thirty minutes," he said. "But we should do lunch soon. Talk about old times."

Ah yes, a not-so-subtle way of saying I wasn't invited.

"I try to focus on the here and now," Calvin answered, accepting the card. "But sure."

Lee smiled again and glanced at me. "Pleasure to meet you, Sebastian."

"Oh, uh. Yeah. You too," I said, stumbling over myself after being a third wheel for most of the interaction.

Lee inclined his head and moved around us both. He paused at the bookshelf beside the door, studied the spines for a moment, then saw himself out.

"Wow," I stated after a long pause.

Calvin grunted. "Sometimes New York is too small of a world."

"Are you okay?"

"I'm fine. Just wasn't… expecting that. Him. *Lee*."

I touched his bare arm and gave it an affectionate rub.

Calvin kissed me. "I'm going to head home."

Home. Hearing that was never going to get old.

"I'll see you this evening," I answered.

"We'll christen the new bed."

The meeting we were scheduled to have in bed was on my mind the rest of the day.

So the second the clock hit six, I all but shoved Max out the door, locked up, brought the gate down, and hoofed it down the block. Of course, first I had to make a deposit at the bank, grab a new box of condoms from the drugstore that weren't the glow-in-the-dark variety because I wasn't okay with Calvin's dick looking like a party favor, and then needed to pick up some takeout since I was certain he'd be too tired to shop and cook dinner again. Especially after we'd both been up and running since four in the morning.

Doing errands was the very essence of delayed gratification, I guess.

I grabbed the receipt from the ATM and turned to exit the after-hours lobby of National Trust. I held the slip of paper close and tried to decipher the tiny print as I shoved the door open with one hand. I felt and heard a loud thud and looked up, expecting a pigeon dive-bombing the glass.

Nope. I just hit a random guy with the door.

"Oh shit, I'm so sorry!" I exclaimed, stepping out of the bank and moving toward him. "Are you okay?" I put a hand on his shoulder and paused. Familiarity hit me hard—years of touches playing through my mind like someone holding a stack of pictures and thumbing the corners to produce moving images. "Neil?"

He winced as he removed his hand from his face. He looked at me, and then his eyes widened a little. "Sebastian?"

Great. First Calvin, now me. Nothing like bumping into an ex in a city of eight million, outside of a crime scene no less, which used to be the only place I had to worry about seeing Neil.

"Is your face okay?"

Neil raised an eyebrow. "Feels like someone hit it with a door."

It wasn't funny.

It really wasn't.

But I started laughing.

And to my surprise, Neil cracked a smile.

"Promise you didn't see me coming," he said.

"And intentionally hit you with a commercial-grade insulated glass door?"

"Yeah."

"I didn't see you."

"Good."

Neil looked great. Well, was looking better than he had back in February, that much I was certain of. He was impeccably dressed and had that same sharp expression and handsome face I used to know so intimately.

During the Curiosities fiasco, we'd been thrust into each other's personal spaces, and it'd been a cop trying to do his job while his pain-in-the-ass ex made everything considerably more difficult. But out here, in front of a bank and next door to a modeling agency and a Greek restaurant, we were just two people. We'd both been off our guard. And for the first time since last Christmas, I was able to look Neil in the face and just feel... okay.

About everything.

"What?" Neil asked.

I blinked. "What, *what*?"

"You're smiling."

"It's nothing."

Neil massaged his forehead for a minute, lowered his arm, and asked, "How have you been?"

"Are you being polite or really asking?"

"I'm really asking."

"Oh…. I've been good," I said, hearing the touch of surprise in my voice.

Neil slid his hands into his trouser pockets, assuming that cool presence he always had and seeming nothing like a man who'd just been whacked with a door. "It's nice to see you."

"Do I need to bring you to the hospital?"

Neil shook his head, looking just the slightest bit amused. He glanced down briefly, scuffing the sidewalk with the toe of his expensive shoe. "Heading home?"

I nodded and countered with "What're you doing around here?"

He looked up and then jutted a thumb over his shoulder at the Greek place. "Picking up a gyro for dinner."

We used to order out from there a lot—50 percent convenience, 50 percent best fucking gyros I'd ever eaten. But since I'd broken up with Neil, I hadn't stepped foot in the Greek shop, despite doing business at my bank nearly every day and being *right next door*. Subconscious thing, I guess.

"Sebby—" Neil paused and then corrected himself. "Sebastian."

I smiled a little. "Yeah?"

"I've been thinking about you a lot lately."

"Neil."

"I mean, it was serendipitous running into you."

"This isn't a 'Between the Devil and the Deep Blue Sea' situation, is it?" I asked.

Neil looked confused.

"Cab Calloway? No? Never mind."

"There's just some things I'd like to say to you. A cup of coffee's worth of conversation."

I let out a breath and consciously relaxed my shoulders. The turbulent relationship I'd had with Neil was the very depiction of what happened when one settled for what they knew in their heart was profoundly wrong for them. That being said, I put the man through hell in February. He'd nearly taken a bullet because of me. A chat over a house brew wasn't going to kill me.

"Okay," I agreed. I fished my cell from my messenger bag. "Let me tell Calvin I'll be home late."

Neil looked at the ground again as he nodded. "Still seeing him?"

"We're living together," I stated.

He raised his head. "Is he treating you right?"

To which I elegantly responded, "Huh?"

I admit, that was not what I was expecting from Neil. In my memories, he was still cold and bitter toward Calvin. I couldn't blame him. We might have been wrong for each other, but hearts were still broken. The comfort and routine of Neil's life had not only been disrupted by me meeting Calvin, but thrown on its head and then out a window.

But he silently waited for my answer.

"Uh… yeah. He does." I smiled a bit serenely. "Like a prince." My phone rang in my hand. "Shit. Sorry, hang on." I raised the screen close, expecting it to read either Calvin or Pop.

It was neither.

I frowned a little and accepted the call. "Hello?"

"This is Tasha Lewis calling with Advice Line. May I speak with Sebastian Snow?"

"That's me. Speaking."

"Sir, your place of business is reporting an unauthorized entry after no security code was entered. Can you confirm if this is you or an employee?"

"No, not at all. My shop is closed for the night."

"I understand. We are notifying the police at once."

I swore loudly and could feel myself starting to shake. I had been at the Emporium *fifteen* minutes ago. It had to be the same person as early this morning. Right? Had they waited in hiding? Or was their plan to come in and make it a face-to-face confrontation, and I'd simply left work more on time than I usually did?

"What's going on?" Neil asked, getting close.

"Someone might be robbing the Emporium again," I said to him. I agreed to whatever Miss Tasha was saying and hung up. "I have to go. I'm sorry, Neil."

"Wait, Seb." He took my arm and pulled me back as I started to move past him.

"Wait for *what*, Neil? For some piece of shit to clean out my place of business? I have to get back there."

"You don't know what the situation is," Neil said firmly. "You don't know if there's one suspect or twelve— if they're armed with a putty knife or a rifle. Is your security company calling the police?"

"Yes."

"Then stay put."

"Like hell I am." I yanked my arm free.

"Sebastian." Neil made a quick movement and cut me off. "Since when have reckless choices gotten you anywhere but in trouble?"

"Well, unless *you* plan on arresting me, I'm going." I took a step to the left, but Neil matched it. "I'm not sticking around for a goddamn dance, Neil. Move."

"What if whoever is there hurts you, Sebastian?"

"Then I'm shit out of luck."

"Don't do that to Winter."

I paused and looked up at Neil.

"If he's treating you right, then you damn well better be doing the same for him. Don't go being an idiot, running headfirst into danger and considering the consequences of it later." He let out a breath that somehow managed to have a tone, then tilted his head toward the side of the road. "I'll drive."

"But—you just—"

"Are you a cop?"

"No."

"Are you armed?"

"No."

"I'm both. Get in." Neil walked to the edge of the sidewalk and opened the passenger door to his car.

I didn't have to be told twice. I quickly climbed in and shut the door as Neil walked around the front and slid into the driver's seat. He merged into uptown traffic, made the next available left, and turned to head back downtown on Second Avenue.

"No way that it might be Max?" he eventually asked.

"He'd never go inside without me."

"Why don't you give him a call. Rule him out." Neil slammed on the brakes when a taxi cut him off. "Stupid son of a…."

I chose Max in my contacts and put the phone to my ear.

"Hi-de-ho, boss," Max answered. "Make it fast, I'm about to go into a tunnel."

"You're not at the Emporium?"

"No?" He sounded confused. "I'm on my way—" The line cut when signal was lost.

I lowered my phone. "He's on the subway."

"And it wouldn't be your father?"

"Of course not."

"Winter?"

"No, Neil."

"I'm just—goddamn it, man, pick a fucking lane—trying to cover all the bases before we get there."

I took a deep breath. "Someone broke in this morning."

"What?"

"At like 4:00 a.m. Calvin installed a dead bolt on the back door today."

"Great," Neil muttered.

He was easily as good a driver as Calvin. Neil wove through New York City rush hour with practiced ease. He might have lacked the patience Calvin had behind the wheel, but he more than made up for it by looking like a hard-boiled detective fresh off the pages of some '40s pulp fiction novel. It was the suit, I think. Neil always had immaculate, if expensive, taste.

He reached the Emporium's block and swerved into a free spot on the side of the road. "Alley door is open."

"Is it?" I looked out the passenger window as I unbuckled my seat belt. "I *definitely* locked it tonight."

"What kind of lock do you have on it?"

"You'd need bolt cutters."

Neil opened the driver's door and got out of the car. I quickly followed.

"Oh no, park your ass in the car," he said as he came around to my side.

"You've got to be kidding me."

"Do I look like I'm joking?"

"You rarely are."

"If you get hurt, that's on me," Neil said.

"I think it'd be my own fault," I countered.

"You can say that because you wouldn't be the one

getting stared down by a combat-trained vet."

Neil walked across the sidewalk, reached into his coat, and pulled his service weapon from the shoulder holster as he got to the alley. He fingered the padlock Beth and I kept on the alley door, then poked his head around the corner. Once Neil disappeared inside, I started across the sidewalk.

I could have listened. But why start now?

I briefly considered that Max might have been right yesterday when he said the Emporium was cursed. Ever since December, it had become a magnet for all things mysterious and murderous. And while that might have been fine and dandy to keep my boredom at bay, I *was* trying to run a business.

I leaned around the corner and peered down the alley. Save for the dumpster pushed up against the left wall, it was empty. The back door of the Emporium was open and seemed to be swinging in the mild, early summer breeze. Neil was inside the store, and I could hear the alarm chirping away.

I stepped in and cautiously moved along the right wall, reached the door, and spared a glance inside. Thank God for my contacts, sunglasses, and a dim shop. I could make out the shapes of furniture, display cases, and the figure, who was most definitely Neil, inspecting corners, under tables, and behind the register counter—gun at the ready.

But that was it.

I didn't see anyone else.

It'd taken us a few minutes to reach the Emporium.... I supposed it was safe to assume the thief wouldn't need more time than that. Because it *had* to be the same person returning for the remaining length of footage they'd failed to obtain earlier. I'd have much preferred a random burglary and be out a mahogany apothecary cabinet, complete with twenty-five glass bottles all with original labels. Or my sword cane. Hell, I'd even be willing to give up the silver pepper shaker in the shape of a pigeon I recently won at an estate sale.

But they'd come looking for the murder portion of the movie, and I just *knew* this wouldn't end well.

"Looks empty," I called.

"I see you're not listening again," Neil answered from within. He strode across the shop to the front door, and after a beat, asked, "Did you change the code for the alarm?"

"You mean, after a vigilante bypassed the system to woo me with the remnants of Barnum's lost museum?"

"Just tell me the new code."

"One, one, four, two."

The alarm silenced, and then Neil turned on a nearby bank lamp. "What's it mean?" he called.

"Hmm?"

"I know you pick numbers that have a meaning so you remember them easier."

"Since when?"

"Since your debit card pin number is your dad's birth year."

"I'll be sure to change it now, thanks."

Another light was turned on as Neil moved around the Emporium, still holding his gun out. "What's the new code mean?"

"I'm a sentimental shithead."

He paused in one of the congested walkways and looked toward me.

"Can I come in or not?" I asked impatiently.

"Wait."

I rolled my eyes and stepped back from the

doorway. I leaned against the exterior bricks and glanced at the dumpster again. The heavy plastic top was open and propped against the wall. Beth and I were sticklers about keeping the lid closed. The last thing anyone wanted was a shop smelling like garbage. And Max should have known better after taking the trash out for the night.

I walked back to the dumpster, grabbed on to the edge, put my foot into a small niche, and hoisted myself up in order to reach the lid.

Inside was a dead man.

CHAPTER SIX

All right.

I wasn't unaccustomed to finding dead bodies.

Man-in-Dumpster marked lucky #5 on my list. And let's not forget, there was once a pig heart stuffed into the floorboards of the Emporium. So this was more like body #5.5, in my opinion.

But still. I had been expecting to see packing peanuts and office trash bags full of coffee grounds and take-out containers. Not a corpse nestled among the debris. And Guy's face was one of shock and horror—eyes wide and mouth hanging open, like he was just as surprised as me to *be* dead. His neck and chest were covered in something dark that at this point I had to simply assume was blood.

I panicked, grabbed to steady myself, touched something wet and slick, screamed, and fell off the side of the dumpster. "Ouch... *fuck*." I slowly sat up as pain shot from my tailbone all the way up my spine.

"Seb?" Neil called from behind me. I could hear the

pounding of his steps on the cement as he ran to join me.

I looked up. "This is blood, isn't it?" I asked, raising my hands for Neil to see.

I'm pretty sure it was cop instinct that made Neil immediately turn to the dumpster. He stepped toward it, taking a moment to study the ground. There must have been blood I hadn't seen and walked right through. Neil held his pistol at low ready as he leaned close enough to peer over the top of the dumpster.

He looked at me again.

"I was just trying to close the lid so the alley didn't smell like leftover spicy tuna rolls," I protested.

Neil turned toward the alley entrance when a patrol car pulled up to the curb, lights flashing but no siren running. He immediately holstered his weapon and pulled out his badge. "Detective Neil Millett, CSU," he said as two uniformed officers entered.

"We got a report of a 10-11—alarm in a commercial building," one of the officers replied.

Neil pocketed his ID. "I've done a walk-through of the location and have found no individuals on the property. The lock on the alley door appears to have been cut, and the back door was already open when I arrived." He took a step toward the dumpster. "We do, however, have a DOA."

The first officer joined Neil and peered over the edge. "*Christ*...."

He turned to his partner and instructed her to do another check of the Emporium, then got on his radio to call in Mr. Dumpster Diver.

I started to get up from the ground.

"Don't move, Seb," Neil instructed.

"What? Why?" I froze in place.

He looked over his shoulder at me. "You're evidence."

The alley was now a crime scene.

An additional CSU detective had arrived and was inspecting the busted back door while Neil was crouched in front of me on the cement, taking photographs of my hands.

"I didn't kill the guy."

"I know that," he murmured before snapping another photo.

"Then why have you pulled out your arsenal?" I nodded to the crime scene kit at Neil's side.

He set his camera down and removed a small paper envelope from the box, as well as a pick. He gently scraped around my nails. "So the evidence backs up that you've just got extraordinary shitty luck."

I looked toward the alley doors before letting out a small sigh. "I don't think you'll need nail scrapings to convince the homicide department of that."

"What do you mean?" Neil asked as he folded the envelope closed.

I hadn't looked away from the doors. "Hi, honey."

Calvin was still dressed for his day off, his hands on his hips and a distinct frown on his face. His partner, Quinn Lancaster, stood at his side, shaking her head.

"I was on my way home," I insisted as they approached. "Cross my heart."

Neil stood. "Detective Winter," he said briskly.

"Detective Millett," Calvin answered.

"So, Sebastian isn't the dead, unidentified male?" Quinn asked, and I couldn't quite tell if she was kidding or not.

"He's in there," I answered, pointing at the dumpster.

"Can I tell you what happened?"

"*Please*," Calvin answered. He didn't sound angry, per se—more like tired and relieved.

Also maybe a little angry.

"I left work," I said. "Doors locked, gate down, the whole shebang. I bumped into Neil outside of the bank. We talked for a minute, and then the security company called to report an unauthorized entrance. Neil drove us here."

Calvin crossed his arms, muscles bulging within the sleeves of his T-shirt. "Did the security company not notify the police?"

"They hadn't arrived yet," Neil replied. "We noticed the lock on the alley doors had been cut, so I went in through the back to check for an intruder. It was all clear."

"Then would someone please tell me why Sebastian is sitting on the ground, covered in someone else's blood?" Calvin asked.

"I was waiting in the alley," I said, staring up at the three. "I saw the dumpster had been left open. I went to close it—boom, dead guy. There's blood on the side. I touched it by accident."

"And stepped in it," Neil concluded.

I frowned and checked the sole of my shoe. It was dark and tacky-looking.

Son of a bitch.

"Never a dull moment with you around, Sebastian," Quinn remarked.

"Thanks, I try," I answered dryly.

Calvin looked down at me. "Was anything inside your store missing?"

"I haven't gotten the chance to look. But I'll give you two guesses as to what they came for."

"I'll only need one," Calvin murmured. He turned

to Neil next. "Finish with him so Sebastian can take a walk through the Emporium."

Neil surprised the shit out of me when he only nodded and said, "Yes, sir."

Calvin took a step closer and squatted down in front of me. "You're okay?" he asked gently.

"Peachy keen."

He kept staring.

"Dead Guy startled me," I admitted. "But other than the bruised ass and ego, I'm fine."

"I wish you had just come home," he murmured.

"Yeah, me too. But I guess we'd have ended up here regardless."

"I suppose," Calvin answered. "But at least you wouldn't have had to wear booties."

"Huh?"

"I need your shoes, Seb," Neil interrupted.

Calvin gave me an apologetic look, as if he knew all along Neil was going to say that.

"They're new, so it figures," I answered.

Calvin stood and went to the dumpster with Quinn. He peered inside with ease, while his partner had to stand on her toes to get a look. Both of them were joined by the city medical examiner while Neil was tugging my shoes off.

"Nice socks," he stated.

"I'd give that a two out of five."

Neil dropped my shoes into a bag, then glanced at me briefly before filling out the form on the front of it. "What?"

"I don't recommend using that pickup line when you start dating again," I continued.

His mouth twitched. Not quite a smile, but it was

something for a guy like Neil. "You used to always wear black socks."

"Oh yeah. I'm turning over a new leaf. What color are they?"

Neil raised an eyebrow but kept writing.

"Apparently I already look like a mess, so hit me," I insisted.

"Red." Neil set the bag aside and held up a pair of crime scene booties.

"Wait. Aren't green and red Christmas colors?"

Neil nodded and put the booties on my feet.

"Great. I dressed myself like a fucking elf and no one said anything."

Neil chuckled. "It's subtle. Don't worry."

I was able to get up after that. Neil instructed me to follow him through the alley. He brought me out to the sidewalk, where a plethora of official vehicles were now parked, and helped get my hands washed and cleaned of the now-dried blood.

"Snow!"

I turned around to see Quinn standing outside the alley. "Yeah?"

"Let's go take a gander inside."

"Thanks, Neil," I said, holding my hands up and wiggling my clean fingers.

"Sure."

I walked to Quinn. "I can open the front door if that's easier."

"No, no. We don't want to contaminate the scene any more than necessary." She nodded for me to follow behind, and we went back through the alley.

The medical examiner was standing inside the dumpster, talking to Calvin as we passed. I overheard her pronouncing the man to be "very dead," and that it appeared to be "blood loss" from a wound to his neck. I slowed down as Calvin murmured a question about the instrument used in the homicide, but Quinn grabbed my arm and hauled me away before I could pick up any more of the conversation.

"So," Quinn began as we approached the open door. "Can anyone confirm seeing you leave for the night?"

"Am I a suspect?"

"You know the routine by now."

"My security cameras would show me leaving."

"Do you have any cameras in the alley?" Quinn asked.

"No." I paused just outside of the doorway. "Can we make the logical assumption that the break-in and homicide are related?"

"We can't assume anything."

"He sure as hell wasn't in the dumpster when I closed up," I stated. "My assistant takes out the trash—he'd have said something. Screamed is more likely—maybe even burned the building down."

Quinn looked expectant.

"The alley was locked when I left. I got to the bank by 6:10 and made a deposit at the ATM, then bumped into Neil outside. We got back here around 6:20—maybe 6:25. You have to take into account that Mr. Dumpster looks to have had his throat cut. Do you know how much of a mess that makes?"

"Yes."

"Er—okay, Quinn, it was a rhetorical question. The point is, I'd be covered in arterial spray. To top it off, I'm not strong enough to toss a full-grown man into a garbage bin that big. I eat too much candy and don't lift nearly enough dumbbells."

"Calvin really isn't kidding when he calls you his Sherlock."

I felt my face get a bit warm.

"You're not a suspect," she concluded. "Not even a rookie detective would think so." She walked into the Emporium. "*But*," Quinn called over her shoulder, "we need to figure out if your dumpster buddy was in here, looking to make a quick buck. And I sure as hell hope you can tell if something is actually missing, because this place is chaos."

"It's *organized* chaos," I corrected. I examined everything as I moved through the store, in the one-in-a-million chance this was totally unrelated to the Kinetoscope. "It had to be more than one guy. He wouldn't have cut his own throat." I crouched to examine a few glass displays, but the contents were undisturbed.

"No honor among thieves," Quinn murmured, moving toward the register. "What in the world is *this*?"

I stood and looked around my Victrola to see Quinn standing at the steps, pointing to the Kinetoscope that Max and I had moved that afternoon. "It's an Edison Kinetoscope."

"What's that?"

"Old movie viewer, before they perfected projectors." I stepped around a few tables and hiked up the steps. I moved to open the cabinet door in order to show her the guts of the machine, but it was wide-open. "Oh boy."

"What's wrong?"

I glanced at her. "Well, uh—it came with a movie. Someone tried to steal it this morning, actually."

"*What?*"

I nodded and pointed to my office door. "But I locked—fuck."

Quinn narrowed her eyes and glanced toward her

left.

The office door was ajar.

I stepped close and pushed it open with my knuckles. The entire room was torn apart.

Three Wise Monkeys.

That's what we looked like, standing around the office doorway. Quinn was pinching the bridge of her nose, gaze cast to the floor. Calvin had his fist resting against his mouth. One arm was crossed over my front and the other rested against the side of my face.

"So you had a movie made by Thomas Edison?" Quinn asked.

"W. K. L. Dickson, actually. But he worked for Edison," I replied.

"And at the end of the film was a murder?"

"That's right."

Quinn raised her head and looked across Calvin to me. "And it wasn't a *movie* murder?"

I jutted a thumb at Calvin. "He saw it."

She turned her gaze to him. "You did?"

Calvin nodded. "Yesterday. Seb called me to come look at it." He crossed his arms, still staring at the mess in my office. "It was authentic, but what can we do about a death that happened over a century ago? It's tragic, but we have dangerous criminals roaming New York in the now. I told Seb there was nothing to be done."

"Perhaps it implicates someone," I said, mostly to myself. I glanced to my left when I felt eyes on me—Calvin and Quinn both staring. "What?"

"You think there's a supercentenarian running around this city, trying to cover up a murder they were guilty of in the nineteenth century?" Quinn remarked.

"Of course not," I replied. "The film itself is just over 120 years old, and I'd give the killer's age at least an additional twenty. The verified oldest human only reached 122 years."

An awkward silence settled around us.

Calvin finally asked, "And who was that, baby?"

"Jeanne Calment," I quickly answered, letting out a held breath. "Thank you for asking."

Calvin nodded.

"What I meant was... maybe someone alive today wants to protect the killer's identity," I suggested. "For *some* reason."

Quinn didn't look impressed. "Or maybe it's just worth money. How much, do you think?"

"Contrary to popular belief, I don't know *everything*," I told her. "Personally, I think the historical value outweighs the monetary, but I'd have to do a bit more research."

"I can honestly say I'm disappointed," Quinn answered.

"Sorry."

Quinn turned her attention to the back door as voices drifted into the shop from the alley. She walked down the steps and made her way through the aisles.

Calvin put a hand on my shoulder. "Where did you put the remaining footage?"

I leaned into the office and turned the low-intensity lamp on. The computer was still there and assembled, although the monitor had been knocked over. Junk from the desk drawers was strewn all over the place, and the fridge door was open—like, yeah, I *totally* hid the film behind a few cans of ginger ale and Max's tuna sandwich from the other day. I looked up at the overhead shelves—

also a mess—and reached forward.

Calvin stopped me from touching anything. He took a latex glove from his back pocket and held it out. "Put this on."

"Please tell me you aren't always carrying these around in your jeans."

"Funny."

I tried to smile, but I just wasn't feeling it. I snapped the glove on and moved a few books from the shelf. I knocked a jar with the spine of one, which in turn rained down a collection of pens and markers on my head. I sighed, ignored the new mess, and stood on my toes to reach for the very back.

The canister was still there.

I held it up and turned to Calvin. "A small miracle."

"They must have hoped it was still in the Kinetoscope," Calvin said.

"Ran out of time searching for it?"

He nodded. "It's a well-thought-out entrance turned messy. I would go so far as to say whoever was in here hadn't considered the possibility that the film could be elsewhere. They didn't know where to look, and the clock was ticking once the alarm went off."

I peeled the glove free and stuffed it into a pocket. "Quinn says I'm not a suspect for the murder."

"Of course you're not."

"Since I'm on camera leaving here, and at the bank."

"And you've got an officer vouching for you," Calvin concluded.

"Who we may or may not have suspected of being a killer in the recent past," I added.

Calvin's posture changed a bit. Self-conscious. "Millett is a good detective. That's the truth."

"You're not mad, are you?"

"To find you at another crime scene?"

"No—well, yes, but—talking to Neil."

Calvin leaned back briefly, checking to confirm the shop was empty, then reached out to cup my jaw in one large hand. "No. He nearly took a bullet for you." He stroked my face for a moment before lowering his hand. "Millett and I have reached an understanding. And I don't want to be the sort of man who's insecure over you having a conversation with an ex."

"Okay."

"All that concerns me is that he shows you respect. If not, then *he and I* will have an issue—not you."

"He was polite," I confirmed.

"Good."

Quinn returned inside just then, with Neil in tow. They were making their way toward us.

"I didn't think my shop was going to be the scene of a murder," I said, changing the subject. "*And* I even stayed in the alley, which was the *safe place* at the time."

"You're really riding those technicalities, aren't you?" Calvin murmured. "Were you able to find the Kinetoscope owner today?"

I shook my head. "I didn't try again. It slipped my mind." I leaned close and whispered, "Do you think these are the same people from this morning?"

He nodded. "I don't like coincidences."

"I think… maybe I'm being set up to be robbed, so the owner can try to hold me financially accountable."

"It seems very likely."

Of course that didn't explain the bloody body in the dumpster.

"Nothing else in the store is missing, right?" Calvin

continued.

"Not that I can tell," I answered.

"Do I have your permission to access the security footage for the shop?"

"Sure. To confirm the break-in and murder are the same event?"

"Yes. And perhaps to catch the partner who got away."

"Exactly," I said quickly. "Because that guy wouldn't have cut his own throat." I motioned excitedly at the back door. "And the new lock you installed could probably be broken by two people. The second individual is likely to be a man as well. They'd have to possess the physical strength necessary to lift the weight of a dead body over their head and toss it into a dumpster."

Calvin listened patiently with a funny little expression on his face. "I agree with you. Did you recognize the victim?"

"I saw *a lot* of blood, screamed, and fell off the dumpster."

"So no?"

"I didn't get a very good look, no," I concluded.

"Would you be willing to look again?"

"Since you asked so nicely."

"Pardon us," Quinn said, motioning Calvin and me to move aside with a wave of her hand. "CSU wants fingerprints."

Calvin stepped down the stairs.

I reluctantly left the office doorway, and Quinn and Neil went to the Kinetoscope. He set his kit down, snapped on a new pair of gloves, and rummaged through his supplies.

"Please be careful," I told him.

"I'm always careful," Neil said, not looking up.

"Yeah, but if you find a print—the tape used to lift it from the cabinet—I don't want it to cause any damage to the finish."

"Seb," Neil said in *that* tone.

Calvin came back up the stairs, took my elbow, guided me through the shop, and out the back door so Neil could do his job.

In the alley, the medical examiner was preparing the body for transport. Calvin led the way to the gurney, said something to the woman, and she pulled back the sheet covering the thief-turned-fatality.

I took a hesitant step closer. Light hair and complexion. Young face, dark clothes—

"I know him!" I clutched the film canister to my chest as if I expected he'd suddenly leap to life and grab for it. "This… this is the brat who was in the shop yesterday. The one who was giving me a hard time over nothing and then stormed—" I paused. If I stared at his upper face… ignored the obscene amount of blood…. "He was at the Javits Center."

Calvin looked at me.

I pointed a finger at the kid. "He bumped into me on our way out."

"This was him? How confident are you?"

I wasn't offended by the question. If a cop was going to take the word of someone with a vision prescription as strong as mine, he needed certainty.

"Positive," I replied. "And yesterday he was examining the Kinetoscope. He was looking for something and got angry at me." I waved the film canister at Calvin— the *something* in question.

"All right," he murmured. He thanked the medical examiner, she tossed the sheet over the body, and he brought me out of the alley and onto the street.

We walked to the end of the block, putting the madness of the crime scene behind us. Without the murder and mayhem to distract me, I realized it was nearly eight o'clock. I was exhausted, hungry, and had an excellent stress headache starting.

"Let me guess," I began, as Calvin raised his arm to flag a taxi. "I'm getting kicked out of the Scooby Gang?"

"That's right."

"I suppose I don't have to remind you to lock up the Emporium when you're done," I said, smiling wryly when Calvin looked at me.

A taxi pulled up to the curb beside us.

Calvin leaned down and gave our apartment address through the open passenger window. The driver nodded and motioned for me to get inside. Calvin opened the back door.

"Will you come home tonight?" I asked.

"I'll do my best." He leaned forward, the car door between us as he kissed my mouth.

"I'm sorry about your day off."

"It's not your fault, sweetheart."

I reluctantly got into the back of the cab. Calvin shut the door, and the driver pulled onto the road.

CHAPTER SEVEN

I wasn't wearing shoes.

My keys were in my messenger bag.

My phone was in my messenger bag.

My messenger bag was in Neil's car.

And I was standing outside of my locked apartment building with nothing but a canister of murder film.

Someday they'd write a book about me. *A Study in Unfortunate Events: The Sebastian Snow Story.*

A lady was exiting the building just then. I grabbed the front door and held it open for her, trying to look as if I had been in the process of entering myself. I think she bought it until she noticed I was only wearing medical booties on my feet.

"It's a long story," I said when she gave me a curious once-over. "I'm the new tenant on the fourth floor."

"I thought that was a redhead who'd moved in."

"I'm his less interesting and more accident-prone other half."

"Oh."

I stepped inside. I was really only half of the way home—what with still having to get into our actual apartment—but at least I wasn't standing on the New York streets without shoes anymore. I couldn't go back to the Emporium, and even if I did, there was no guarantee that either Calvin or Neil would still be there in order for me to bum keys or pick up my bag. And showing up at Calvin's precinct because I was locked out was... embarrassing.

I supposed I could ask a neighbor to call the super.

I reached into my back pocket for my wallet as I trudged up the last set of stairs. I heard someone else— about a flight behind me. While our apartment might have been refurbished into a chic loft, the building itself creaked and groaned and sighed with the ghosts of a previous century. I pulled out a credit card as I reached the top floor and walked to the end of the hallway. I stopped outside the door and stuck the flimsy plastic against the frame and dead bolt.

The odds were not in my favor.

I heard Dillon patter to the other side of the door and bark after a minute.

"Don't worry, bud. It's Dad's dumbass boyfriend, not a rob—"

The canister, held between my arm and body, was suddenly snatched from behind. An arm wrapped around my neck, forced me back against the firm body of a man, and started choking me. I dropped my wallet and card and grabbed on to the bicep with both hands. I coughed and fought for air. I clawed at his arm to free myself as black spots seeped into the corners of my vision.

I kicked a foot out and slammed my heel into the door.

The assailant grunted and adjusted his hold.

"Where're the other movies?" he growled, breath hot and wet against my ear. It smelled sickly sweet, like some kind of candy.

Other movies?

Dillon was barking more incessantly.

I wheezed and gagged as the assailant cut off my air, and in a last-ditch effort, pounded my foot against the door again. This time I got enough leverage that it sent the stranger backward, and he hit hard against the opposite apartment door.

"H-help!" I half screamed, half coughed.

"*Where are they?*" he shouted with renewed vigor, shaking me.

I heard a dead bolt turn and then the door behind us opened. "What the hell is—*whoa*!"

I met my new neighbor when Mr. Movie Aficionado and I tumbled into the apartment, knocked into him, and the three of us crashed to the floor. I flailed like a fish out of water as I escaped Movie Guy's hold. He was up and on his feet before I had a chance to catch my breath. He stumbled through the doorway, grabbed the fallen canister from the floor, and ran down the hall.

"Call the police," I told my neighbor, voice raspy sounding.

"What?"

Jesus Christ, were three words too many?

"*Police! Call!*" I ran into the hallway, feet slipping and sliding across the worn, polished wood.

Always wear your PPE! Unless you're chasing after some nutcase—then it might become a hindrance.

I danced from foot to foot as I yanked the booties off, then ran toward the stairs. I thundered down the steps, holding on to the railing with one hand and the wall with the other so I wouldn't go careening head over heels. I shoved the front door open and burst onto the sidewalk, looking to the left and to the right.

But there was no sign of my attacker on the busy streets of New York.

"Sebastian *Snow*?" Officer Shapiro repeated.

"Yeah. Snow. Not Sneeze, or Sleaze, or any combination thereof."

"I just meant—you're that guy."

"I might be."

"The one who stopped the dirty cop in February."

"Oh. Technically that was a detective with a gun," I replied.

"I know. Detective Winter. Popped that scum in the kneecaps." She looked me over briefly. "They say you're a bit crazy."

I sighed.

Shapiro returned to taking her report. "So how are you?"

"As the indifferent children of the earth."

"What's that?" she asked, pen hovering over the notebook.

"*Hamlet*," I replied.

"I'll assume it means you're fine." She took a breath and looked at me again. "Can you describe the assailant?"

"He came up behind me.... Taller, maybe six feet. Pretty damn strong. When we crashed into 4A over there," I continued, pointing across the hall at my neighbor, who was being interviewed by Shapiro's partner, "he got up and ran off before I could see his face."

"Hair color?"

"I'm color-blind."

"Okay…. Then can you describe what he was wearing?" she tried.

I shrugged. "It happened pretty fast. I don't have very good vision. I saw a hoodie."

She pursed her lips. "Anything else you can remember?"

I rubbed my chin. "He had a growly voice, but I think it was intentional. And his breath smelled like red licorice."

Shapiro didn't write the licorice thing down. "Would you be able to confidently pick him out of a lineup?"

"No," I admitted.

"What's this? Who called me?" My scary super was walking toward us from the staircase, arms spread out in a questioning manner.

4A raised his hand and pointed at me. "He's locked out of his apartment."

Super, seemingly unfazed by the presence of police, asked, "You lost key already? It's been *one* day." He held up a finger on his paw of a hand and waved it menacingly at me.

"I didn't lose it," I quickly answered.

"Then where is it?" Super asked.

"A crime scene."

Both officers looked at me.

"Why you not call Boyfriend?" Super continued. "I am *emergency only*."

"Boyfriend is at the crime scene with my key," I tried. "And my phone. And my shoes. Please unlock the door. I've had a day like you wouldn't believe."

Shapiro looked down at the mention of my shoes. "You've got some piss-poor luck."

"I know," I agreed.

But I finally got into my apartment.

After two break-ins, a dead body, no keys, an assault, police questioning, an angry neighbor who would probably never let me borrow a cup of sugar after tonight, and a regular workday that had included migraine-inducing Pete White and a former military fuck-buddy of Calvin's—I was *finally* home.

I shut the door, crawled onto the floor, and lay facedown.

Dillon barked at me.

My stomach growled in response.

And I never did pick up dinner.

Or condoms.

"Fuck," I said, voice muffled against the wood.

Dillon got closer and sniffed the side of my face.

"All right, all right." I heaved myself up to my knees and took a look around.

At least our furniture had been delivered. The new couch was pushed up against the windowed wall. The little dining table for two was assembled and standing beside a big pile of broken-down cardboard, thick plastic sheets, and discarded pamphlets on how to assemble affordable European furniture. Near the loft stairs was a partially constructed bookshelf, which I was sure was what Calvin had been doing before he was called into work. I wondered if the bed had arrived.

My shoes were upstairs anyway, so I climbed to my feet and headed in that direction. The last thing I wanted to do was leave the house after the energy I'd exerted to get here, but if I didn't take Dillon out soon, I'd spend the night cleaning up dog piss.

I paused as I reached the top of the stairs. The bed. Oh God damn, after months of sleeping on a couch or Calvin's too-small-for-two bed, this was a sight to behold.

It was huge and inviting—with lots of pillows and a fluffy-looking comforter. I sighed pathetically but stood my ground against its siren song and proceeded to dig out shoes from a still-packed duffel bag in the closet. I tugged the backs over my heels and made a quick exit down the stairs.

I picked up the landline phone sitting on an end table beside the sofa. Yes, I was fully aware that the necessity for a home telephone these days was quite miniscule. But I also knew my technologically inept self would come to depend on it eventually.

And by eventually, I mean the day after I had it installed.

I dialed Calvin's cell. He didn't pick up. I doubt he'd even programmed our home number into his address book.

"Hey," I said, once I'd been instructed to leave a message. "It's me." I held the phone between my ear and shoulder and rummaged through the table drawers. "Sebastian—obviously."

I moved to the matching table on the other side of the couch and pulled those drawers open. "This is the landline you swore was a silly purchase. I left my bag in Neil's car. I don't have my phone or keys—trying to find that spare—never mind, found it."

I straightened and tucked the extra set of keys into my pocket. "If an Officer Shapiro calls you…," I began, before deciding, no, no, discussing an assault over the phone would not bode well. "You know, I'll tell you about it when you get home. If you call back and I don't answer, I went for a walk with Dillon. Love you."

I ended the call and glanced across the room. Dillon was sitting in the middle of the packing mess, staring at me, his tail swishing back and forth.

With the feeling that Calvin's dog was eavesdropping, I held the phone close once more and dialed another cell. I sort of thought it'd be a combination of random numbers I'd have forgotten months ago, but muscle memory had kicked in, and before I knew it—

"Neil Millett. Please leave a message."

"Uh, hi. It's Sebastian. So, I left my bag in your car. Not that I need my cane right now, but it makes for a decent weapon and I've had a less-than-stellar night." I cleared my throat. "Anyway. If you see Calvin again this evening, could you give it to him? Thanks. Bye." I ended the call and set the receiver back on the charger. I looked at Dillon.

He cocked his head to the side.

"I found a body in a dumpster tonight, dog."

Dillon barked in response and stood.

"Then some guy tried to choke me out."

Dillon ran to the door, tail wagging.

"What's this world coming to?" I asked, following him. I grabbed his leash from a pile of junk, hooked it to Dillon's collar, and reluctantly left the house.

With the dog leash in one hand, I unlocked the door with the other, held a take-out bag between my teeth, and was greeted to a ringing phone.

"Errph—'ol ahn!" I shut the door behind us, removed the leash from Dillon, and tripped over the piled cardboard as I kicked off my shoes. The bag of Chinese food fell to the floor. I left it, rushing for the phone before whoever— most likely Calvin—hung up.

"Cal?" I answered breathlessly.

A moment of silence. "It's Neil."

"Oh. Sorry."

"It's fine."

I walked back to the abused sweet and sour chicken. I picked up the bag, and the plastic container of sauce spilled open all over the floor. I stared at the mess for a hot second before I just started *laughing*.

"Are... you okay?" Neil asked.

"No," I said between hysterical chuckles. "I'm exhausted, alone, CSU has my shoes, and I'm wondering if I can put ketchup on Chinese food."

"You sound hangry."

"*I am!*"

"I have your messenger bag," Neil said after a beat.

I grabbed a wad of napkins from the takeout and sopped up the sticky mess while simultaneously shoving Dillon away as he tried to lick the floor.

"I can drop it off," Neil continued.

"You don't have to do that," I muttered.

"Winter isn't around, so your options are limited."

"You drive a hard bargain."

"I should have been a prosecutor."

"Wow, did Neil Millett just crack a joke?"

"What's your new address?"

I gave Neil the street number and told him to buzz the apartment when he arrived. I set the phone aside after he ended the call, finished cleaning the sauce, and took the mess into the kitchen. I dumped the container and napkins into the trash, then went to the fridge. Usually the light from inside, combined with a dark room, hurt my eyes, but seeing as how I was still wearing my sunglasses because, *bag*! I grabbed the last bottle of beer, decided against using ketchup on the chicken, and left the room.

Since the table was inaccessible due to the mountain of shit, and with my luck, I'd spill what remained of dinner all over our new I-paid-*how-much*-for-it sofa—I opted for sitting on the floor. And there I remained, sipping beer, eating greasy chicken, and finally letting myself reflect on… well, everything.

Edison's brilliant assistant, W. K. L. Dickson, built the Kinetoscope. And someone, likely the crew behind the invention, shot footage of a man being brutally murdered.

Fast forward a century later, and that movie ends up in my shop. And in one day, the Emporium was broken into *twice*, someone had stolen half of the reel, left a kid dead in my alley, I was attacked, and the second portion of the film was snatched right from my own hands.

Where're the other movies?

I glared at the far brick wall, where the partial bookshelf was, and took another long swig of beer. Mr. Licorice must have been the dead kid's partner-in-crime, and he'd followed me home from the Emporium. What was important to note was that he'd snagged the reel of footage before he'd even grabbed me, which said something about his priorities. And when he did speak, he could have demanded anything from me—phone, wallet, blood type, my hand in marriage—but he asked for movies.

The *other* movies, to be precise.

So, did that imply the Kinetoscope had come with more than one canister? But it hadn't. Max and I had checked that crate inside and out. Or did—did he perhaps know about the murder spliced on the end? Were there more than one of *those*? Did that bring legitimacy to my suggestion that someone in modern times was somehow concerned about the content—be it uncovering who the victim and killer were, or perhaps even keeping those identities concealed? Or was this all nothing more than an elaborate attempt to hold me accountable for lost property?

I huffed to myself.

But why kill that kid? Brat though he might have been, no one deserved the fate he had. No one deserved to have their fucking body dumped as if it were actual trash. Maybe the kid wanted to call the whole thing off. Or maybe his partner didn't want to share the potential cash I'd be liable for?

And who was Mr. Licorice? I thought our suspicions of Pete had seemed legitimate. No one outside of my little circle knew about this footage except him. And Pete was well aware of what the Kinetoscope was. But even if he'd been working with the kid killed tonight… he hadn't been the one to attack me. Pete looked fairly strong, sure, but he wasn't tall enough. That, and while I hadn't seen Mr. Licorice's face, he'd gotten close enough that I'd have felt a beard on my ear, should it have been Pete.

Was there a third person involved? Or was I suspicious of Pete just because I didn't like him?

I shuddered when a very real thought occurred to me: If Mr. Licorice expected me to have more movies—which I did not—was my fate going to be found inside of a dumpster too?

The door buzzer nearly scared the shit out of me when it sounded, bouncing and echoing off the still-empty walls of the apartment. Dillon stood as I did and followed me to the door. He was a good dog. He'd protect me until Calvin got home. And be handsomely rewarded in biscuits.

I tapped the intercom button. "Hello?"

"It's Neil."

"Hang on." I hit the door buzzer, holding it down for a few seconds before letting go. I didn't unlock the door until he knocked, and I checked the peephole to be *certain* it was actually Neil.

Paranoid?

A little, yeah.

I opened the door, and Neil held out my messenger bag in one hand. "Thanks for coming all the way over." I accepted the bag and dug inside for my glasses case.

"I wasn't far away," he answered. "What happened to you?"

"Hmm?" I looked up as I removed my sunglasses. He became a blurry gray blob before I slid my regular glasses on. "What do you mean?"

Neil motioned to his own neck. "Are those bruises?"

"What?" I instinctively touched my neck and felt that telltale tenderness just under the skin. "*Christ*...." I dropped my bag on top of Junk Mountain to my left. "It's a convoluted story." I held the door open wider.

Neil glanced over my shoulder, likely surveying the living room, before reluctantly stepping inside. "What happened?" he asked again. He slid his hands into his trouser pockets.

I shut the door and turned.

Dillon was sniffing at Neil's leg and hesitantly wagging his tail. Neil didn't offer the pup any behind-the-ear scratches.

"Want a drink?" I asked. "We have tap water."

"No."

"Sit down?"

"I probably shouldn't," Neil stated.

I opened my mouth, ready to accuse him of pulling some alpha male bullshit and to knock it off because it's just a *chair*, but it occurred to me that Neil was simply being respectful. This wasn't *my* house. It was *our* house. And he was being very mindful of Calvin's personal, private space.

"We never did have that cup of coffee," I stated, voice sounding loud after the silence.

His smile was distant. "Another time."

Doubtful. I knew Neil would never be in the same headspace to say what he wanted when we'd been standing in front of the bank. And maybe it was for the best.

I simply nodded and soldiered on. "Someone attacked me."

His posture changed, and Neil grew more alert. "Someone—what the hell?"

"Calvin put me in a cab home, I got inside when a neighbor was leaving the building, and he must have slipped in behind me before the door shut. I got all the way up here, and when I was trying to figure out how to get inside without my keys, he grabbed me from behind and started choking me."

"Sebastian. Jesus! Did you—"

"The police were already here," I interrupted.

"And?"

"I filed a report, but he'd run off before I got much of a look."

"Did he rob you?"

"No. Well, yes, technically. I had a canister of film. He took that and wanted more movies."

Neil stared blankly.

"That machine you were fingerprinting at the Emporium is a movie viewer."

Neil took a hand from his pocket and held it up. "So this may have been the man who killed Dumpster John Doe?"

"He certainly wasn't after my Buster Keaton collection," I answered. Which, mind you, I'd lost when my apartment went up in flames. Calvin had recently replaced it for me. I think he enjoys silent comedies more than he cares to admit.

Neil walked toward me. "Show me your hands."

"What?" I held them both up.

"Out. Palms down."

I did as instructed.

"Do you know if you happened to scratch the assailant?" Neil carefully put his fingertips on my palms and raised my hands up for closer inspection.

"I don't think so. He wore a long-sleeve shirt—a hoodie."

"You keep your nails too short."

"For collecting the DNA of strange and unhinged men? My bad."

"Not now, Sebastian."

I sighed.

He let go of my hands and said, "Give me your clothes."

"I'm in a relationship that utilizes an ampersand. But thank you."

Neil pinched the bridge of his nose. "I know you're being a smart-ass because you're scared—"

"Whoa, who said I was scared?" I said, speaking over him.

Neil raised an eyebrow. "We dated for four years, Seb. It's not like we forgot each other's habits upon breaking up—the good, bad, and ugly ones. I'm trying to help, okay? Spare me the attitude."

I *was* scared.

Shit scared, if I was being honest.

I'd wanted to throw up most of the night.

My business had been invaded. My home wasn't safe. I felt *helpless*—like I was standing at the East River Greenway with a gun to my head all over again.

I needed Calvin. I needed him to wrap his arms around me, hold me against his chest, and whisper, "I'll protect you." Because Calvin never broke his word. But the world simply doesn't have enough heroes, and he was needed elsewhere tonight.

So if I was calm enough—*smart enough*—I'd be okay.

I could watch my own ass.

I'd managed to get this far in life.

I was just feeling… a moment of insecurity.

That was all.

I cleared my throat and took a step back. "I'll go change."

I walked through the living room and heard Dillon patter behind me, then stop at the bottom of the stairs as I went up. Once I reached the loft, I stood at the foot of the bed and undressed. I made a folded pile before finding my pajamas pants and tugging those on. I sifted through the T-shirts hanging up in the closet, picked one of Calvin's, and pulled it over my head. The scent was a brief comfort, but my reflection in the mirror on the door was a fucking joke, shattering the respite my partner's clothing had given. Calvin was a brick wall, all height and muscle. I looked like I was drowning in his shirt.

Too many cookies. A sedentary lifestyle. Soft hands from working with pages instead of firearms.

Maroon sweater.

Red socks.

"Stupid…."

Suck it up.

It would be okay.

Just another moment of insecurity.

That was all.

I yanked the shirt off, grabbed one of my own, and put it on. I found a paper bag on the floor from part of the moving mess, stuffed the day's clothing into it, took Calvin's shirt into my other hand, and went downstairs.

"Here." I held out the bag as I reached Neil once

again.

He took it and glanced at Calvin's shirt in my hand. "That too?"

I shook my head. "It's Calvin's."

"All right." Neil turned a bit, then paused. "Are you okay?"

"Yeah."

He knew. "If you want—no one will blame—" Neil paused and collected his thoughts. "I'll stay, if you want company. I'll call Winter and let him know so he's not, you know, taken off guard or something."

"Thanks... but... I think I'll be fine."

"You sure?"

I smiled and waved my free hand in an "ehhh" fashion.

Neil looked down at the bag of clothes. "I'll have these checked out for trace evidence."

"There's probably nothing," I said. "I went for a walk afterward and picked up dinner."

"Better to be safe." Neil started for the door. "Come lock this behind me."

I followed, murmured a goodbye, and shut the door. I glanced through the peephole. Neil was standing in the hall. I turned the dead bolt on the door, and when he heard it, he left.

Silence settled on my shoulders like heavy weights.

I wished my ego hadn't sent Neil away. I was sure he wanted to go to bed after a long day, but he'd offered to stay. And this apartment was new. Unfamiliar. I was still learning the sounds the building and its occupants made.

I walked across the room, and Dillon followed. I picked up a few throw pillows from the couch and tucked them under one arm. I grabbed one of the chairs from the partially buried table with the other, and dragged it to the door. I shoved the chair under the knob, made sure it was secure, then got down on the floor.

I put my head on one of the pillows and pressed Calvin's shirt against my chest.

Dillon lay down at my side.

If I was calm enough—*smart enough*—I'd be okay.

CHAPTER EIGHT

In that distant, hazy place where reality began to seep into dreams, I heard a key unlock a door. Then a knob turned—a thump and a creak.

I cracked open an eye and watched Dillon jump to his feet, staring at the front door just behind me. I sat up, fixed my glasses, and looked to see the chair holding firmly in place, despite someone trying to get into the apartment.

A knock.

Wait....

And another.

"Sebastian?"

The knob was twisted again.

I got up, dragged the chair away, and threw the door open. Calvin looked up, holding his cell to his ear.

The house phone on the opposite side of the apartment rang. Without a single second of hesitation, I leaped forward and wrapped my arms around Calvin's neck. The phone stopped ringing. His arms locked around me.

I took a deep breath, picking up notes of cinnamon breath mints, the lingering whispers of his cologne, and the city night. "I'm really glad you're home," I mumbled.

Calvin lifted me off my feet and silently walked us into the apartment. He set me down and, with one hand, shut the door and threw the dead bolt.

"What time is it?" I whispered, still holding on to him. The heat radiating from Calvin's body, the gentle *thump, thump, thump* of his heart against my own chest— they were a soothing balm over my stressed soul.

"Three in the morning," he answered, just as quiet. Calvin tilted his head and kissed my hair. "What's wrong?"

"Nothing that can't wait until daylight," I said, finally taking a step back. "Can we go to bed?"

It was sort of obvious I'd been scared—what with the chair—but Calvin looked as exhausted as I felt. He simply nodded and followed me through the dark apartment to the loft.

I set my glasses on the nightstand, pulled back the blankets on the bed, and collapsed on the new mattress. Calvin undressed and left his clothes on the floor to be dealt with later. He climbed in beside me in nothing but boxer briefs, tugged me closer, and wrapped his arms around me.

Heaven.

My arm was asleep.

I yanked it free from underneath Calvin and rolled over. My fingertips tingled as blood pumped back into them.

Calvin moved with me. He slid an arm underneath mine and pressed himself against the length of my back.

Waking up to fresh bedding and a powerful, living body at my side made me feel strong. Fear that had been worming its way back into my heart last night scurried away like a mouse after hearing the roar of a lion. It was a good thing. The insecurity and worthlessness that had cropped up alongside the very real concern for my safety had been almost too much.

I grunted. "No."

"No, what?" Calvin murmured.

"If you're awake, that means it's time to get up."

"We don't have to get up yet," he said, breath ghosting across the back of my neck.

"I don't want to get up *ever*," I corrected, speaking into the pillow.

"How're we supposed to eat?" Calvin asked, words still a little slurred from sleep.

"Delivery."

He chuckled and tightened his hold on me. "Pretty sure they don't offer in-bed service."

"An untapped market."

Calvin reached underneath my shirt and trailed his hand up my chest.

"Don't say it," I warned.

Calvin sat up on his elbow and kissed my ear. "I'll service you in bed," he said, voice deep and sexy, but I could hear the smile in his tone.

I laughed and looked over my shoulder. "What did I just say?"

"It was too easy."

"Usually I'd take you up on it, bad joke and all," I said as I rolled onto my back.

"You slept with your contacts in again."

"Fuck, I know." I rubbed one eye. "But we can't," I

continued.

"Why's that?" Calvin asked. He propped his head up and let his free hand caress my exposed stomach and hip.

"I threw out the condoms." I blinked a few times as the red-tinted contact adjusted itself.

"That was silly."

"It was like being stabbed in the ass by a lightsaber."

Calvin snorted and pressed his face against my shoulder. "Jesus, baby."

"And I never made it to the drugstore yesterday," I finished before glancing at him. "Unless you've stashed one somewhere for emergencies?"

"Sure, in my shoulder holster."

I cocked my head to the side. "What? Really?"

"You know what they say about protection."

I rolled my eyes and shoved Calvin. "You're so full of shit this morning."

He smiled and slipped his hand under the waistband of my pajama bottoms, then leaned in and kissed me. Deeply. Exploringly. Like we had forever and his alarm wasn't going to beep soon and demand the start of another day.

It was just me and him, and we were about to lose control.

Calvin broke the kiss, shoved the blankets off us, and held my arms as he rolled onto his back. He reached up, yanked my shirt over my head, and tossed it in the general direction of the laundry pile he started last night. He sat up and took my mouth again—harder, like a man who survived on kisses alone and he was starving.

Calvin bit my lower lip before pulling away. "I want to suck your cock," he groaned. "Do you want that? To fuck my face?"

"Have I ever turned down the offer?"

Calvin leaned forward and started nipping my neck, biting the spot that made my eyes cross.

The one thing I wasn't in the mood for that morning was dirty talk. From *me*—I should reiterate. I'd had enough blows to my ego in the last twenty-four hours. I really wasn't up to feeling like an awkward fool this early, even if Calvin insisted it was good for him.

"I want to suck you too," I said quickly. "How about at the same time?"

Calvin let up on my neck. He gave me the sexiest goddamn smile I've ever had the honor of being on the receiving end of, then threw me onto my back. I let out a yelp as I fell backward on the mattress. Calvin leaned over me—all muscles, freckles, thigh-hugging briefs, and *Christ*… I was going to bust a nut then and there.

"Can you stop being gorgeous?" I asked. "For like—ten seconds. Hold on." I closed my eyes and reached down to give my dick a firm *don't misfire* squeeze.

Calvin chuckled. His voice was so deep and beautiful that a conversation about toothpaste usually left my gut doing somersaults. Imagine how my balls felt when he was actually *trying* to be sexy?

"No talking either," I added before taking a deep breath.

The mattress shifted, and when I opened my eyes again, Calvin was entirely naked.

Fuck. I'd been looking forward to getting him in bed since yesterday. I was so amped up now, I wasn't going to last.

"I'm going to beat the alarm clock," I stated.

"That's all right." Calvin tapped my hips and pulled my pajamas off when I raised them.

"All the self-control of a teenager with their first dirty magazine. Flip right to the centerfold."

Calvin leaned over me. "My first was *Blueboy* and I spent on the cover."

"I had *Playgirl* hand-me-downs from onetime handjob buddy, Ethan Cohen."

"Yikes."

"Tell me about it. Some of those pages were stuck together. Man of the Month for February tore."

"Are you sufficiently distracted?" Calvin asked after a beat.

"What? Oh—oh yeah. I'm good."

He smiled and lay on his back. "Come up here."

Sometimes getting into positions necessary for letting someone put their mouth in interesting areas wasn't so much a game of sexy Twister, but one of "oops, sorry," "closer," and "ouch, fuck—no, I'm fine." In past relationships, I'd always felt embarrassed in those moments. I still did. But... less so, I guess. Sometimes. My subtle growth in self-confidence had been warring with my tendency to self-deprecate as of late.

It made being me more stressful than usual.

But then Calvin was underneath me, running his powerful hands up and down my asscheeks while sucking on the head of my cock, and I was stretched out across his body, holding his impressive girth in one hand and eyeing his dick like it was a first-place trophy in a competition I hadn't expected to even place in. There wasn't any room left for thinky-thoughts at that point.

I flattened my tongue and dragged it up the length and over the head of Calvin's cock. I wrapped my mouth around it, pumping the base in one hand and stroking his balls with the other. Calvin flexed and gently thrust his hips upward, groaning all the while. The sensation vibrated along my own cock, and *goddamn* did it feel so good.

Calvin dug his blunt fingertips into my ass, hard

enough to make me whimper, then smacked both cheeks.

"Oh fuck!" I cried out when his dick slipped free from my mouth. "*Cal*."

Don't stop, don't stop—don't make me say it.

He let up on me, took a breath, and asked, "Again?"

I leaned my head against his thigh and nodded vigorously.

Calvin gripped both cheeks. "Ask for it," he ordered.

The reason I'd even suggested this convoluted position in which there was a cock in both mouths was so I didn't *have* to speak. Hell, the only reason I tried sexy talk at all was because Calvin got off on it, and love was a two-way street. But even the promise of a delicious orgasm wasn't enough for me. I needed to be drunk in order to pull out the dirty words right now. And seeing how it wasn't even seven o'clock....

Damn it. I *had* been getting better at all of this. I'd gotten more confident in asking for what I wanted during sex because it *wasn't* something to be embarrassed by, and I had a partner who enjoyed it as much as I did. I hated that I was doubting myself so much lately.

And yesterday's events certainly weren't helping.

I swear I was a man of simple needs. All I wanted was to be able to say "please spank me" without having an existential crisis over it.

I opened my mouth to speak—but just couldn't. I was a mess.

"It's all right, baby," Calvin murmured. "Keep sucking."

So I did, and tried to put out of my mind that this was supposed to be awesome, christening-the-new-apartment sex, and that I'd ruined it.

"That's it," Calvin said, thrusting his cock deeper down my throat. "Such a sweet mouth." He smoothed his big hands over my ass before smacking it again. "You look so pretty—that ass in the air."

Calvin repeated the motion several more times, until my cheeks burned and stung and I was moaning and writhing on top of him. He grabbed on to my hips once more, guided me back enough so he could reach my dick, and took it into his mouth.

I let go of his cock with a wet pop, saliva glistening on his skin. Calvin was so fucking good at giving head—I wasn't going to—!

"*Cal!*"

He slapped my ass one more time, and a bullet of fiery-hot passion ran from my toes to my balls before I came hard enough to see stars. I dropped back down, resting my forehead on his muscular thigh as Calvin milked my orgasm for all it was worth. His cock was huge and erect beside my face, pulsing in time with his rapid heartbeat.

I shifted a bit, pulled myself free from Calvin's mouth, and started sucking on the head of his dick in between desperate attempts to get enough oxygen to my brain.

"Ah, yeah…. You like that big cock, don't you?" Calvin's voice was getting hoarse. He dug his fingers into my stinging, sensitive asscheeks and thrust up into my mouth. "Fuck, your mouth is so good—*shit*—baby!"

The first spurt of salty cum landed on my tongue, the second dribbling down my fist after I pulled my mouth off. I stroked Calvin until his groans had subsided. Awkwardly getting off him, I collapsed sideways on the bed, shifted to my side, and stared at the rumpled pillows by the headboard.

Calvin moved about on the mattress, pressed up against my back, and kissed my shoulder a few times. "That was good," he whispered. He reached his hand out for mine and threaded our fingers together.

"No, it wasn't."

He kissed my shoulder again. "I'll stop talking during sex."

"That's *not* the problem," I said firmly. "I like when you—I like it. Seriously."

Calvin waited.

"Never mind."

"I love you," he said.

"Yeah."

"There's nothing you say or do or need that's going to be embarrassing." Calvin pried his hand free from my death grip to stroke my hair briefly. "Having you truly enjoy yourself gets me off. I mean that."

"All right," I said, but my throat was weirdly tight and it came out more like a choked whisper.

The alarm clock started beeping.

Calvin climbed from the bed, turned the alarm off, and put on his dirty clothes from yesterday. "I'm going to take Dillon out."

I nodded but didn't get up until Calvin reached the stairs and started down. "Calvin?"

He paused and looked over his shoulder.

"I love you too."

He was too far away to make out clearly, but I was pretty sure he smiled. "I'll be right back."

I sat there, naked and still, until I heard the front door close. "I love you," I said again, louder. "And I'm sorry for the lackluster performances."

I stared at the floor as I came to the sad realization that what was really causing the self-doubt was the fact we'd moved in together. I'd moved in with Neil, after all, and that relationship had become a beautiful tragedy almost overnight. What if—? I squeezed my eyes shut and pressed the heels of my hands against them. No. I deserved better than to think what we had wasn't strong enough to achieve a Happily Ever After. *Calvin* deserved better.

I climbed off the bed, grabbed my glasses, and went to the bathroom. I left them on the counter, got into the shower, and let the room get warm and steamy as I tried to scrub myself clean of sweat and dirt and fear and copious amounts of insecurity. There were more pressing matters that morning—namely my unknown attacker, the story behind the Kinetoscope footage, and the fact that the Emporium was closed *again* due to a mystery.

I was out of the shower and shaving my face when Calvin appeared in the reflection. "That took a while," I said, trying to use a casual tone that suggested we'd woken, had *great* sex, and were continuing our morning routine as if nothing unpleasant had happened.

He grunted as he pulled his T-shirt and pants off and walked naked into the bathroom. "I think Dillon had to sniff every tree between here and Astor Place."

I raised my chin and felt underneath my jaw. Missed a spot. I turned the electric razor on again. "He seems to be real partial to the one outside of—"

"What's that?"

I glanced at Calvin in the reflection. "What's what?"

He came up behind me and pointed at my neck while meeting my gaze in the mirror.

"That's a hickey," I said with a smirk. "Which, thank you, by the way. Now I can look forward to side-eye and snickers from Max, and my father's chastising 'Don't let Calvin suck your neck' comments."

Calvin poked the bruise and frowned when I flinched. "I meant this."

"Er, well, that has a rather long story to it."

He let out a breath through his nose while staring at the ceiling. "God help me." He turned and stepped into the shower. "Is this in regards to whoever Officer Shapiro is?" he asked over the spray of water.

"Uh, yeah."

"Start talking."

"Well, you got my message then, about not having my phone or keys," I said as I continued getting ready for the day.

"Yes."

"Someone followed me into the building after the taxi dropped me off. I was standing outside of our door and this… guy attacked me."

Calvin pulled back the curtain. "He what? Who *the fuck* was it?"

I'll be honest—the slip of Calvin's, showing his defensive boyfriend side that was usually so well controlled, made me feel a little better.

I turned to him and made a shooing motion. "Finish." When Calvin closed the curtain once more, I continued regaling him with the tale of being choked, meeting 4A, and giving my statement to a cop who laughed at my luck—or lack thereof.

"*Other movies*," Calvin said at the end of my story, climbing out of the shower.

"That's why I'm convinced he was the second person at the Emporium," I clarified. "Otherwise, what the hell, you know?"

"And that's all he said to you?"

I shrugged. "Pretty much. Took the canister and ran away."

Calvin grew silent as he toweled off.

I left the bathroom, went to the closet, and found some clean underwear in one of my bags. "Neil came over," I continued, speaking loud enough for him to hear me. "He dropped off my bag. I told him what happened, and he took my clothes. Trace evidence." I dug out a pair of jeans and did the twist-and-shimmy to get into them.

Calvin walked naked across the bedroom. He reached around me at the closet to pull out a suit. "Did you get a badge number on Shapiro?" he asked.

"Oh, yeah. I figured you'd want to get the statement I gave her."

Calvin didn't respond immediately. He tossed his clothes on the bed, put his hands on my shoulders, and gently turned me to look at him. "I'm sorry."

"Why?"

"This is my fault."

"Calvin," I said firmly. "This is no one's fault, least of all yours. Hell, we could blame *me*. Usually I don't listen to you. The one time I did, I got into trouble."

He frowned. Calvin's sense of humor about these things was a bit lacking before coffee.

I reached up and put both hands on his face, pulling him close enough to press our foreheads together. "This is not your fault. Period. You sent me somewhere I should have been safe. No one could have predicted that the second guy was hanging close enough to the scene that he was able to follow me. I'm okay," I insisted. "Shaken up, but… *hey*, have you met the detective on the case? Mr. Invincible, I think the other cops call him. A real hero."

This close, I watched the muscles in Calvin's face soften. Just a little.

"*My* hero," I reiterated.

He finally smiled.

"Get dressed, handsome." I let go of him and grabbed a T-shirt from the closet. I studied it for a moment, then looked over my shoulder.

Calvin was staring.

"Blue?" I inquired, holding it up.

"Gray," he corrected.

"Oh thank goodness." I yanked it over my head and went downstairs.

I walked through the dim living room, the blackout curtains doing a fantastic job at blotting out the intense May morning light. Dillon got up from his haphazardly placed dog bed in front of the couch and obediently followed me to the kitchen. I ignored the awful, fluorescent overhead that needed replacing, in favor of a small lamp on the counter. I switched it to the lowest setting, poured kibble into Dillon's bowl, and then started a pot of coffee.

I spread some cream cheese on a day-old sort-of-stale bagel and took a bite. When I heard Calvin coming down the stairs, I grabbed a second bagel from the bag on the counter and dropped it into the toaster. God forgive me, I loved a man who preferred his bagels toasted. I opened a cupboard—no—another—for fuck's—and found coffee mugs in the one farthest to the left. I set two beside the pot, poured cream into each, and glanced up when Calvin entered the doorway.

"About today," he began, pulling his shoulder holster on.

"Emporium is closed, I know," I said.

"No," Calvin answered.

I perked up and turned around. "*Really.*"

He adjusted his pistol. "But I have some regulations about returning to work."

"Of course you do." Not that I was going to fight him—not after how sincerely scared I'd been last night.

"You're not to be alone. I mean it, Sebastian."

"Okay," I said. "I'll hold on to Max with my free hand in the bathroom."

Calvin ignored the smart-assery. "Don't stay late either. When you close, leave together."

"Fine."

"Keep your phone on you at all times."

"Calvin. I get it."

"This man from last night is dangerous," Calvin replied sternly. "He could have killed you."

"I don't need to be reminded of that," I muttered, pouring coffee into both mugs.

"After work, will you go to your father's for the evening?"

I put the pot back on the burner a bit harder than intended. "I live here. *With you*."

"Whoever this person is, they've zeroed in on you, baby. He knows where we live," Calvin continued. "He knows where and when to find you. You're not staying here alone until I catch this son of a bitch."

He was right, of course. And last night, more than anything, I'd wanted Calvin's protection and safety. I still did. But when he talked in his cop voice—I just couldn't help myself. It was like a knee-jerk reaction to ward off any perceived attack against my battered self-worth.

"My dad has a life," I answered. "He can't keep playing babysitter to his *thirty-three-year-old* son. I know what happened was bad, but you can't lock me up in a bunker."

"Sebastian, in the six months I've known you, you've been stalked, shot at, blown up, run-over, and nearly bludgeoned with a hammer," Calvin retorted, ticking the points off on his fingers.

"I didn't go looking for—"

"You sure as hell did," he interrupted.

I opened my mouth, closed it, then sputtered, "W-well, I didn't *this* time."

"I'm not arguing with you," Calvin said with a tone of finality.

"Yes, you are."

"*Sebastian*—!"

The bagel popped from the toaster. Calvin startled suddenly at the noise, almost comically so. But there was *never* anything funny when moments like this happened. The oddest sounds still shook him, especially when he was stressed or running on fumes. Something as innocent as a fucking toaster could spark Calvin's PTSD, send him back in time to witness a horror from war all over again.

He'd been seeing a therapist for a few months now, but let's be honest. It could take years before Calvin was able to swallow the guilt he carried with him and admit the lives lost overseas were not his burden to bear. This disorder might always be a part of him. The best we could hope for was managing it. A shouting match over the same old bullshit was not the way to go about keeping Calvin from slipping into the bad habits we'd both been working so hard to eradicate from his routine.

"Calvin." I immediately reached out to take his face into my hands.

He startled again.

"Stay here with me." I pulled him flush against myself. "Where are you?"

Calvin swallowed and took a deep breath. His eyes were a little glassy. "With you," he whispered.

"In our kitchen."

"In our kitchen," he agreed.

"In New York."

Calvin nodded. "New York," he echoed. He swallowed hard a few more times, as if he'd just been in a fight for his very life. A tear rolled down one cheek. "New York," he said again, a bit louder. He pushed his arms through mine and wrapped them around my back, letting his forehead rest on my shoulder.

I rubbed his back. "I'm sorry."

Calvin squeezed me tighter in response. His big frame and powerful muscles all but engulfed me. Dillon whined, and I craned my head to see him staring up at us. He raised a paw and scratched at Calvin's leg a few times.

I bent my knees and eased us both to the floor. "Sit right here." I waited for Calvin to rest his back against the bottom cupboards before I straightened. I put his bagel on a plate and offered it. "Take this." I grabbed our mugs next, then settled beside him. "And this."

Dillon had moved to Calvin's right side and put his head down on his thigh. That dog *knew* when he needed help being secured in the present. Pop couldn't have picked Calvin a better companion.

Neither of us said anything for a moment. I held Calvin's bicep and kept my head on his shoulder. Anchoring. Like Dillon.

Calvin petted Dillon with one hand. His other, wrapped around the mug, twitched. "It startled me," he finally said, before adding unnecessary clarification. "The toaster."

I nodded.

"I *know* it doesn't sound anything like gunfire," he continued, his voice thick.

"Being Detective Winter is easier," I said for him.

Calvin made a sound that was a mixture of a grunt and humorless laugh. "Yes."

I squeezed his arm. "I'm pretty fond of Calvin, though."

"I've been trying."

"You've been doing so well," I insisted, sitting up straight.

Calvin finally looked at me. "You think so?"

"I think so."

He took a deep, cleansing breath, set the mug on the floor, and picked up the now-cold bagel from his plate. "I don't think you're helpless."

"I know that."

"You're frustratingly competent."

"You're making me blush."

That made Calvin smile. "I didn't mean to get angry with you."

"Me neither." I leaned over and kissed his smooth, freckled cheek. "You're trying to do your job. I know that. I was just—" I swallowed the urge to lie. "Scared and overcompensating."

Calvin took a bite of his breakfast.

I sipped my coffee.

A silence settled between us again.

"What're you thinking about?" he eventually asked.

I raised my eyebrows and tapped the side of my head with a finger. "It's pandemonium up here. Sure you want to know?"

"It's remarkable," Calvin corrected.

Aw, shucks.

"I have an idea."

CHAPTER NINE

"A year ago I'd have said this was absurd," Calvin stated.

"You didn't know *me* a year ago."

Calvin checked his mirrors before making a turn at the end of the block. "You really want to go all the way to Queens?"

"That's where the Museum of the Moving Image is."

"You don't have to take the train, though. I can drive you."

"They don't open until after ten," I replied. "And I've no desire to wait around in the desolate, ass-end of Astoria with a bunch of overworked and undercaffeinated filmmakers. I'll go this afternoon. It's no problem."

"Whatever you want," Calvin answered.

I looked at his profile. "I appreciate the offer, though."

Calvin nodded, eyes on the road as he made his

way through morning traffic to the Emporium. "I guess I shouldn't be surprised there's a film history museum in the city." He drove past an open spot on the side of the road before quickly backing up to parallel park.

"Just be happy the Kinetoscope didn't come with a stag film," I stated.

"Why's that?" Calvin put a hand on the back of my seat and looked behind him as he worked his magic.

"It might have required a trip to the Museum of Sex instead."

"Gotta love New York," he murmured before putting the car in Park and turning off the engine.

I climbed out of the passenger seat and looked at the storefront.

The gate was down and the interior lights appeared off.

All was seemingly well.

Calvin stepped between bumpers, came onto the sidewalk, and opened the back door to let Dillon out. He handed me the leash, leaned against the car, and crossed his arms. God, he looked so cool without even trying.

"Max is on his way?" he asked.

"Yeah."

"You told him what happened?"

"Uh-huh."

Calvin retrieved a near-empty tin of mints from his coat pocket and popped a few into his mouth.

"Hey. What do you want for your birthday?"

Calvin crunched down on the cinnamon treats. He shook his head. "Nothing."

"Come on. It's *tomorrow*, and I'm a terrible present-picker-outer."

He crossed his arms again. "I don't need a gift."

"*Need* wasn't part of the question."

"I already have everything I could possibly want," he corrected.

I scoffed. "Aren't you romantic."

Calvin smiled.

"If you end up with a watch, it's your fault I panicked and bought something generic," I continued.

Calvin raised his arm and pulled the sleeve back to show me his nicer-than-I-probably-would-have-picked-out-anyway watch. "I already have one."

"Coffee mug."

"We just bought that new set."

"Shaving kit."

"I've been shaving for nearly thirty years. Safe to assume I've already got the necessary grooming products."

"How about a tie?"

Calvin glanced down at the one he was wearing.

"You're killing me," I stated.

"Boss!"

I turned to my right, recognizing Max's voice before I was able to correctly identify his shape on the sidewalk. Summer sunshine's a real bitch. "Hey," I called.

He jogged toward us, gave Calvin a high five, then looked at me. "How're you?"

"Fine. Thanks for coming."

"Well… I work here," Max said as he pointed at the Emporium. "Admittedly some days I'm less excited about that than others."

I made a face.

"Can we sage this place before opening?"

"No."

"Or call a priest," Max continued.

"Max."

"Because I am *so out* if Linda Blair shit starts happening next."

I ignored Max's commentary and walked to the gate. I unlocked it, and then Calvin came up behind me and hoisted the woven metal upward before I had a chance to. I unlocked the front door next, leaned inside to tap in the security code on the wall panel, and moved out of the way.

"Armed boyfriends first," I said.

Calvin stepped inside. He flipped the overheads on and started down one of the aisles. Max and I peered through the open doorway, waiting until Calvin deemed the shop clear of thieves and killers.

"The police department put a padlock on the back door," he said.

After letting the pup inside, I took Dillon's leash off, killed the overheads, and switched on some bank lamps. "Keep it on for now?"

"If you don't mind."

"No problem. I won't be able to accept any more oversized crates full of murder and mystery."

Calvin shook his head, pushed his suit coat back, and put his hands on his hips. "God, I love you," he said dryly.

I smirked. "Love you too."

Calvin stepped forward and kissed me. "No sleuthing today."

"Museums don't count," I said. For clarification purposes.

"Only barely." He looked over his shoulder at Max, returning from the counter. "Keep him on the straight and narrow," he said while pointing at me. "Or I'm arresting you too."

"Straight isn't gonna happen. But I'll call if he runs off with only his magnifying glass and delusions of being the World's Greatest Detective."

"Traitor," I muttered.

"I'm leaving," Calvin stated. He gave me one more look. "Will you go to your father's afterward?"

"Only if you promise not to pull an all-nighter. I mean it."

Calvin took a breath and nodded. "Promise." He reached down to give Dillon a few scratches behind one ear before he saw himself out.

After we opened for business, I was a bit distracted.

Not that anyone could really blame me.

I stood in front of the Kinetoscope, behind the counter, coffee cup in one hand, the other rubbing my chin. I scowled at the viewfinder, lost in thought. I was trying to convince myself I had simply been set up to be swindled, and that somehow those plans had gone astray after one of the contenders wound up dead in my dumpster. But the film itself was the object of desire, and it just wasn't worth anything in comparison to the Kinetoscope. And that was a four-foot-tall, heavy, old cabinet. It wasn't like the owner would have been stupid enough to think it could be hijacked from the Emporium and wheeled down Second Avenue with people none the wiser.

So it was definitely the footage they wanted. I supposed the owner could argue the historical value alone made it priceless, but it just seemed like an odd way to try to suck my wallet dry.

I glared harder at the Kinetoscope.

It did nothing in return.

"I figured out what you should get Calvin for his birthday," Max muttered, suddenly hovering beside me.

I jumped, spilled coffee, and spun. "*Jesus*. Don't

130

sneak up on me like that." I wiped my hand on my jeans.

"I had to break you out of that obsessive zone you get into." He pointed to his own forehead. "You've got that thinking-too-hard crease between your eyes."

I rubbed at my forehead, like the wrinkle was a stain I could wipe away. "What were you saying?"

"Birthday gift for Tall, Pale, and Ginger."

"And what's that?"

"Concealer."

"Conceal—huh?"

Max pointed at my neck. "To hide that *wicked hickey* he gave you."

"Make yourself useful. Go dust something." I turned back to the Kinetoscope.

Max left when the bell over the front door chimed. He welcomed the customer to the Emporium, and I stopped listening.

I'd have to call the shipping company again. As much as I wanted to believe a murder long-since past was what this all revolved around, solving it seemed about as likely as obtaining the little golden key had been for Alice after she shrank to only ten inches high. So I'd mostly focus on the present and help Calvin obtain a name to put to the Kinetoscope. I just hoped I didn't get Cindy on the phone again.

I crouched down in front of the Kinetoscope and leaned close. "Shit." I'd gotten coffee on the wood finish. I set the cup on the floor and wiped the base with the sleeve of my sweater.

My idea to visit the Moving Image museum wouldn't be of any real use to Calvin. It was mostly to satisfy my own curiosity about the footage and to gather historical facts about the Kinetoscope. Despite not having the film on hand to show curators, I hoped there was still an opportunity to glean *something* of mild interest relating to the boxing match. Or the murder.

You know. Either-or.

Believe it or not, I was quite happy with my recently acquired domestic setup. I wasn't looking to set my life on fire. But at the same time, this was a mystery *within* a mystery. If Calvin was taking care of today's murder, then who else was there to look into the one of another era but me? Even if I never got to the bottom of the long-ago death, I couldn't just ignore it indefinitely. Once upon a time, that victim had been someone. He had a story. And as a researcher, historian, and recovering sleuth, it was my job to share that story so he wasn't forgotten.

Near the base of the cabinet, where I'd been wiping the wood, a corner piece suddenly shifted.

"Oh no." I reached back, pulled my magnifying glass from my pocket, and got on my hands and knees to inspect the possible damage. "Don't you dare be broken," I said in a threatening tone. I touched the wood, and it gave way a bit more. I sat back on my knees quickly. "Max!"

"Boss," he answered from somewhere near the front displays.

"Come here."

"Ah, you should probably come here first."

Immediately, all I could imagine was my assailant inside, with a weapon, threatening Max. I jumped to my feet, turned, and saw a man with him near the door. The spike of adrenaline took a second to ease upon recognition.

I walked toward Max and patted his shoulder. "It's okay."

He looked at me like I was crazy. "You sure?"

"Yeah." I stared at Neil. When Max took an exit, I said, "Hey."

"Morning."

"If you've come for more of my clothes, take a hike."

I wouldn't say a smile crossed Neil's face—too strong of a description— but the glimmer of one perhaps. The sort of smile you could only see from the corner of your eye.

"I was driving by and saw you were open."

"You don't drive this way to work," I replied.

He put his hands into his pockets. "I wanted to make sure you were okay."

"Why wouldn't I be?"

"After last night."

"Everyone has a moment of weakness," I answered with a stiff upper lip.

Neil nodded. "I know."

He didn't say anything else, and I didn't offer further insight.

The tension between us at that moment could have been cut with a knife.

Finally, Neil exhaled. "All right."

"Fine."

We kept staring at each other.

"Good talk," I concluded. I started to leave.

"Sebastian, hold on."

I looked at Neil again.

"*Is* everything okay here?"

"Yes. Calvin even opened with me." I cocked my head to the side and shifted focus, going from Point A to Point Q, as Calvin liked to say. "When you were collecting fingerprints from the Kinetoscope, you didn't damage it, did you?"

"Oh hell, Seb. Do you think I got this job yesterday?"

Whatever sort of shaky truce there had been between

us was gone just like that.

"No. I mean—the bottom corner looks to be loose."

"The whole cabinet appeared to be wiped down," Neil said, not really answering my question.

"Uh, yeah. I did that after Max and I moved it behind the counter."

He frowned. "I only pulled a partial from the door."

"Get a hit on it yet?"

"Nothing from AFIS," Neil replied thoughtfully. Then he looked at me and held a hand out. "I'm not talking about an open investigation with you."

"What about an ID on Dumpster Kid?" I continued.

Neil crossed his arms. "I know there's nothing wrong with your hearing."

"It'd be nice if you'd tell me."

"So Winter can kick my ass seven ways to Sunday?"

"I'm trying to help."

"Helping never helps," Neil answered.

"You should be a motivational speaker," I replied.

Neil shook his head. "I'd nearly forgotten what a salty son of a bitch you could be."

"You started it."

A chuckle came from an unaccounted-for voice. I'd missed the bell over the front door entirely and was surprised to see Lee Straus, in another good-looking suit, standing not too far away.

He held up a hand. "I'm sorry for interrupting. You guys are funny."

Neil and I looked at each other.

"A real riot," Neil muttered, deadpan.

Lee made a beeline for me, forcing Neil to take a step out of the way. "I don't mean to be a bother two days in a row."

"Oh. Uh—no." I glanced at Neil and then back at Lee. I noticed he had a lanyard with a custom design around his neck and an ID card hanging from it. It stood out against his light-colored suit. I squinted a bit to make out—ah, his teacher's badge, I thought it was. With a motif of a sun rising over a hill? Not a school logo I was familiar with. "It's fine. Did you need something?"

"Calvin isn't here, is he?" Lee absently tucked the badge into his breast pocket.

"He's at work."

"I felt I came on a little strong yesterday," Lee continued. "Seeing Calvin was a bit of a shock. He all but vanished when we got out of the Army. I couldn't even find him through his family. We saw a lot. Together. I've always been a little worried about his transition to civilian life."

It's not that I disliked Lee as a human being. If Calvin had kept his company, he must have been okay. It was that I disliked Lee as a—a guy. He'd been out of the picture for far too long, and yet spoke like he and Calvin were still tight as hell. I mean, I got it. He was possessive, a bit jealous, and definitely offended that he was him and I was me and Calvin chose Frumpy Dumpy Sebastian Snow. But he wasn't sorry for how strong he had come on.

He was there to rub salt in my wounds.

"A lot of the guys used to say he was heartless— nothing shook him. But that isn't always a valuable skill in the real world," Lee murmured.

I remembered one of the photographs Calvin kept hidden in a box.

Of him in uniform, dirty and missing his helmet, holding a crying child.

"Heartless is going out of style here in New York," I

replied. "Mr. Invincible is more popular these days."

Lee smiled. "Yeah? Suits him." He made a flippant gesture with his hand. "Anyway. He seems happy with you, so I wanted to give my blessing."

I narrowed my eyes. "I wasn't aware I needed your approval." Okay, maybe that came off a bit dickish. But my choice in words didn't seem to bother Lee.

"Calvin used to be my boy—well, we used to see each other."

Over Lee's shoulder, Neil slowly leaned into my line of sight.

"It was pretty serious," Lee continued.

Neil had an eyebrow raised as he made eye contact with me. I could almost hear him asking, "Want me to butt in?"

It was nice of him.

I took a deep breath and gave Lee a fake smile. "What's past is past."

Lee met my fakeness. "I suppose so."

Neil cleared his throat. "Mr. Snow and I were discussing business."

Lee looked behind him, like he'd completely forgotten Neil was there. "Oh! I'm sorry. I believe you two were somewhere around 'salty son of a bitch,'" he said in amusement.

I *really* didn't like Lee.

Neil pushed past him. God bless the man, his pricklier-than-a-cactus personality was turning out to be beneficial for once. He stood sideways to look at Lee. "We're capable of insulting each other without assistance."

Before any of us could speak again, there was a shot.

Cracking glass.

And the front window of the Emporium exploded.

CHAPTER TEN

I hit the floor hard enough to have the wind knocked from my lungs.

Neil had his body draped over my own, his head lowered beside mine.

Another shot splintered the air.

"*Holy shit*!" Max screamed from somewhere.

"Stay down!" Neil bellowed in response.

A third round sounded louder. Closer. Like it'd ricocheted off the pillar beside the register. Neil tensed above me. A fourth hit the distinct sound of hard plastic and gadgetry. Somewhere in the back of my mind, I realized the security camera near the door had been shot.

Then... I heard nothing.

Nothing but ringing and blood pumping in my ears.

Neil raised his head, looking down at me with an intensity I'm not sure I'd ever seen before. "Are you okay?"

"I think so."

He sat back on his knees and looked over his shoulder. I sat up on my elbows. The front window was gone, broken and shattered into a hundred thousand little pieces across the floor and nearby displays. New York City ambience drifted into the shop.

At least it wasn't raining this time.

Neil got to his feet and held a hand out. "Call 911," he said as he helped me stand.

"I already am," Max's scared voice said from somewhere behind the counter.

"Winter, then," Neil told me before stepping away.

"Wait, Neil!" I grabbed his arm. "It's dangerous."

He pulled his pistol from his holster. "Sebastian," he said in a quiet, unreasonably calm tone. "Call Calvin."

I blinked a few times and nodded. I reached into my pocket for my phone, chose Calvin in the contacts, and put it to my ear.

Neil was walking to the front door. Lee got off the floor, said something to him, and followed close behind. Ex-Army did what ex-Army wanted, I supposed.

Calvin didn't answer and I got his voicemail.

"Shit. Shit." I hung up and tried Quinn next. I started moving down aisles and checking behind displays. "Dillon? Come here, buddy," I called as the line rang.

"Hel—"

"Quinn," I said, cutting her off. "I need to talk to Calvin."

"*Yeah*… then you called the wrong number, didn't you?" she countered.

"He wasn't answering."

"He's on the other line. *Working*. Stop shouting, Sebastian."

"I need you guys at the Emporium." I got down

on the floor when I found Dillon hiding behind a table. I reached out, let him sniff my hand, then gently petted his head. "Someone just shot the place up."

"Dude, no offense, but today fucking sucks," Max said.

"No offense taken."

I stood at the counter, assistant on one side of me, dog on the other. Dispatch had sent more cops than I could count, and the dimly lit Emporium was strobing like a rave party from all the cruisers parked outside. Lee was near the pillar, and a uniformed officer was taking his statement. Neil was standing outside on the sidewalk, talking with a few more cops.

"Someone's out for you, Seb," Max muttered after another minute had passed.

"Figures."

"What do you mean?"

"Oh, just, you know. If it's not some nutcase stalker or vigilante, it's this." I held my hands out toward the shop floor. "Whatever *this* is." I looked at Max. "What do you think of the possibility of someone trying to sue me for their property being stolen?"

Max made a face and jutted a thumb over his shoulder. "What, the Kinetoscope?"

"Yeah."

He didn't seem convinced, but said, "I guess it's a possibility."

"It's the only one that doesn't seem too fantastical to be true," I answered. "The 1890s murder is fascinating, but there was a killing in the alley that takes a bit more precedence."

"One of us could be next," Max said with an audible

swallow.

I cleared my own throat. "Last night, when that fuckface asked for the other movies… maybe there was a second package that was delayed or lost by the delivery company—what? Why're you smirking?"

Max leaned forward to rest his elbows on the counter. "You said fuckface."

Lee climbed the stairs just then to stand on my left at the counter. "I was told we can't leave until the lead investigator gets here."

"Fantastic," I muttered. I'd really had all I could stomach of Lee.

Lee looked at me, away, then back. "What's wrong with your eyes?"

"Nothing." I took off my glasses, set them aside, and tilted my head a bit to try to stop the shaking. "Nystagmus."

My dancing-eyes condition was nowhere near as bad as when I was a kid. These days it was hardly noticeable unless I got really stressed out. And I was usually pretty chill, almost to a fault. Although, at that moment, I could do without Calvin's ex in my personal space, being a living reminder of everything I wasn't.

The cordless phone beside the register rang.

Max just laughed. "We're closed," he said at it.

I reached for the phone, missed, fumbled, and grabbed it. I put my glasses back on before hitting a button. Among all the cops and chaos surrounding me, I said, "Snow's Antique Emporium."

My ear was immediately filled with Glenn Miller's "Moonlight Serenade." I could hear someone mutter and the handset of a phone get jumbled around.

"Ah—hello? Hello? My name's James Robert. Can you hear me now?"

"Yes, sir. How can I help you?"

"I'm looking for the owner," he said, a bit too loudly, and I had to pull the phone back.

"That's me. Sebastian Snow."

"Did you get my package?" he asked next, barely letting a breath settle between introductions and the heart of the matter.

"Excuse me?"

"My package, boy!"

All right, Jim Bob. No one but my pop gets to refer to me as a kid.

"Would you mind being a bit more precise, Mr. Robert?"

"The Kinetoscope!"

I felt my heart beat a little faster. "You're—wait, you're the owner of the Kinetoscope?"

"*Seb*," Max murmured, nudging my arm.

"Hold on," I hissed. "Sir, it's sort of difficult for me to talk at the moment—"

"That's all right," he answered. "I have more tin cans to show you."

"Tin—film reels?" I asked. I could hear someone to my left crunching through glass strewn across the floor.

"It'd be easier on an old man if you came to my place."

"Okay… uh… today?"

"I'm ancient. I sure as fuck ain't got faith in tomorrows."

He started reciting an address, and I dived for the nearest writing implement. I grabbed a marker, yanked the top off, and looked around for something to write on, before I began scribbling on the back of my hand.

"Building's got a red door."

"Red door," I repeated, like that meant something

to me.

Max nudged me hard in the ribs.

I ignored him. "I'll be there as soon as I can, Mr. Robert."

"See you, kid." There were a few obnoxiously loud beeps in my ear before he figured out how to end the call.

I set the phone down, planted both hands on the counter, and looked at Max. "*What*?"

He stared at me while pointing at the opposite side of the counter.

I followed his motion and saw none other than Calvin. Relief flooded every muscle in my body, nearly causing my knees to buckle. "Cal." I moved around Max and went down the opposite set of stairs from Lee.

Calvin had that expression I didn't like—the one I'd be only too happy to never see again for the rest of my life. Jaw clenched too tight, lines in his face a bit too pronounced, his pretty, crystalline gray eyes murky, like river water after a storm.

"Hey." I reached out and gave his hand a squeeze.

Calvin sighed. It was such a gentle sound—I could nearly hear the heartbreak in it. As if he'd truly been expecting the worst upon entering the shop. His sigh pierced my skin, cracked bone, and impaled my heart as if it were all no stronger than the flesh of an apple.

"Hey," he said in return, voice a bit gruff. He gripped my fingers tight and raked his free hand through his hair. "Everyone's okay? No one needs to see an EMT?"

"We're fine," I insisted.

He nodded. Calvin looked up at Max and panned to Lee. "What're you doing here?" he asked, a bit of surprise betraying the authoritative cop tone he put back on.

"Hoping to leave," Lee replied with a small chuckle. "Are you the lead investigator we're waiting on?"

"Did you give a statement yet?"

"Of course."

Calvin let go of my hand and flagged a uniformed officer over. "Mr. Straus is good. Arrange to have him driven home."

The cop motioned for Lee to follow. "Right this way, sir."

Lee glanced at the three of us before letting his shoulders drop a bit. "Stay safe, Mr. Snow. It sounds as though you've stuck to someone like a tick and they're trying to burn you off."

"How kind of you," I said.

"Max," Calvin ordered next as Lee headed toward the door.

I turned and patted Max's shoulder as he stepped down to my side. "I'll call you."

He surprised me with a back-breaking hug. "Don't get yourself killed, boss."

"*Me?*" I managed to wheeze. "Never."

Max reluctantly let go. He walked toward the door and followed an officer outside.

Calvin looked at me. "Let's go."

He wasn't going to get a single complaint out of me.

I went into the office, switched to sunglasses, collected my bag and Dillon's leash, then returned to the register. I picked up the dog and followed Calvin across the glass-strewn floor. The May sun was blinding when we stepped outside. I looked down at the ground, following close behind Calvin's steps as he led the way down the block. I nearly gave him a flat tire when he stopped abruptly.

"—Completely different MO than yesterday." That was Neil's voice.

I set Dillon down on the sidewalk and shielded my

eyes as I looked up. Neil stopped talking and turned to look at me and Calvin. Quinn stood beside him, rolling an unlit cigarillo between two fingers.

"The murder and shooting are related," I said.

Neil's gaze shifted to Calvin and he remained silent.

I looked at Calvin too.

"Let me find a black-and-white to drive you—" he started.

"That seems more plausible to me than two completely unrelated incidents taking place less than a day apart at the same location," I started.

"But there's no evidence they're related," Neil answered.

"Sure there is," I replied. "We know there's *at least* two people involved."

"One's dead," Quinn pointed out.

"When someone kills with a knife, it's up close and personal," Calvin added. "The mindset is different from standing outside the Emporium and shooting through the windows."

"So maybe there are three people involved," I answered. "One is dead, one prefers knives, the third a gun."

The three detectives stared at me, and let me tell you, even having done absolutely nothing wrong, it was unnerving when their expressions were *all for you.*

"No?" I asked at length.

Neil shook his head.

"Highly improbable," Calvin answered.

"Sebastian may be onto something, though," Quinn said. "Not three suspects, but that the events are indeed related." She looked up at Calvin. "We know whoever killed John Doe doesn't have a weak stomach. And how easy would it have been to do the same to Sebastian last night?"

I swallowed the distinct taste of bile trying to come up my throat, and caught Neil looking at me. I squared my shoulders and said nothing.

"But it sounds like they want more from Sebastian," Quinn continued. "And that they're convinced these *movies* must be obtained through him. Shooting up the Emporium may in fact be dangerous escalation—scaring him into cooperating, perhaps."

"Except I don't have any other movies," I pointed out.

Quinn shook her head. "They might not be aware of that fact."

"Why is this footage so valuable to the suspect?" Neil asked. "Was it dipped in gold?"

"Blood is more likely," I answered. "The way I see it, if we want to follow the clues in a conservative manner, this has a money-making scheme written all over it. And the poor kid in the dumpster may be nothing more than the victim of a greedy partner unwilling to share whatever cash the Kinetoscope owner tries to hold me accountable for. But if you're willing to suspend your belief a bit, my assailant, who we suspect may also be the murderer, came after me to steal the second portion of the footage that had a century-old killing on it. It had nothing to do with the Leonard-Cushing boxing match. So what if there is a connection between the past and the extremely shitty events happening right now?"

Neil rubbed his forehead like he had a headache, then made a gesture at Calvin. "He's all yours."

I gave him an annoyed look. "*Pig heart*, Neil."

Calvin put a thumb and finger to his mouth, whistled loudly, and waved at what I guessed was a patrol car parked across the street. He turned to face me. "I'll make sure the Emporium is taken care of."

"If you believe I'm not going to research this, you think far higher of me than you ought to," I replied.

"Research to your heart's content," Calvin said. The patrol car pulled up to the curb behind him. He took me into his arms and hugged me tight. "Just do it from your father's couch."

"Kiddo!" William Snow exclaimed as he opened the door to see me hiking the stairs to his apartment.

"Hey, Pop," I replied. I gave him a hug in the doorway. My police escort had made certain this time that I got inside safely, and without an attacker on my heels.

"What're you doing here?" He stepped aside and let me enter the home.

"I've had a long day," I answered, crouching to unclasp Dillon's leash. He immediately ran to Maggie, both wagging tails and sniffing butts.

Pop was consulting his watch as he shut the door. "It's not quite noon."

My shoulders drooped. "Fuck."

He came up behind me, took my shoulder, spun me around, then started patting my hair down. "You're a grown man, Sebastian. Comb your hair."

"I was recently rolling on the floor."

"I can see that. Don't let Calvin suck your neck."

"What? No. No—I was on the floor with Neil. I mean—*not*…. Can I have a beer?"

Pop took a step back and gave me The Look. "Not at 11:45."

I pulled my messenger bag off my shoulder and set it on the back of the couch. I walked to the table near the windows. The blinds were drawn—the home always dim and welcoming as if Pop could just sense I was dropping by. I collapsed into a chair and pulled my sunglasses back to rest on my head. Pop joined me a moment later. He put his hands on the back of a chair beside me but remained standing.

I glanced up at his detailless, blurry figure.

"Oh, Sebastian."

"*How*?" I protested. "How do you know without me having said anything?"

"I'm your father."

"Does that mean you were bestowed clairvoyance upon the auspicious day of my birth?"

"Despite having a detective and sleuth in the family, I don't have to be either to know when something's wrong."

"Uh-huh."

"And when it comes to you, kiddo…."

"I know." I leaned back in the chair.

"Are you in trouble?" Pop asked.

I slipped the sunglasses down again so I could actually see Pop's expression. "Everything will be okay. Calvin's on the case."

"Sebastian."

"Someone broke into the Emporium yesterday and ended up dead in the alley."

His eyes grew wide. "Oh my God."

I stood, stepped toward him, and put my hands on Pop's shoulders. "*I'm* fine, though." No way in hell could I or would I tell Pop the full story. I was not looking to put my father into an early grave.

Pop was quiet for a moment. He reached up and put his hand over mine, giving it a squeeze. "I'm going to make us some tea."

Yuck.

He stepped back and wandered into the kitchen. I lazily followed. Pop was filling a kettle with tap water when I joined him at the long counter space.

"How's Neil involved in all of this?"

"CSU has less than fifty detectives working all the boroughs, Dad. He was bound to end up on Calvin's cases sooner or later."

Pop put the kettle on the stovetop and gave me a brief look.

"I hit Neil with a door yesterday."

He quickly put a hand over his mouth, and I realized after a moment that he was suppressing a laugh. "Is he okay?"

"Actually, I don't know. He was almost pleasant today. I could practically stand him. I might have knocked something loose."

"Sometimes you'll never love someone, kiddo. But when you stop forcing it, you might end up liking them instead." Pop took some mugs from the cupboard and dropped a tea bag into each. "Maybe that's all your relationship was meant to be." He looked at me again. "Friends."

"Let's not get carried away." I turned, opened the cupboard in front of me, and moved aside cereal and granola bar boxes, hunting for my dad's candy stash.

"With all of this happening, have you boys even gotten to enjoy the new apartment?"

"Not really." I shut the cupboard and tried the next one. "Pop?"

"Hmm?" He reached out, closed the cupboard I was pawing through, then opened a drawer, revealing bags of hard candies and taffy.

"Thanks."

"*Pop*, what?" he prompted.

I glanced up from spinning the wax paper. I pulled the single piece of taffy free while mulling over my choice of words. "Never mind." I put the candy in my mouth.

Pop reached out and patted my cheek. "What's on your mind?"

I laughed because, Jesus Christ, was *that* a loaded question. I started folding the paper into a tight wad. "I should double-check the mail forwarding because I haven't gotten even a single preapproved credit card at the new apartment. I hate the Emporium's new landlord—I'm still waiting for him to cash the rent check. Did I turn off the kitchen light before leaving the house this morning? Was that recently acquired ambrotype photograph of a boy in a tartan hand-tinted? I'll have to ask Max because I can't see color. I should start working out, except I hate strenuous activity. I do like sex, though. I'm probably the worst lay Calvin's ever had."

"Whoa, whoa," Pop said, quickly putting his hands up.

But there was no stopping it. Just all at once, everything that'd been pent up for weeks—months. *Fucking decades*—just came out like a tidal wave.

"I'm such a hypocrite," I continued, feeling hot tears pour down my cheeks. "Demanding Calvin be honest with me and I can't even tell him what I'm thinking. I lie and make some smart-ass comment to hide every single insecurity I have, because if he had any idea, God knows he would have never gotten involved."

"Sebastian," Pop tried.

"But I can't fucking hide it anymore. Even Neil's noticed. I'm not as brave as I pretend to be. Last night—last night I was so scared. I wanted Calvin to come home and *hold me*, and I told Neil, oh no, I'm okay. Just a little itty-bitty moment of weakness!

"I'm lame in the sack. No matter how hard I try, I know I'm not sexy. I know I sound stupid and look stupid, and Calvin's just being polite. I wore *red and green* yesterday. I met Calvin's ex, and he's stylish and handsome and—and I just love Calvin *so much!*" I wrapped my arms around Pop's neck and sobbed out every single dark and bitter emotion I had in my heart. "I feel like it's only a matter of time before our relationship ends like the rest of mine have."

My dad ran his hand up and down my back, like he used to when I was a kid, coming home from school—bullied and alone. I'd later perfected the art of pretending like I didn't give a shit.

Except that had been a lie. I always gave a shit.

I liked myself when I was happy and confident. I liked when the world wasn't gray—no pun intended. I wasn't looking to make a one-eighty in personality. I was always going to be a bit of a crotchety grump. But the self-loathing as of late? The buildup had been worse than I'd ever cared to admit. After last night's scare and the extreme emotions of inadequacy that'd accompanied it, I wanted it to stop but felt caught up in a vicious cycle. I hated it.

Pop stepped back, gently pulled off my sunglasses, and set them aside. He took my face into both hands. "I love you so much, son. No matter how alone or hopeless or rejected I felt after your mom left, there you were to always guide me home."

I swallowed and concentrated on breathing.

In.

Out.

Again.

"Calvin has probably let you see him at some of his darkest moments, would you agree?"

Thrashing in his sleep. Sobbing in a diner bathroom. The fearful, faraway look before being brought back to reality.

I bit my lip as it quivered, and nodded.

Breathe.

In.

Out.

Again.

"And you've probably held him and comforted him?"

"Y-yes."

"Why won't you trust him to do that for you?"

"Because it's not the same," I whispered. My throat hurt.

"Never compare pains, Sebastian," Pop said. "Yours are just as real."

Remember to breathe.

In.

Out.

Again.

Pop reached for something on the counter, then wiped my cheeks dry with a napkin. "Let him be a lighthouse when things get dark. When you have doubt and fear, tell him. What was it you call him?"

"Knight."

Pop nodded. "You have to tell him what you need to be protected from. Otherwise he'll fight any and everything trying to figure it out. That'll only sow the seeds of contempt."

"What if he doesn't care?"

And there it was. Through all the waste and filth— the kernel of truth.

What if Calvin didn't care?

No one else ever had. Every man I'd been romantically engaged with, at the end of the day, just *hadn't cared.*

Pop took my face into his hands again. "If more people had partners that looked at them the way Calvin looks at you, kiddo, the world would have far more love and less hate in it."

Breathe.

I took in a deep, gasping breath and felt my insides alight.

"It's okay to not be the strongest or the bravest," Pop continued. "It really is. He loves you for your wit and intelligence. Your humor and your charm."

"I'm not handsome."

"Beauty is in the eye of the beholder." He smiled and let go of my face. "And of course you're handsome. Look whose genes you have."

I laughed, although it sounded kind of pathetic, and carefully dabbed at the corners of my eyes. "I'm so sorry you had to see that." My mouth worked, but even though I felt drained and oddly clean inside after that sobfest, my lip wouldn't stop quivering. "I feel better, though," I added.

"I'm glad."

The kettle started whistling loudly. Pop moved to take it off the burner.

I used my T-shirt to wipe my face dry one more time. "I know he loves me." I looked up at the fuzzy outline of Pop. "He came out for me." "That's true," Pop said, pouring the water into the mugs. He set the kettle down and faced me again. "And did you ever stop to think, his ex is precisely that?"

"An ex?"

Pop nodded. "Instead of comparing yourself to

153

someone who came before you, consider the reasons why what the two of you have works better."

Huh.

"What does Calvin think of you talking to Neil?"

"He doesn't care."

"Probably because he focuses on the fact that you two function in sync and not against each other, like you had with Neil."

I leaned back against the counter. "Straus and Winter sounds like a tax firm."

Pop laughed softly. "A bit."

"Snow and Winter sounds like…."

"A happy accident?" Pop supplied.

I picked up my sunglasses and fiddled with them for a moment. "Sounds like forever."

CHAPTER ELEVEN

"Is it okay with you if I stay the night?"

Pop set down his empty mug and reached across the table for one of the last cookies on the plate. "If I knew you liked the couch so much, I'd have given it to you as a housewarming gift."

"The request comes from Calvin," I clarified.

"Do *you* want to stay the night?"

"A little." Calvin was right to be wary of the apartment. My gut was telling me to steer clear without some sort of backup, and my gut had kept me alive this long. "Just until Calvin gets off work," I added.

"Then, of course."

My cell rang. I picked it up from the tabletop. "One sec, Dad." I stood and answered the call. "Hey."

"Hey, sweetheart. I'm sorry I only have a minute—I'm between locations."

"It'll be the best sixty seconds of my day."

"Is that so?"

I shoved my free hand into my pocket as I wandered across the living room. "Really needed to hear your voice."

Calvin paused for a beat. "Are you all right?"

"Yeah," I answered quickly. I paused at the couch, raised my eyes to the ceiling, and blew out a breath. "No. I will be."

"Sebastian?"

"Don't worry," I continued. "All limbs are accounted for and I'm not bleeding profusely. Can't ask for much more than that, can you?" I walked a bit farther away from the table at my back and said in a low voice, "I just mean—I like you, you know?"

I could feel the tension over the line ease a bit.

"I like you too."

"What're you doing?"

"Heading back to the precinct."

"Were you able to collect any shell casings? In my statement, I said there were four shots."

"Nothing was found," Calvin said.

"That's weird. Maybe it's an old gun?"

"To not leave behind casings?" Calvin asked. "We'd be looking at black gunpowder and lead balls. Which would have been how long ago?"

"Prior to the 1860s."

"Thank you. It's more likely the shooter collected them."

"I don't think there was enough time for that. Neil and your—uh—Lee, went after the suspect."

I think Calvin caught that, but he didn't remark on it. "We'll find out soon enough. Millett's digging one of the bullets out from the pillar near the register."

"I've been thinking of changing up the shop interior, but the rejection of aesthetics is a little bit too Dada for me."

"I'll only start to worry if you install a urinal on the showroom floor and call it art."

I chuckled.

"I'm not totally ignorant of your world."

"You've no idea how happy it makes me."

I could hear Quinn mutter in the background, followed by the blaring of a few car horns.

"I need the name of that shipping company used for the Kinetoscope," Calvin said.

"Why's that?"

"So I can get a warrant and obtain the shipper's information—since they gave you the runaround."

I glanced down at my hand. Jim Bob's address was still scribbled on the back, albeit a little smudged after all the tears from earlier. "Uhm… Barnes Brothers Shipping."

"Thanks."

"What about the kid?" I asked.

"What about him?"

"Any idea who he is?"

"I'm still waiting to hear if he has any official connection to the Javits Center Antique Fair. All the people who can answer questions are 'unavailable.' He had some sort of ID on him, but it wasn't plastic."

"A paper ID?"

"Mm-hm. Folded one too many times and stuffed into a sweaty back pocket."

"Fabulous."

"Forensics is trying to decipher it." A car door opened and shut. "I've got to go."

"Sure. I'll see you tonight."

"Bye, Seb."

"Bye, Cal."

I lowered the phone, pressed End Call, then turned and walked back to the table.

"How's Calvin?" Pop asked.

"Good. Just checking in between crime scene and precinct. Dad, do you know of any schools in the city that supply paper IDs to their students?"

"Like colleges?"

"I'm thinking so." I'd pegged the kid as being eighteen—twenty, tops. Pop leaned back in his chair. "I can't think of any. The plastic ones obviously last longer. Plus, they have the barcodes on the back so students can make purchases or check books out of the library with ease. You had one like that. My old teacher's ID was the same."

I nodded thoughtfully. "What about those academies you see advertisements for in the subway? That host summer workshops or those intensive two-week courses."

Pop put his hands behind his head. "I'm not sure. Some may supply paper IDs—what with the high turnover rate of students. Why?"

I looked down at my hand, tapping the address with my finger. "Just thinking out loud. Do you mind watching Dillon for a few hours?"

"Of course not. I was thinking of bringing Maggie to the dog run anyway. Do you have somewhere to be?"

I hated the subway.

It wasn't the heat, stale air, smell of piss and garbage, or that the rats were big enough to wield knives. The tunnels were over a hundred years old and the system was in use 24-7. *That* was an impressive feat of engineering which I tried to always marvel when I was underground.

And it wasn't the lack of personal space that

bothered me either—I was a born-and-bred New Yorker. If I didn't have someone's armpit in my face during rush hour on the Uptown 6, I'd be concerned I'd gotten on the wrong train. It was the lighting inside the train cars that I despised. The newer ones were so goddamn bright that even with sunglasses, the world was washed out to white and the faintest of grays. If I was alone, it meant having to rely on my walking cane.

Usually I'd have opted for a taxi, but after first and last month's rent, plus a security deposit on the new apartment, let alone Calvin and I basically buying all new furniture, I was dead broke. So the choice between using my MTA card, which had a balance of nine dollars on it, or paying upward of thirty bucks for a taxi to take me seventy blocks to the Upper East Side… it was sort of a no-brainer.

But still.

I hated the subway.

I hiked the stairs out of the Seventy-Seventh Street station, collapsing my cane as I did. I walked toward Seventy-Eighth Street, stuffing the stick into my messenger bag. The smell of a halal food cart at the end of the block made my stomach growl painfully loud, reminding me it was now after 1:00 p.m. I gave the street meat a longing glance, sighed, and turned right to Third Avenue.

I came across a row of brownstones between avenues and consulted the address on my hand. In my rushed conversation with Mr. Robert, I'd actually written down "red door." Helpful. I scanned the million-dollar homes for addresses.

31… *S*. It was probably a five.

Or was it a six?

I was too far away, and hiking up the stairs to each door to read the numbers would get old real quick.

I looked around, backtracked, and approached a

teenager standing under a tree, texting away on his cell phone. "Excuse me?"

He glanced up, reached inside his hoodie to remove an earbud, and asked, "Yeah?"

I pointed to the brownstones. "Do any of these have a red door?"

He immediately pointed over my shoulder to a door I'd walked by twice now. "That one there."

"Second one down?"

"Uh-huh."

"Thanks."

"Sure." He returned to texting.

I went to the house in question, opened the gate, and hurried up the steps to the stoop. I hit the buzzer to the right of the frosted glass door and waited. I shoved my hands into my pockets and rocked back and forth on the balls of my feet. I'd been to plenty of these gorgeous old homes since opening the Emporium—whether as part of an estate sale or because the client was far too old to deal with the hassle of transporting antiques—but I still got excited. I'd never be able to afford such a property, so I lived a bit vicariously through my customers when I was offered such invites.

Frowning, I pressed the buzzer again.

I should have asked Mr. Robert for his telephone number. Cupping my hands around my face, I leaned into the glass but couldn't make anything out through the texture.

I tried the buzzer a third time.

"I fucking hear you!" an angry voice suddenly answered, crackling through the intercom.

I jumped and looked at it. "Uh—sorry, sir."

"Who're you? You're not a delivery man."

Nice. Jim Bob the Grouch had a camera system.

"No. I'm Sebastian Snow. You called me earlier. I own the Emporium in the East Village."

"Oh right. You. Hang on."

I hung on for at least another minute before I heard the inner door open. The front door was unlocked, and a shrunken, balding man with wild hair and wilder eyebrows shuffled back a few steps. He was wearing a plaid bathrobe, slippers, and had a lit pipe clenched between his teeth.

What the fuck? *This* was the owner? I suddenly didn't feel the need to keep my guard up. No way was Mr. Robert involved in this mess. Which meant this *wasn't* about extortion, but the *content* of the films.

"I was on the john," he explained. "Come in, come in."

"Er—thanks. Sorry it took a while to get here."

"Take your shoes off," he warned, pointing at my feet.

"What—oh—okay." I reached down and tugged the loafers off, setting them to the side in the short hall between the doors.

Mr. Robert chewed on the end of his pipe, shook his head, and shuffled through the door. "Kid's got the same shoes I do…."

I pretended not to hear that and followed him to the parlor floor of the house. "Wow." I paused in the threshold between the staircase and the living area.

The room was chock-full of antiques—Victrolas, cabinets of silver and china, grandfather clocks, musical instruments, and a penny-farthing bicycle pushed up against one wall behind a pair of parlor chairs with what I suspected was the original fabric and cushioning. Every square inch of the walls was covered with paintings, mirrors, pistols, and swords, as well as odds and ends that Mr. Robert had obviously run out of room to store in a more traditional means.

He turned to look up at me, puffing on his pipe in such a determined manner that he was doing a decent job of emulating a chimney. "Like it, eh?"

"It's a very impressive collection you have."

"So why didn't you call me when you got the damn Kinetoscope?"

"The shipping company you hired didn't provide your name or address on the contact sheet, just their own office."

"Piss," Mr. Robert muttered. He turned and began the shuffling journey to the next room.

"What can you tell me about the Kinetoscope?" I called, following after him. I stepped into a kitchen just as full of awesome gizmos and gadgets as the previous room. Everywhere I looked, vintage and antique baking tools, mixing bowls, and advertisements on the walls. "Jesus," I muttered.

Mr. Robert opened the fridge and removed a container. He slowly made his way across the room to the counter. "I got a lot of shit," he said, as if in agreement.

I went to a shelf that had an old flour sifter, rotary egg beater, hand-crank coffee grinder, and even an array of Christmas cookie cutters. It reminded me of the collection of kitchen tools I'd kept for Calvin after an estate sale in late January. He'd seemed so genuinely into them, and I thought at the time that maybe they would encourage his potential cooking habit.

But I'd lost those in the explosion too.

"My boyfriend would really like these," I said.

"He cooks?" Mr. Robert asked.

I looked away from the items and watched my crotchety host pour himself a small glass of some dark-looking liquid. "When he has free time."

"Any good?" he asked before downing the drink and making a disgusted face. "Prune juice," he told me.

"Uh, yeah. He made lasagna the other night."

"Marry him."

"Pardon?"

Mr. Robert put the glass in the sink and returned the jug to the fridge. "Gay marriage is federal law now, ain't it?" He put his pipe back in his mouth.

"Yes...."

"Then if he cooks, marry him. Or you'll end up like me, eating runny eggs every day of the week that ends in *y*."

"I'll... thanks." I was, in absolutely no way whatsoever, discussing my romantic hopes and dreams with Jim Bob. "So, about the Kinetoscope?"

Mr. Robert walked past me, back to the living room, while waving his hand. "I sent it to you for safekeeping."

Crap.

"Sir, that's not what my business—"

"I was looking for the cat this morning," he continued, picking up a paper bag sitting on a chair, "and found the other two reels. Then I remembered I didn't have a goddamn cat, and called you about the films."

What the...?

Mr. Robert turned and smirked. "Laugh, boy! It's a joke. I'm old, but I know I haven't owned a pussy cat since 1935." He pointed the pipe at me. "Siamese. Agatha."

"Lovely."

He put the pipe back and held the bag out.

"Why did you decide to send it to me?" I asked as I moved forward, took the bag, and set it on the nearest semiclear spot I could find. In this case, a piano.

"Found you on Google."

"Oh." I reached inside and pulled out the cans of footage. One had a small dent in the lid. "Do you mind if I open them?"

"I didn't bring you here for sightseeing. Go on." He sat down in the now-empty chair.

I reached into my messenger bag, which was slung over a shoulder, felt around, and retrieved cloth gloves. "But why did you give me the Kinetoscope for safekeeping?"

"Ah, well, my grandson, that little brat, has been acting strange."

I looked up. "Strange like…?"

"He wanted me to give him the Kinetoscope. Where would that boy keep it? He rents a bedroom in Bushwick. I didn't trust him, so I pretended to get rid of it. Until he calms down."

Suddenly I was thankful I hadn't indulged in a falafel over rice on the street corner. My stomach churned uncomfortably. "You were afraid he'd… steal it from you?"

Mr. Robert nodded. "That's right."

"The machine itself or the film?" I held up both cans.

"Couldn't be sure. So the other day, I unspooled it all, packed it into one of those cans, and sent it to you. I knew I had more movies. It took me two days to find where I'd stored them."

I looked down at the worn, slightly beaten-up cans. "Sir, are you aware that there's some disturbing footage at the end of the Leonard-Cushing boxing match?"

"The murder?"

"Yes!" I said quickly. I put the cans in the bag and walked to the chair Mr. Robert sat in. I crouched beside him to be closer to eye level. "What can you tell me about that?"

"I was born in 1928. Fuck you if you think I'm old enough to have been a witness."

"No, I—" I tried not to laugh. "Do you know who it was *in* the film? The man killed?"

He puffed on his pipe thoughtfully, a cloud of cherry smoke settling around us. "I bought the Kinetoscope from a man who said it'd belonged to his father—Tom Something-Or-Other. His father worked alongside W. K. L. Dickson. Do you know who that is?"

"Dickson was the chief inventor of the Kinetoscope," I replied. "But who was this Tom person?"

"Oh, who the hell knows. An assistant at Black Maria—lost to history. You know what the Black Maria was, don't you, kid?"

Again with the "boy" and "kid" shit.

"Edison's film studio in Jersey," I answered. "Also designed by Dickson. The building had the ability to rotate in order to utilize the sunlight—" I caught myself from going off the rails. "Sorry. Uh, this long-lost assistant, Tom—was *he* involved in the murder? What did his son tell you about the footage when you bought it?"

Mr. Robert stroked one out-of-control eyebrow. "Just to keep it safe."

"Safe from what?"

Mr. Robert looked at me. "Not what, boy. *Who*."

My skin prickled, and I felt the hairs on my arms stand up underneath my sweater. "Who, then?"

"Someone who wanted to do harm to Dickson. That's all I know. Tom supposedly suspected one of their own on the film crew was out to sabotage Dickson. And as long as the Kinetoscope and footage were kept hidden, everything would be okay."

"Dickson is dead, though," I stated before standing,

knees cracking. "He passed away in the 1930s. In London, no less. If someone was out to hurt him, they never succeeded."

"Well, of course not. The Kinetoscope was being hidden by that Tom fella."

Okay.

William Dickson, chief inventor of the Kinetograph camera and Scope viewer. Alongside Georges Méliès and the Lumière brothers of France, Dickson was truly one of the grandfathers of modern cinema as we knew it today. He worked for Thomas Edison, who—because of the media, patents office in DC, and history at large—had been credited for the invention of these wonderful machines. Dickson was more or less ignored. In 1894, the Kinetoscope was all the rage across the country, with parlors opening up in New York City for the everyday man to enjoy this newfangled piece of entertainment.

And sometime between then and whenever Dickson left Edison's company, someone at Black Maria tried to… kill him? I didn't see a connection. A conspiracy to take down Dickson in the 1890s was one thing, but how did that tie in with the murder movie and the particular Kinetoscope machine sitting in the Emporium? It could be that the answer to the events of both the past and present lay within these newly acquired film reels. To me it was more than plausible, considering how adamant my assailant had been about obtaining the *other movies*.

Of course, that would also mean the motive for killing the teenager would be on these movies, and I wasn't so sure I wanted to know….

I began walking back to the bag on the piano. "Why'd you want me to view the rest of your film collection?"

Mr. Robert set his pipe on the small table beside the chair. "I don't remember if I've ever watched these two films. But I can't now because you've got the movie viewer. Find out why my grandson wants it so badly. I'll pay you for your time—just send me an invoice."

I turned around. "You believe the reason he wants them is going to be obvious once I watch these movies?"

"I think so."

"Sir, do you...?" I took a breath and asked about the connection I hadn't wanted to make. "Do you have a picture of your grandson?"

"I got lots of pictures."

"Could I borrow one?" That sounded creepy. "I, uh... a teenager came in the other day who seemed interested in the Kinetoscope."

"That little shit. He didn't bother you, did he? I'll tell you—he's gotten real strange lately."

Oh no.

"I'll just hold on to the photo until I'm done looking at the film. You know, in case I see him... I can call you."

Mr. Robert didn't seem to think the request was terribly strange. He slowly got out of his chair and shuffled to the room's fireplace. He stared at the mantel for a moment, hand hovering over a variety of framed photos, before he plucked one from the back. He wiped it off with the sleeve of his robe and held it out.

I took the picture and steeled myself to look at it.

Fuck....

I didn't call Calvin until I'd reached Queens.

I'd felt sick to my stomach on the train ride to Astoria. I ducked into the Starbucks just outside of Moving Image. Not that a sugary coffee was a suitable lunch, but it was better than the murder of a misfit teenager churning up stomach acid all day.

I stood outside the coffee shop under the awning, leaning against the railing, with my phone smooshed between my ear and shoulder. Although it was far too sunny for my liking, it was an otherwise balmy, perfect day. The warm weather had caused me to panic at the counter, and like a dummy, I had ordered one of the Frappuccino drinks Max always chose. I ended up sipping on some white chocolate, caramel, java thing that I wasn't so sure had actual coffee in it. I might have had an insatiable sweet tooth, but when it came to coffee, I preferred it dark and bitter.

No answer from Calvin.

I ended the call. I considered trying Quinn, but was certain she could and would beat the crap out of me for interrupting their job as much as I did. I eventually decided on the old-fashioned method. I called the precinct, requested Detective Winter, and was patched through to his extension.

The phone rang a few times, and then he answered. "Detective Winter."

"Hi."

"Seb?"

"I tried your cell first."

"Sorry. I was grabbing a coffee in the break room."

"I bet it's better than the sweet mess I have."

"I think this was brewed last night. Tastes like burned engine oil."

"And the mystery behind your fixation with cinnamon mints is finally revealed."

"You've got me worried. You're not bleeding profusely *now*, are you?" There was a smile in Calvin's tone.

Best to just come clean. Fast, like ripping off a Band-Aid.

"I've got the name of Dumpster Diver."

Silence.

"Casey Robert," I said.

"Sebastian."

"I was only sleuthing a little."

"Explain how you've gotten the name of the victim before the police."

"Small World Syndrome strikes again."

The bandage was off, but it had left that tacky Band-Aid-shaped residue.

"Would you believe he's the grandson of the Kinetoscope owner?" I continued.

"No, I wouldn't."

"He is," I insisted. "I met the owner today."

"*What*? Why did you—Sebastian, if this person has been setting you up and had the balls to murder—"

"James Robert is the name of the grandfather," I interrupted. "And he's ninety years old. I don't think the guy can climb stairs, let alone cut the throat of his own grandson and then toss his body in a dumpster. He sure as hell wasn't the man who attacked me," I said in a rush.

I could practically hear Calvin silently counting to ten.

"James called me. He suspected his grandson wanted to steal his Kinetoscope, so he'd looked me up on the internet and shipped it to the Emporium for safekeeping. To make a long story short, when he mentioned that, I asked for a photo of his grandson. Minus the fixed gaze and copious amount of blood—same kid from the alley."

Calvin didn't respond.

"So… I don't think the grandfather is involved. I think Casey was definitely looking to steal from him, though. My attacker might be a friend of his. They're a bit taller than me. I'd also look for someone who likes candy. Red licorice. I'm telling you, his breath—"

"Seb."

"What?"

"It never occurred to you that the grandfather might have orchestrated this? That he could be involved without being *physically* involved? *Christ*, baby. You could have been in serious danger."

Okay… that hadn't occurred to me.

"I didn't—" I frowned and stared at the ground. "Sorry."

"Where are you?" Calvin asked. "Are you still with the grandfather?"

"I'm in Queens."

"Why?"

"Moving Image."

"Is that really necessary anymore?" Calvin asked.

"I really don't think Mr. Robert was involved at all, not even as a puppet master."

"You don't know that."

"No, that's true. But I'm convinced, now more than ever, the clues are in the past."

Calvin let out a frustrated breath.

"I swear I'm totally safe. And I didn't say anything about Casey being dead to the grandfather."

"Good."

"Do you want me to text you his information?"

"Yes, please."

"Will do, Detective." I said goodbye and sent Calvin a text. Luckily I'd thought to get Jim Bob's house number before I left.

Jamess Robert
316e 78, reed door

555-23688

Calvin replied before I finished off my Frappiyucko. *That phone number has too many digits.*

What? Oh. Oops.

1 8

Wait. That made it more confusing.

No.

555-2368

Srry

I tossed my empty drink into a nearby trash can, dug out the photo of Casey from my bag of goodies, and took a picture of it with my phone. I sent it to Calvin.

Now I was ready for some movie magic.

CHAPTER TWELVE

I stepped through the large glass doors of the museum and walked to the counter. "Hi. I have a question about your core exhibit."

A young guy sitting behind the desk began reciting a canned response. "Our Behind the Screen exhibit features fourteen hundred artifacts from the culture of the moving image. It includes cameras, projectors, costumes, props, and more. General admission is fifteen dollars."

"Thanks," I drew out. "But my question was, do you have a Kinetoscope as part of the exhibit?"

He laughed. "Oh, I have no idea about any of that old stuff." He spun in his chair. "Greta! Do you know if there's a—what'd you say it was?" he asked, twirling to look at me again.

"Kinetoscope," I grumbled.

"A Kinetoscope upstairs?"

A woman, presumably Greta, joined my clueless friend a moment later. She had at least two decades on me

172

but held herself with more elegance and grace than most people could ever hope for at their youngest and hottest. She was my height, with salt-and-pepper-looking afro hair, glasses, and a sharp ensemble.

"Is there a Kinetoscope?" She echoed before facing me. "Yes, there is."

"Great," I said, reaching for my wallet. "What about a curator to speak with regarding some of the artifacts?"

"Museum educators are available for group tours."

"It's just me," I replied.

She looked sympathetic. "Unfortunately the educators are only available for preorganized tours. You're welcome to call and book a date. Otherwise it's a self-visit."

Well, shit.

"My name's Sebastian Snow, and I own Snow's Antique Emporium in Manhattan," I began, holding a hand out.

"Greta Harris," she said, shaking it. "I'm one of the museum directors."

"Pleasure," I said. "I'm actually here for research, which is why I was hoping to speak—"

The guy shoved a business card across the counter. "You can contact our research department," he offered—trying to be helpful.

I picked up the card.

"They respond to all inquiries within two weeks."

I handed the card back. "I don't have two weeks. It's sort of an... odd situation I'm in, and I can't provide a lot of explanation," I continued, turning back to Greta. "I know a fair amount about the Kinetoscope and Graph themselves, but I need details about the man behind the inventions—"

"William Kennedy-Laurie Dickson," Greta supplied.

"Yes!" I felt myself getting excited and—daresay—hopeful. "And if I could learn more about him and the early films he did for Edison, let's just say the NYPD would be thankful."

She looked a bit intrigued. Maybe in pursuit of curiosity she'd killed a cat or two in her lifetime too. But she didn't say anything for a long, uncomfortable minute.

I looked down, opened my messenger bag, and pulled out the paper bag Mr. Robert had supplied me with. "I have these," I said.

"Have what?" she asked.

"Original Kinetoscope footage."

Greta leaned forward. "Which movies?"

"Honestly? I've no idea. I haven't been able to look at them." I lowered the bag. "I have a Kinetoscope in my possession, and the knockout round of the Leonard-Cushing fight. But... er... it's at my shop, which is... inaccessible at the moment."

"There's no surviving footage of the knockout round," she replied.

I smiled. "There wasn't until this week, when it fell into my lap."

Greta tapped the counter with a finger. "There's simply no way we can play your footage in our machine, if that's what you hoped for. It's a replica. And the museum cannot be held accountable for any damage done."

"I just need to talk to someone who knows more than me," I said, an underlying tone of desperation in my words.

Greta gave me a look of conflicting emotions. I wasn't entirely sure what it was supposed to mean. "I'm sorry, Mr. Snow. The best I can offer is contacting our research department or a group tour on a future date."

Sucker punched.

I felt myself deflate a little. "All right," I finally said. "Thank you for your time." I turned, walked back to the door, and stepped out into the summer sun.

I moved to stand under the shade of a tree beside the road. If I smoked, I was pretty sure right about then was when I'd be stuffing the entire pack into my mouth.

I looked down at the paper bag and pulled out the canister with the dented lid. There were secrets on these reels. Secrets that would shed light on the break-ins.

The murder.

The attack on me.

Today's shooting.

And perhaps even the identity of the poor bastard killed a century ago, and why *Dickson's* own life was in danger from these films being in existence.

"Guess that's that," I said to myself.

"Mr. Snow?"

I turned around, pushed my sunglasses up, and watched Greta Harris come out the museum doors. She had her purse hanging from an arm and walked with purpose toward the end of the block.

"I'm going on lunch," she stated, passing me. "Do you like beer?"

So, the plus to visiting Astoria was the amazing German beer garden only two blocks away from Kaufman Studios and the museum. It had a huge outdoor seating arrangement, with a speaker system for live music and a massive screen for sporting events. Inside, the light was subdued and it was illuminated mostly by the dozen flat-screens playing different soccer and baseball matches. The exception being one television in the far corner of the drinking hall that seemed to have been left on the soap opera channel by mistake.

Steinway Bierhaus definitely made their money off the film and television crowd. This I'd pieced together by the fact that the bar near the door had specialty drinks with names like Rosebud or 123 Sesame Shot, and that every Monday night was Producer's Night. I figured that was the same thing as ladies' night, but you had to be a producer.... Luckily for Greta and I, it was the middle of the afternoon on a Thursday, so we shared the communal tables with no one but our pints and two exceptionally large pretzels.

"There isn't a lot I can do for you," Greta said. She took a sip of beer. "Officially through the museum, at least. We have strict policies in place, especially for information. I can't even guarantee we'd have what you're looking for, on top of having to wait and paying the research fees."

I nodded.

"And the guided tours, while they are quite good, they're ninety minutes and cover the entire Behind the Screen exhibit. Our educators likely won't know the nitty-gritty."

"But you do?"

Greta broke her pretzel into a few pieces. "I have an MFA in film studies and worked as a television producer for twenty years. I know some things."

I smiled. I liked her.

"Hopefully I know what you're on the hunt to learn."

"Have you ever heard of, while Dickson was employed for Edison, some attack on his life?"

"Oh no." Greta frowned and shook her head. "Never. *Granted*... the past gets a bit hinky around the birth of the Kinetoscope."

"How so?" I took a long, refreshing drink.

"Scholars to this day debate how much involvement Edison had with the physical construction of the camera and viewer. He patented it, sure, but he and Dickson parted ways in '95 with a rather strained relationship. Documents have been conveniently lost, changed, opinions have soured personal accounts.... It's hard to get a concise view of this period in film history."

"But one thing for certain is that Dickson *was* the primary inventor," I said.

"Without a doubt," she agreed. "Cinema history was made with Dickson."

"What was the reason for his leaving the company and Black Maria?" I asked around a bite of pretzel. It was still warm, and the spicy mustard dip... I almost made an orgasmic sound but managed to stifle it.

Greta held up a finger as she made good headway on her beer. "This is a moment I find particularly fascinating. William Edward Gilmore was appointed general manager of the Edison Manufacturing Company in 1894, and by most accounts, was a tough businessman. By then, Dickson had begun moonlighting for the Latham brothers. They owned a Kinetoscope parlor in New York City and were instrumental in pioneering one of the first machines to project footage for an audience. Such parlors wouldn't need half a dozen Edison machines at start-up, and instead could create a business with a single unit."

"Cost-effective," I said.

"Very much so," she agreed. "And although most of their work was engineered by Eugène Lauste, Dickson *did* help. Edison's manager became suspicious of Dickson and, in April of 1895, orchestrated his exit from the company."

"What put Gilmore on Dickson's scent?" I asked.

"That I can't be certain of," Greta answered. "Some suggest Dickson was overly confident—that Edison would sooner toss out the general manager than the man who'd put the Kinetoscope on the map—but such was not the case."

"Truth is stranger than fiction," I stated.

She nodded. "It's a story perfect for a movie, don't you think?"

"Which some screenwriter would inevitably destroy by inserting made-up drama or a romantic side plot that never existed," I replied.

Greta laughed, deep and hearty. "Don't I know it."

We ate in a companionable silence for a few moments.

"I was told a story," I finally said. "It's hearsay at least three times over."

"Those are always fun."

"The Kinetoscope I'm currently in possession of is a working original. The owner is the one who supplied me with these reels," I said as I patted the paper bag at my side. "He says he purchased it all from the son of a man claiming to be one of Dickson's original assistants on the Kinetoscope."

Greta raised an eyebrow.

"I know," I replied to her suspicious expression. "He couldn't supply any proof of the claim—but the story he was told was that there was a betrayal from within the circle, and it had put Dickson in danger. So long as the Kinetoscope and movies were kept hidden, Dickson would be safe."

"*That* sounds like the unnecessary addition by the screenwriter," Greta stated.

"Could be," I said. "But maybe the danger was Gilmore?"

"Gilmore didn't try to *kill* Dickson," she said. "He just had him fired. What was this 'assistant's' name?"

"Tom."

"Just Tom?"

"That's all I was told."

"I'll admit, I don't know the names of every man involved," Greta finished. "Maybe there was a Tom. *Maybe*." She perked up a bit, grabbed her purse, and began to rummage about. "I actually know who to ask. If there *ever* was a Tom or a threat against Dickson, this man would have the story."

I grabbed my magnifying glass from my bag, took the business card she offered a moment later, and brought it close to read. "Dr. Bill Freidman."

"He teaches—"

"At NYU," I said, glancing at Greta. "I had him for Film History, and Theory and Criticism my junior year." I looked at the card again. "I can't believe he's still teaching."

"Oh yes. He now brings his history class to the museum once a year."

"Guess I missed that fieldtrip," I said, stuffing the card into my messenger bag. "But thanks. I don't think it'd have ever occurred to me to ask him. We, uh—we butted heads a bit when I was in college."

"He can be rather strict with students," she agreed.

"And I was a smart-ass know-it-all, so you can imagine."

Greta laughed and wiped her hands on a napkin. "So. Are we going to take a look?" She nodded at the paper bag.

"At the still frames?"

"Better than nothing." She leaned forward. "I've got to know what footage it is. Perhaps it's additional reels from the Leonard-Cushing fight, since you somehow got your hands on round six."

That was a probability. I dug into my messenger bag to take out the cloth gloves. "I only have one pair," I said, waving them. "It's best to avoid touching—"

179

"You don't think I'm prepared?" She clucked her tongue and retrieved a similar pair from her purse.

I smiled and offered her one of the two cans from the bag. I put on my gloves, shimmied the lid free from my container, and carefully held up the film strip. "Single perforations puts this before 1894," I said. "This movie is definitely earlier than the catalog available to the public."

"Test footage?" Greta asked as she worked the lid from her can.

"Yeah. But this is *after* they discarded cylinder experiments. Which would make it around 1891?" I held the roll of still frames upward, letting the flashing light of a nearby television backlight it. I narrowed my eyes and brought the still-pliable film closer. "I think this is Dickson."

"What? Really?"

"I'm not crazy about the fantastic mustaches men had back then, but he's a handsome guy. This *is* Dickson. I'm certain. Wasn't 1891 when they held a public demonstration?"

"For the National Federation of Women's Clubs, if I'm not mistaken," Greta replied. "But that would make it the *Dickson Greeting*, and that's not possible."

"Why?" I lowered the film briefly.

"Only a three-second fragment exists today. The *New York Sun* described the entire reel as a man who bowed, smiled, waved his hands, and removed his hat. But if I recall, only the bit of Dickson holding his hat has survived."

I raised the strip again and gently unspooled it. "This is the *Dickson Greeting*," I insisted in a low tone. "He's doing everything you've just described."

"That needs to be brought to the attention of the National Film Registry. It's without a doubt historically significant."

I looked at Greta as she gently unspooled a bit of her film and studied it. I sifted toward the end of my own footage. The fact that I had in my hands another piece of history thought lost to time was incredible. But like the boxing match, I was suspecting there was more hidden toward the end. And sure enough, there was a bump where two pieces had been haphazardly spliced together.

The second piece of film was perforated on both sides, which put it several years after the original *Dickson Greeting* movie. And that was brilliant, because now I had a working timeline. Whoever had been tacking the mysterious murder footage to the end of the reels likely did so between 1894, when the team had perfected the 35mm film used in the machines, and 1895, when Dickson left the company.

"This one is awfully hard to make out," Greta murmured. She was doing the same as me, holding the still frames up to the light of the television. "Looks like a young boy—almost like he's conducting music or something. You know that hand motion?"

"That doesn't sound familiar," I said, distracted.

"I'm sure there's plenty Dickson's team did that we'll never know about."

I brought my magnifying glass up to the film. It seemed to be the same outdoor setting—the Flatiron site—but in daylight. The figures were much easier to make out. One man stood before the camera, pointing up and behind. He must have been referencing the magic lantern used on site. I took a leap and made the educated guess that the team had been testing recording at night and wanted to use the city lights, like the magic lantern, for exposing the film. When he looked directly at the camera in another frame, I realized he was the murderer. Muttonchops with the gut.

I fed more footage through my hand, approaching the end of the reel, when two additional men finally stepped into the frame. The minute details of the individuals were impossible to make out, but the angle of the hat worn on one suggested Dickson himself. The second might have actually been the man who died hours later in the nighttime scene.

So if I understood these two scenes correctly, I had four characters involved in the murder: Heise, who was the cameraman of the crew, Dickson himself, the killer—Muttonchops—and the unknown victim.

I leaned to the side and took my phone out of my pocket. They wouldn't be the greatest photos, not by a long shot, but I had one half-baked idea on how I could go about trying to identify the killer with no information to work with except his face. I let the phone's camera focus on the tiny frame, magnified it, and snapped a few pictures of Muttonchops.

Greta swore to herself.

"What is it?" I asked, beginning to carefully wind the film up.

"It's a club in the boy's hand, not a baton. You've got three movies that are said not to exist."

I finished with my film and set it in the bag, then reached out when she offered me the reel. "I'm not familiar with the footage," I said.

"*Newark Athlete*. It's the oldest film in the Registry," she continued. "Only existed as stills that were reanimated."

"Like *Fred Ott's Sneeze*," I mumbled.

Greta made a sound of agreement.

I reached the now-expected bump of the old single perforation merged with newer, double-perforated film. I put the magnifying glass to the stills. It was shot at the Black Maria in Jersey, for sure. There was Muttonchops again. He was standing before the camera, making exaggerated movements.

More testing, I'd bet.

In the background of the scene was a damn Kinetoscope. Something— no, *someone*, was crouched in front of it, but I couldn't be sure what they were doing.

I started moving through the stills a bit faster, and persistence of vision nearly made the past come to life in my hands. I stopped when another object entered the frame and viewed it under magnification. That was Victim. He got into Muttonchops's face. Maybe they were arguing?

Some of the stills were black and destroyed with age and poor exposure, but right at the end, Dickson appeared, like he was trying to break up a potential fight. So whatever the conflict had been in regards to, it was undoubtedly the fuel that fed the fire for murder.

What the hell happened between this group of talented men?

Had it been so awful that murder was the only recourse?

And how did it all tie in to Dickson then and the person who'd shot up the Emporium now?

"This is a Brooklyn Bridge–bound 6 train. The next stop is Astor Place." I held on to the overhead railing with one hand and kept a grip on my cane with the other. I stared at the floor, avoiding the overblown lights of the subway car. Incoming riders moved around me to find places to sit or stand.

After our lunch and discussion of celluloid corruption and crime, I'd left Greta Harris and headed back to the city. I was overwhelmed with questions, but at least I had a consistent cast of faces to work with on my quest for answers. And putting names to the unknowns—Muttonchops, Victim, and that man who'd been fiddling with the Kinetoscope in the background of the last movie—was of the upmost importance. Knowing who all of the film assistants were, being able to correctly assign their roles in the unfolding story, that was where I hoped I'd discover a clue to today's tribulations.

Not that I was basing this hope on any particular piece of evidence, just the stories from a foul-mouthed old man and an assailant with a penchant for candy who'd been ready to kill me for the rest of the movies I *now* had in my possession. But what I did know was that if I could untangle this historical web of contradictions, betrayal, and human ingenuity, I would close the case on a century-old murder and *perhaps* even alter the course of cinema history. And in so doing both of those things, might also be able to handcuff the person who killed Casey Robert.

Talk about killing two birds with one stone.

Maybe that wasn't the best metaphor to use at the moment....

"This is Astor Place," the automated system announced.

I put the cane in front of me and moved toward the doors. Someone to my left stepped aside. As the train slowed at the station, and pillars and people passed by the window in a blur, another passenger moved to stand beside me at the door. He leaned in close, surpassing those three inches of New Yorker personal space. I hated people like that. I wanted to get off the train too, guy, but there wasn't much I could do before we'd even parked in the station.

The brakes screeched, and I shifted my weight to move with the motion of the halting train. The doors opened, and I took a step forward before the creep to my right shoved hard into my shoulder. My foot caught in the gap between the train and platform, causing me to flail and crash to the ground.

"*Fuck*!" My sunglasses flew off and I tried to break my fall, but I was too late and only managed to slam my face into the tacky, filthy cement floor and scrape up the heels of my hands.

After a moment of feeling around, I reached out, snagged my glasses, and put them on with shaking hands. I looked around the dimly lit platform for who'd tripped me, then zoned in on a teenage brat picking up my messenger bag. I made eye contact with him.

I knew him.

He'd been the one I'd asked regarding the brownstone with a red door.

"*You*!" I exclaimed.

He immediately took off toward the turnstile exits.

"H-hey! You little shit." I grabbed my cane, scrambled to my feet, and chased after him. "Stop! Fuck—*thief*!" I screamed, hoping like hell a Good Samaritan would jump into his path and... *no one was stopping him.* Are you *kidding* me?

"I said stop," I shouted one more time.

The guy reached the exit, skidded to a halt, then jumped the nearest turnstile. I got there a few seconds later but was blocked as passengers were swiping cards to enter the platform. I swore and slammed my bruised hands into the bar of the emergency exit door, alarm wailing as I ran out. I didn't recognize the back of the kid's head so much as I recognized my bag being flung around in the crowd as he continued to outrun me. I'd learned my lesson about keeping all of my necessities in the bag, and so had kept my phone and keys in my jeans. But the goddamn Kinetoscope footage was safely tucked inside!

The teen was slowed by the afternoon foot traffic on the stairs, and I took the only chance I had. I lunged forward, using my cane to knock between his knees and trip the little shithead. As he fell, I surged toward him. I grabbed the back of the thin hoodie he was wearing, but as quickly as I thought I had him, he yanked his arms free of the clothing, took the bag again, and raced up the stairs.

"You asshole!" I tripped my way up to ground level after him. But outside the Downtown 6, I stood bruised, out of breath, and empty-handed.

CHAPTER THIRTEEN

"Sebby. What the hell's with all the police activity at the Emporium?" Beth paused and gave me a long, critical look from head to toe. "What the fuck happened to *you*?" she corrected.

I stood in the doorway of Good Books, holding my disassembled cane and a bag from a nearby drugstore in one hand, and the hoodie of my thief in the other, like it was the head of my slayed enemy. The shop stereo was tuned to some shitty radio station playing a slew of cringe-worthy local advertisements.

"Are there customers in here?" I asked.

Beth turned and peered down the aisles from where she stood at the register. "A few down in the travel section. Why?"

I walked toward her. "I need your help." I set my things on the counter, dug into the plastic bag, and held up a bottle of concealer. "I don't know how to put this on."

Beth eyed the makeup with a glimmer of distain.

187

"Do I look like the sort of old broad who wears concealer? I worked for these age spots."

"Just help me," I protested. "My face is bruised and I want to cover it."

She snatched the bottle. "This is about half a dozen shades too dark for your complexion, Sebby."

"What?"

"And to cover a bruise, you'll need more than—" She shook her head when she paused to stare at the makeup again. "A $4.99 bottle of CVS brand liquid concealer. Good grief." She took the plastic bag and looked inside. "Is that the only one you bought?" Beth removed a box of condoms and tin of cinnamon mints. She held them both up and gave me the hairy eyeball. "*Really?*"

"Calvin's almost out of mints," I replied.

She jiggled the condom box.

"Please stop waving that around."

Beth rolled her eyes and shoved them back into the bag. "Your priorities are something else."

I snatched the concealer and stared hard at it. "So this won't work?"

"No. Unless you want a giant brown smudge on your face and makeup-caked whiskers."

"Great."

Beth tossed the bottle into the waste bin for me. "Been sleuthing, have you?"

"Not really."

"Liar."

"Only a little. But it's regarding that film from Tuesday, so I'm not meddling in police business."

"Then why have there been cops outside your store all day?"

"The window got shot out," I said, maybe a bit too

calmly.

"That was next door?" she protested. "Holy hell. I thought it came from down the street."

I shook my head.

"So… *why*?" Beth put her hands on the counter and leaned forward.

"Someone—" I looked over my shoulder to make sure the future vacationers hadn't moved close enough to overhear. "Someone stole that footage from my shop and a teenager was found dead in our dumpster. I think whoever did those acts tried to scare me this morning into handing over more footage."

"D-did you?" Beth asked, stumbling over her words.

"I didn't have anything *to* hand over," I replied. "But afterward—"

Wait a minute.

Wait a damn minute.

Calvin might have been right. Fuck!

After the shots at the Emporium, Mr. Robert had called. He'd called, enticed me to come grab more footage, and then I'd had it stolen less than three hours later by another *teenager*. And the gun that had been fired at the front window…. Calvin suspected the casings had been collected prior to the attacker running off, but what if….

Mr. Robert had antique weapons at his house. They were hanging on the walls for me to see—single-action revolvers from the 1830s and '40s. And those didn't have bullets like we know them today. I hadn't made any mental notes about a space on a wall missing a gun, but that house looked like what I suspected my own would be like in a decade or two. There could have easily been a pistol unaccounted for.

I looked down at the hoodie on the countertop.

That teenager who escaped with my fucking bag

was taller than me. Not a huge guy, but he had seemed healthy, especially since I'd no chance of catching him. *He* might have been the partner-in-crime to Casey Robert…. Which meant he'd followed me home last night.

And today, by the time I'd visited the grandfather's house. Maybe even prior to that. Since I left the Emporium for Pop's? Regardless, he'd have confirmed by Astoria that I had more footage, and must have been waiting for the perfect moment to jump me. It wasn't a random attack at all.

Was I *honestly* being set up by a prune juice-drinking, ninety-year-old man who was using his own grandson to do the dirty work? I couldn't be sure if Casey's murder was part of the plan, but… this was bad. Outward appearance was that Mr. Robert certainly wasn't hurting for cash. He lived in a gorgeous brownstone in a highly desirable neighborhood, with a house full of shit that'd make him the most popular seller at an auction.

But who knows. Maybe he was destitute. What the fuck did I know about his financial situation?

Was it just bad luck that he'd chosen my antique store from a Google search instead of my asshole competition, Marshall's Oddities? And if that were all true, did that mean the Dickson footage meant jack squat in this modern-day mystery?

No. I refused to believe these long-lost movies were red herrings.

Beth snapped her fingers in front of my face. "Earth to Sebastian."

I blinked and looked at her. "S-sorry. What was I saying?"

"I'm not sure," she replied. "How'd you bruise your cheek?"

I furrowed my brow. "Someone tripped me getting off the subway." I stared at her for a beat. "I have to go."

"Of course you do."

I grabbed my things, took a step away, then paused. "Do you have a pair of glasses I can borrow? Mine were stolen."

She raised an eyebrow and pulled off the ones she wore, the rhinestone chain hanging from them. "Want these?"

I winced. Not my style. "What about more Miss Butterwith books? I still need *Miss Butterwith Plants a Clue*."

Beth had been helping me reassemble my extensive, old-lady sleuth series I'd lost in February.

"Nada."

"Gay cops?" I tried.

She reached under the counter briefly, then stood with two paperbacks in her hands. "I knew I'd convert you to romances eventually."

I leaned closer. "Miss Butterwith will always be my number-one gal."

"Sure."

I snatched one of the offerings. "But this looks promising." I slid it into my plastic bag.

"Get out of here, troublemaker."

"I'll see you later."

I stepped outside and let the door fall shut behind me. I was considering if, in my current state, it was possible to go home to grab my extra pair of glasses while remaining safe and under the radar, when I spotted Neil's car still parked across the street. I guess multiple shots and shattered glass was more than enough to keep an evidence-gathering detective busy for the better part of a day.

I marched toward the taped-off area surrounding my

shop. I peered around a uniformed officer who moved to block me. I only made out a few people through the open door, and there were definitely less cars than earlier in the morning.

"Almost done?" I asked.

"You'll have to use the sidewalk across the street, sir," the officer replied.

"Is Detective Millett still inside?"

"Sir."

"I'm the owner," I said, waving a hand at the store. "Could you just check if he's available for thirty seconds?"

"I believe the detectives left a few hours ago."

"He's CSU," I corrected.

She put her hands on her utility belt.

"Please?" I looked over her shoulder again as two people stepped out of the Emporium, carrying evidence kits. "Hey!" I called. "Neil."

Both detectives stopped and looked at me. Neil said something to the other man, handed over his gear, and then walked toward the police tape.

I moved away from the officer and met Neil about ten feet away from her. "I have a question," I stated.

Neil took in my rumpled, bruised appearance. "And I have several," he countered. He reached out, touched the side of my head, and pulled his still-gloved hand back. He held up his fingers to show a dark stain on the latex. "What the hell is in your hair?"

"I was on the subway floor."

"That does *not* narrow the list in any way whatsoever. When's the last time you had a tetanus shot?"

"I'll take a shower."

"Make it a good one," he agreed, yanking off the glove and checking his watch. "You're a mess, and it's been, like, five hours since I last saw you, Sebastian."

"A lot can happen in five hours."

"Jesus," Neil swore under his breath. "What's your question?"

"What kind of bullet did you get out of my wall?"

He put his hands up. "No. No case questions."

"But I—"

"No." He turned around and was already walking away.

"Was it a lead ball?" I called after him.

Neil stopped. He looked over his shoulder.

That was a yes.

"Lead balls look like pancakes after being fired," I continued.

Neil glanced at the officer to my left before he returned to loom over me.

"We know it wasn't a musket," I said, trying to sound helpful. "That'd have drawn attention. But on the other hand, those shots were in pretty quick succession."

"Yes," Neil reluctantly admitted. "It'd need to be something with a revolving cylinder. How do you know this?"

"I have a suspicion an antique collector I visited today may be behind everything happening. He had a lot of well-kept weapons on the walls."

"That's not proof."

"No, I guess not. But I challenge you to a scavenger hunt. First one to find someone in New York City who owns a nineteenth-century pistol with a stock of black gunpowder and lead balls wins."

"*Sebastian.*"

"Who's also the grandfather of the kid in the dumpster."

Neil's features softened into curiosity. "*What*? Does Winter know?"

"I told him," I agreed. "About the family relation. The gun realization just occurred to me a few minutes ago. I know Calvin's going to talk to Mr. Robert at some point."

Neil was already pulling his cell out. "I'll tell him about the bullet so he can ask the grandfather about his collection."

"He should get a warrant to test Mr. Robert's firearms."

Neil put his hand over the mouthpiece. "Go home." He then moved it and said, "It's Millett."

"Tell Calvin I said hi."

Neil made a shooing motion.

Adrenaline crashes were hell.

After a successful, though nerve-racking, pit stop at home to find my backup glasses, stuff a backpack with clean clothes, and borrow Calvin's tablet, I hightailed it to Pop's. I had no idea if this was the last I'd see of the second teenager, but I was fairly confident he was working in conjunction with Mr. Robert. And if that was the case, I wasn't looking to be caught alone with a guy who was brutal enough to slit a friend's throat.

So I got reacquainted with Pop's couch.

And promptly fell asleep about forty pages into my hot cops book.

"—sorry to wake you, William."

"Hush, hush. Sebastian warned me you would be late. He's been asleep since seven. Stay the night."

"Are you sure? Thank you."

My brain was a bit sluggish on the uptake—unable

to successfully identify the whispering voices near the front door until the sounds had migrated behind me. I recognized Pop's bedroom door shutting. Then I heard another door farther away—Calvin in the bathroom.

I opened my eyes, wiping my mouth while sitting up.

I drooled. Great.

I leaned forward, took my glasses from the coffee table, and put them on. The near-dark room came into focus. The curtains were all drawn, both pups were attempting to sleep on Maggie's bed across the room, and at some point in the night, my dad had put some pillows on the couch and covered me with a light blanket.

I hoped he hadn't gotten an eyeful of the page I fell asleep reading.

That'd been a damn fine sex scene.

I picked the book up from where it'd fallen to the floor and set it on the table. I turned my head to the right and stared down the dark hall with the small bit of light peeking out from under the bathroom door. I can't be sure what prompted me to stand and walk down the hall just then. Maybe it was confidence shining through after the late spring cleaning of my heart. Maybe it was the desire to feel *alive* after the morning's shoot-out. Hell. Maybe it was just the lingering effects of the scorching-hot read.

But I stopped outside the bathroom, knocked on the door, and opened it.

Calvin turned as he dried his face with a towel. His sleeves were rolled back, showing the cords of muscle in his arms, and his tie was loosened, with the first button of his shirt undone. "Hey, baby. I'm sorry I woke—"

I pushed the door shut, took a few steps forward, grabbed Calvin by the tie, and pulled him down into a kiss. And it wasn't just *any kiss*. It was everything that I was—

everything that made him and me, *us*. It was affection, trust, surprise, want, and need. It was pure, undiluted joy, uncertainty, weakness, and strength.

It was every promise I'd made. Every apology owed. Every vow to do better.

It was every last ounce of love I had for Calvin Winter.

He broke the kiss first with an audible gasp.

I reached around Calvin's neck and let him pull me closer. "I know Lee used to be an old boyfriend."

He looked surprised that was my conversation starter. "That was a long—"

"Hang on. Just let me… I don't care," I said quietly. "I don't. I've been a mess lately. I know that. Trying to convince myself that *this* will somehow end because I'm not a good enough catch for you."

"Sebastian."

"Listen," I insisted, looking up at him. "I get self-conscious. There are some days… when I'm wearing mismatched clothes, have crumbs on my sweater, and the clerk at CVS gives me a dubious look when I buy condoms because she'd sooner believe I'm making balloon animals out of them than getting laid. And it gets to me. Sometimes not so much. Sometimes it's worse. But I want to apologize to you. Because for months I've asked you to be honest with me and talk with me when you're hurting, and I haven't had the balls to do the same."

Calvin's face softened. His arms wrapped a little tighter around me.

"And I let Mr. Suave and Handsome get under my skin. But he's an ex."

"Yes."

"And I'm not."

Calvin smiled lightly and shook his head. "No,

you're not."

"And... and I think we're imperfectly perfect for each other. Like, peanut butter is too savory alone, and jelly's too sweet, but we...." I started laughing. "We make a great sandwich."

Calvin smiled with his entire face. He leaned down and kissed my forehead.

"You picked me," I continued. "Despite all the warning signs that I'm an obnoxious know-it-all on even my best days, you're here now. You could be anywhere in the world. And you're *right here*. So maybe I'll never be wholly confident in life. But when it's just you, and just me, I know I have nothing to be afraid of. You're not going anywhere."

"I'm not," Calvin said. "I love you."

"I love you too," I answered before kissing him again.

I pushed Calvin back against the sink, grabbed his arms, and guided them down my body until his hands settled on my ass. I slipped his tie from around his neck, tossed it to the floor, and fumbled with the buttons down his chest as we continued kissing.

Calvin slid his hands into my pajama bottoms and gripped my ass hard, forcing me up against him. His erection pressed against his suit trousers and nudged my lower belly.

I tugged Calvin's shirt free and pushed it from his shoulders, before it got caught around his lower arms. He laughed against my mouth and broke the kiss in order to finished pulling off his shirt. Calvin quickly threw it to the floor, took my face into his hands, and kissed me hard. He tasted like too much cheap coffee and never enough sleep. But he also tasted like love and life, and I was woefully addicted.

I reached between us and stroked Calvin through his clothes. I cupped him in one hand and gave a squeeze as I kissed his neck. He sighed and put a hand on the back of my head, keeping me in place. I licked from the hollow of his throat to his Adam's apple, and he swallowed hard in response.

I said, with a surprising amount of confidence in my tone, "I want you to fuck me."

Calvin leaned back a bit and raised my chin. "We're in your father's bathroom."

"We can have sex on the couch if you'd rather, but I'd prefer not to subject my dad to front-row seats of his son getting plowed."

"God, you're so romantic." Calvin held my face in both hands again. "Finish getting undressed."

I untangled myself from Calvin and went to the door.

"Where're you going?"

"Getting a condom."

"You brought condoms?"

I stepped into the hall and looked over my shoulder. "Balloon animals—remember?" I smiled and hurried back to the living room.

I grabbed the backpack beside the couch and dug through it to retrieve the plastic bag from the store. After fighting with the wrapping around the box, I yanked it open, tore a condom free, and returned to the bathroom. I slipped inside and locked the door behind me.

The bathroom was small, but luckily there was enough space for the thick towel Calvin had put on the floor. He'd ditched his pants, too, but was still wearing boxer briefs when I entered.

"I hope you thought to pack lube as well, because I'm not using a makeshift product that'll inevitably not work and/or leave us smelling like peaches and daffodils," he said.

"Luckily for you, my dad has neither peach- nor daffodil-scented lotion." I gave him the condom and opened the cupboard under the sink. "I left a small bottle here from, like, a month ago." I felt around for a minute before finding it still safely tucked away behind the neat little baskets Pop used to keep items organized. I held it up triumphantly.

"You're insane," Calvin said with an amused smile.

"Yeah. And horny as hell. So ditch the briefs."

When both of us were naked, Calvin took the lube and indicated with a finger for me to turn around. He leaned me over the sink, pressed his body against the length of mine, and slid a wet, slippery finger between my asscheeks. I took a few deep breaths and consciously relaxed to accept the slow, deliberate ministrations.

Calvin kissed my spine. "Feel good?" he murmured.

"Yeah."

"Spread your legs a bit more."

I did as instructed and gasped when Calvin started pumping two fingers into me. Of all times to feel enthusiastic about offering up some dirty talk, of course it was the middle of the night at my father's house. But whatever. Sexy whispers were nearly as good, right?

"I want your cock… please, Cal…."

His hand faltered for a brief second.

Yup, good enough for Calvin.

Calvin reached with his free hand to carefully wrap it around my throat. He pulled me back into a straight standing position with his fingers still pushing in and out of my ass. Calvin tightened his grip enough on my neck to make me gasp again. He looked at our reflections in the mirror above the sink.

"Say it again."

I swallowed against the palm of his hand and met his gaze. "I want your cock," I repeated, maybe quieter than before, but hey, at least I said it.

Calvin, who usually had to get me considerably further along in the exploration of an orgasm before I was willing to grit any words out, looked fucking beside himself with happiness. He pulled his fingers free, took my hips with both hands, and rubbed his dick against the cleft of my ass. "This cock?"

I leaned my head back against his shoulder. "Yes." I closed my eyes as Calvin kissed my neck and continued teasing my hole. It was now or never, I supposed. "Cal?"

"Hmm?"

"Would—will you spank me?"

He stopped moving completely. And for one second, embarrassment like I had never known threatened to swallow me whole. But Calvin took my chin and turned it enough to kiss me hard, leaving me breathless.

"Baby, I'd love to smack your ass until you can't sit tomorrow without being reminded of me."

I felt my entire body shudder in response.

"But I'm fairly certain that'll wake the third occupant in this house."

"Oh. Right." *Motherfu—*

He smiled and caressed one asscheek. "When I get you home, though…." Calvin leaned close, bit my earlobe, and whispered, "I'll spank you until it makes you come."

Sweet Jesus.

Calvin gently let go of me, and I found I had to grab the sink to stay steady. I watched him take a moment to unwrap the condom and roll it over himself.

He picked up the lube, moved to the towel, and got down on the floor. Calvin stroked a good amount of the liquid over his cock. "Come here," he said, shifting a bit on his back.

My knees gave their telltale old-man crack as I got down beside him. I climbed over Calvin, putting a leg on either side of his body. He gripped my ass tight, then spread my cheeks. I reached back, held the base of his cock, and eased myself onto the head. I sucked in a sharp breath—those first seconds, every time it was like, whoa now, was I sure about this? But Calvin always made it good. He kept still, let me find a comfortable pace, and instead focused on giving my own cock delicious, lazy strokes.

"You okay, sweetheart?" Calvin whispered, his voice a little shaky.

I nodded. "Sorry. Yeah." After pausing to adjust to having my ass stretched to maximum capacity, I sat down the rest of the way.

Calvin swore under his breath. My thighs were already shaking a little from the position, but I was just going to have to deal with it. I had my gorgeous boyfriend buried balls-deep in me. I wasn't about to ruin that for an only slightly less cumbersome position.

Calvin ran his hands up my chest and down my arms. "You look so perfect right now. Come on. Let me watch you fuck yourself on my cock."

I smiled, albeit awkwardly, and lifted. That pull up, the push down—it was an instinctive rhythm that even a dorky guy like me didn't need to be taught. Every deep stroke of his dick felt like an ember was being lit in my belly. The erotic sound of sweat-slick skin meeting each time I sat was making my toes curl. Calvin held on to my hips and adjusted the way I came down, causing a zing of pleasure to nearly throw me off him. I only managed to half stifle the cry that tore out of my throat.

"*Shh*…. Come here," Calvin whispered. He took my

shoulders and guided me to lean over him, arms braced on either side of his head. He grabbed on to my ass, held me still, and lifted his hips to pound into me. "You've got such a sweet, tight ass."

I dropped my head down beside his, panting and whimpering with every thrust. The sensation had morphed into what felt like an electric arc discharging across my entire body.

"Harder," I gritted out.

"You sure?"

"Please," I begged. "Please… don't stop. Make me feel it."

Calvin growled in my ear and slammed into me, giving exactly what I'd asked for.

"I want to come," I said, moving to kiss Calvin.

"Yeah," he said between kisses. "I want to see you get off with my cock still in your ass. Touch yourself, baby."

I sat up a little, gripping the tile floor with my fingertips. I grabbed my dick with my other hand and jacked off while receiving the pounding of a lifetime. Just a little more. Nearly there. *Almost*. I wanted to close my eyes so I could pretend Calvin wasn't totally absorbed in watching my gawky-self stumble to the finish line, but I didn't.

Because there was nothing to hide from him.

"That's right," he said, managing to keep his voice relatively low. "You love my cock, don't you?"

"Y-yes—Calvin. I love it so much. Please—*please* come in my ass." My body was as taut as a rubber band just before it reached its breaking point. And then I was awash in utter delight—nothing but orgasmic bliss.

Cum dribbled down my fist. I stroked out the last of that high until I felt like I was about to black out. I let go of my hypersensitive cock, touched a fingertip to some of the splattering on Calvin's abs, then slid it into his mouth. He sucked my finger hard and shuddered. Calvin's thrusts faltered, he ground out a few smoking-hot expletives, and then he was coming.

I dropped down on top of him afterward, and Calvin wrapped his arms tight around my back. We were a sweaty, sticky mess of tangled limbs on the bathroom floor, and I could have died happy then and there.

Calvin gently stroked the back of my head. "That was incredible."

"Tell me about it." I raised my head and fixed my glasses.

He kissed me lightly. "What part of the sandwich am I?"

"Huh?"

"The peanut butter and jelly sandwich. Which am I?"

"Jelly, definitely," I answered.

"You think I'm the sweet one?"

"I'm way too salty to be."

Calvin smiled and petted my hair. "We really are better together."

Even though he'd been running on only a few hours of sleep pretty much every night this week, Calvin was an early riser. Granted, being squished onto a couch with me sprawled across his chest like deadweight probably hadn't encouraged him to sleep in much. We were both up before my dad, taking turns showering and changing into the clothes I'd packed the night before.

I sat on the floor in Pop's office, head tilted to the side to read the spines of the books on the bottom shelf of one of several bookshelves. The office had actually been my childhood bedroom, which when I moved out, I helped convert into something more useful for my dad. Of course, since his retirement from teaching, Pop was rarely in there for more than grabbing a book to read, storing holiday decorations, or hiding the ever-growing mass of dog toys currently out of rotation.

Despite my fear that the content of those Dickson films were irrelevant to the crimes taking place in *this* time period, I'd be lying if I said it was reason enough to give up the mystery. There had still been a murder. There had still been a conspiracy against Dickson. If I didn't shine light on what had happened all those years ago, who would?

I plucked a textbook and read the cover. *From Edison to Hollywood, A History of American Cinema*. I set it aside and removed a tome of a book next: *A Study of Silence, Storytelling Before Talkies*. The last of my film course books I'd kept from college, mostly because I couldn't bear parting with something that had cost an arm and a leg to purchase, was called *Cinema Truth, Before Chaplin, Keaton, & Lloyd*.

"Morning."

I glanced up to see Calvin leaning against the doorway. He was dressed and ready for the day in a dark suit. I felt a flutter of butterflies in my gut when I met his smile. Despite dating for months now, and having been naked and intimate more times than I could count, it sort of felt like those first-time jitters all over again. You know, now that I was being up front and honest about life, sex, death, and everything in between.

"Happy birthday," I said, by way of greeting.

Calvin smiled a little. "Thank you."

"I—er—I don't have your birthday present here. With me." Okay, I was being honest with him about everything *but* the fact I still hadn't found a gift.

"That's okay," he said.

"Feel forty-three?"

Calvin rubbed the back of his neck. "A bit. I think I'm a year or two too old for sex on the linoleum floor." He slid his hands into his pockets and inclined his head at the books. "What're those?"

"Textbooks from college."

"A Complete History of Romanticism?" he guessed.

"From my Film History, and Theory and Criticism classes."

"Sounds like some real page turners."

I bit back a laugh. "I'm going to call my old professor and see if he'll meet with me today."

"Ah. About the footage?"

I nodded, stacked the books in one arm, and stood.

"How'd you get the shiner?" he asked next, touching his own cheekbone.

"*Oh*."

Calvin raised his eyebrows.

"Something happened yesterday."

"I gathered as much." He reached out as I moved toward him and put his arm around my shoulders. "Does it have anything to do with an antique revolver?"

"Sort of."

"Let's grab breakfast."

CHAPTER FOURTEEN

"I thought you wanted waffles?"

"I do, but I'm still paying off student loans. I don't want to go into debt over breakfast confections too." I shifted my books to one arm and tapped the outdoor case displaying an outrageously priced menu.

"Don't worry about the price." Calvin leaned close, kissed me, took one of the doorstops from my arms, and walked into the café.

"But it's your birthday!" I protested.

"And I want to eat here," he called from inside.

I grumbled and followed him through the open doorway. The little restaurant had fewer than a dozen tables, giving it a sort of sweet, intimate vibe. All of the storefront windows were open to accept the cool morning breeze, although I'm sure it was also to entice those passing by to duck inside and have a quick meal after smelling the crackling bacon and sizzling eggs.

Calvin was already getting a table. When the hostess

motioned to free seats by the far-right window, he pointed farther in the back where it wasn't so bright.

I sighed kind of dreamily. Calvin always considered the needs I had that most people never thought twice about. If I wasn't already dating him, so help me, I'd be on him like syrup on—okay, I definitely wanted some waffles.

I followed them toward a small table near a counter with a sign advertising brunch cocktails. I sat down across from Calvin and put the books on the table, up against the wall. A waiter came by with fresh cups of coffee and menus, then left us.

I pointed at the sign. "Want to play hooky and get drunk on blackberry mint mimosas all morning?"

Calvin smiled at me. "Maybe if I didn't have an open case affecting my boyfriend's safety."

"It's always something, huh?"

"So what happened?"

"Mr. Robert gave me two more movies for the Kinetoscope. He claimed to have not found where he'd stored them until the first package had been mailed. On my way back from Queens, some punk got the upper hand on me in the subway and stole my bag with the footage in it. It wasn't a random occurrence—that kid followed me."

Calvin narrowed his eyes. "You're certain of that?"

"He was outside the brownstone. I asked him what door on the street was red."

Calvin reached into his inner coat pocket and took out a small notepad. "What did he look like?"

"Nothing particularly unique stands out."

"I need more than that."

I shrugged, closed my eyes, and tried to recall the details outside Mr. Robert's house, when I'd gotten the best view of the teen. "Casey Robert's age—twenty, max. Clean shaven, maybe a tan? Tall, average build."

"Glasses? Tattoos? Scars?" Calvin prompted.

I shook my head. "No. Nothing like that." I opened my eyes and looked at him. "He had to have been working with Casey. Don't you think?"

Calvin set the notebook down. "This individual is certainly a person of interest now."

"What have you found out about the grandson?" I asked.

Calvin opened his mouth, then closed it when our waiter returned. We each gave our orders—omelet for him, waffles for me—and were left alone again. "Nondriver's ID for New York State with an address in Bushwick."

"That corroborates what his grandfather said."

"I've a meeting with his roommates this morning and the grandfather later in the day." Calvin poured some cream into his mug. "No missing person's report has been filed for Casey."

"Huh. Maybe he's not close with family."

"Doesn't seem to be."

"Considering his grandfather thinks he's a thief."

"If the grandfather is even telling the truth himself," Calvin added before sipping his coffee.

"True...." Frowning, I reached for the little cup of cream but paused. "Whatever came of that paper ID in Casey's pocket?"

Calvin set his mug down. "School ID."

"And the school hasn't reported him missing?" I asked, a bit surprised.

"It's one of those academies in Midtown. I requested a transcript from the enrollment office late yesterday evening."

"Still waiting on it?"

"They go home at five o'clock on the dot. Even so,

from what I gather, the school pumps out 'graduates' so fast, I doubt teachers bother to learn their names."

"So one missing student wouldn't exactly cause alarm."

"Unfortunately, I don't think so."

I leaned back in my chair, staring at Calvin.

He raised a light-colored eyebrow. "What?"

"Which academy is it?"

"You know I'm not supposed to tell you any of this."

"But you will," I said, smiling a little.

Calvin held my gaze.

"Please," I added.

He threaded his fingers together and rested them on the tabletop.

"You're the most handsome detective to ever grace the NYPD," I concluded.

"Flattery will get you nowhere."

"Doesn't mean it isn't true."

Calvin finally smiled, like he couldn't hold it back anymore. "Smooth."

"Thanks," I said, grinning.

"Sunrise Film Academy," he said before pointing a finger at me. "And don't you dare go there to snoop around."

"Sunrise *Film* Academy?" I repeated.

"Yes, that was not lost on me," Calvin answered.

"Hold on." I raised both hands in sudden excitement, knocking one into my coffee mug. "Oh shit!" I grabbed the cup, spilling half the drink onto my hands and the tabletop. "*Hot*. Motherf—*ffft!*"

Calvin grabbed his cloth napkin, took my hands, and blotted them dry.

I clenched my jaw and hissed, "*Thank you.*"

He let go and sopped up the mess on the table before the dark liquid could reach my books.

"What's their school logo look like?" I shook my hands and wiggled my fingers a bit.

"Here we are, gentlemen," our waiter said, returning to the table. "Omelet and waffles." He set the plates down and refilled the mugs. "Anything else I can—*oh.*" He took a rolled napkin from his apron pocket and gave it to Calvin before picking up the soiled one from between our plates.

"This is great, thank you," Calvin answered. He waited until our server left, then reached into his coat pocket to remove his cell. He poked at the screen, turned it around, and said, "Here's their homepage."

I pushed my glasses up and leaned in close. It looked like a sun rising over a hillside. Or rather, a film reel with a bit of celluloid probably meant to emulate the sun's rays. "Holy shit."

"What?"

I pointed at the phone and looked up at Calvin. "Do you know who goes to this school?"

"I'm certain you'll tell me."

"Lee Straus."

"What're you talking about?" Calvin tucked the phone into his pocket.

"When he came to the Emporium yesterday, I noticed a lanyard around his neck. The logo is the same."

"Lee said he was an adjunct professor." Calvin picked up his utensils and cut into the omelet.

"Yeah, so?"

"I don't think these academies have *professors,*" he continued.

"So Lee's got an ego."

Calvin gave me a look.

"He does," I replied. "I'm not trying to be a jerk about it."

"Seb."

"Do you still have the business card he gave you the other day?" I asked.

Calvin looked a bit surprised as he took a bite of food. He set his fork down, reached for his wallet, and sifted through a few cards. He plucked one, stared at it, then set it on the tabletop.

I put a finger on it and dragged the card closer.

Sunrise Film Academy

Lee Straus, Instructor

East 28th Street, New York, New York

"He might know these teens," I stated.

"And he might not," Calvin replied. He took another bite.

I frowned and poured syrup onto my waffles. "I think it's more than coincidence," I mumbled. "Especially seeing how it'd be hard for him to walk by the Emporium on his lunch break when I'm twenty blocks away from the academy." I looked up and stuffed a hunk of waffle in my mouth.

Calvin set his fork down again and stared at me. "What do you expect me to say to that? Lee is now a suspect because he teaches at the school Casey attended and he made the mistake of visiting your shop?"

I held up a finger, taking a longer-than-intended moment to chew the huge piece of waffle. "*No*," I said around the last bits. "Unless you have reason to think—"

"I don't have reason to think Lee is a suspect," Calvin said firmly.

We grew silent.

I wasn't trying to accuse Lee of anything. I didn't think. I only wanted to point out that… that… maybe we were both wrong about Mr. Robert.

Fuck.

Because while James Robert was definitely many things, a liar just *hadn't* struck me as being one of them. I'd believed him when he said his grandson Casey was trying to rob him. Probably with the help of this friend I'd unfortunately met a few times. And no matter how much I tried to convince myself to the contrary, I *absolutely* believed unlocking the mystery of the Dickson footage would reveal the reason for the thefts.

Logically, thefts equated to money.

But the movies themselves were simply not worth all this trouble. And Mr. Robert's brownstone had been full of so many other gorgeous and rare items that would have fetched a far prettier penny and been less of a pain in the ass to obtain.

It was what was *on* the film that was worth it in someone's mind to lie, steal, and kill.

I didn't think these two teenagers were working alone either. Yesterday it'd almost made sense that the grandfather was pulling the strings and this was a far less convoluted mystery. But now? Nothing was ever cut-and-dry where I was involved. I don't doubt for a minute that there were kids who loved art and history like I did and had learned about Dickson at an early age. But it simply wasn't the norm. Students learned about his accomplishments, if at all, in college.

Usually in a specific field of study.

Like moviemaking.

"It's never good when you're quiet," Calvin murmured. He didn't look up from his food.

"It's never good when I talk either," I countered.

He smiled.

"Look," I began. "I'm not trying to make this uncomfortable for you. But I think we need to discuss something about Lee—like, how yesterday when the grandfather called the Emporium after the shooting, I wrote his address on my hand." I raised it to show Calvin the faint outline of letters that hadn't come off in the shower. "And the people with me when that happened were Max and Lee."

"Lee was in the shop when the shooting happened," Calvin replied. "And you identified a teenager outside of James's house and in the subway—"

"Exactly. I don't think those kids were acting of their own volition. I think someone's preyed on two susceptible teenagers and convinced them to commit terrible acts in the hunt for those film reels."

"Why *Lee*?"

"Because there's no way Casey or this unidentified assailant are Dickson fans trying to collect long-lost footage to hand over to museums. Someone in a higher position than a student, with knowledge of the movies, is orchestrating this. The logical assumption is a teacher. Lee works with students. At the Emporium, he would have had time to call this second kid and give him the address I'd written down. I didn't hide the fact I was going to visit the grandfather."

"You're coming to conclusions without evidence, Sebastian." Calvin pushed his plate away. "Before you jump off the deep end, let's wait until I receive a copy of Casey's transcript. *If* Lee is one of his instructors, then I have reason to interview him."

"Lee is definitely a big enough guy—"

Calvin held his hand up. "Stop theorizing and eat your waffles. *Please*."

I slumped into my chair, picked up my fork, and hacked off a chunk of syrup-soaked waffle.

Calvin pointed at his tablet on top of my book tower. "Researching recipes?" he asked, cutting through that awkward "we're not angry at each other, but sort of annoyed and unwilling to apologize" silence.

"No," I muttered. "I wanted to borrow your copy of *Professional Criminals of America*."

He looked interested at that. "And why does my boyfriend require a handguide written by the controversial Chief of Detectives of New York City in 1886?"

I smiled a little and pushed pieces of waffle around my plate. "Who was that again?"

"Thomas Byrnes."

"Careful or you're going to give me a chub."

Calvin laughed under his breath.

I took a few bites of the soggy waffle and grabbed the tablet. "Before I was robbed in the subway," I began, searching through Calvin's e-books, which were, in fact, mostly cookbooks, "I spooled through the film."

"And?"

"It was the same as with the Leonard-Cushing fight—footage thought lost to time. But there were more spliced test pieces attached. One was the same outdoor scene—could have been a few hours before the killing. The other was definitely shot inside at Edison's lab, earlier in the murder timeline."

"So what's it all mean?"

I chose Byrnes's comprehensive book on criminals, tweaked the brightness level on the screen, and started scrolling through pages. "Supposedly, someone was after Dickson in 1895, and these movies were a crucial element to his safety. Since the only damning footage I've seen so far is the murder, I suspect if we can identify the men

214

involved, we'll understand why Dickson was in peril. *And* why I ended up with a Kinetoscope that's killed a kid." I looked at Calvin.

He puffed his cheeks as he blew out a big breath of air. "In all my career, I've never heard of anything quite like the cases I've picked up since meeting you."

"I wasn't kidding when I said antiquing was murder."

"And curiosity kills."

"Not yet, it hasn't," I answered. I put my phone on the crowded tabletop. "I took a picture of one of the stills that had Muttonchops—the murderer."

"Are you going to utilize the mugshots?"

"Bingo."

Calvin took a sip of coffee. "There are only about 200 mugshots in the book."

"The New York rogue's gallery had a lot more, yeah?" I glanced up.

Calvin made a so-so motion with his hand. "Byrnes *claimed* he had documented over seven thousand criminals."

"Well, if I had access to *that* registry, that'd be one thing. But it no longer exists, and I'm not sure how else to obtain a story about Muttonchops," I said. "So much of what Dickson did has been lost. Finding the names of the even lesser-known assistants is all but an impossible task. Especially if they killed a man."

"But a book of century-old mugshots?"

"It can't hurt to look," I said in return. "I know the timelines don't exactly add up, but there's always a chance that he committed less-violent crimes before he had it in himself to kill. If that were the case, maybe he ended up in here," I continued, tapping the tablet.

"You think Thomas Edison would have hired a

committed criminal?" Calvin picked up my phone and opened the photos.

"It was considerably easier to become a new person back then."

"That's true, I suppose."

I was scrolling through photographs of forgers, pickpockets, and bank robbers, and paused at a woman known as the Confidence Queen. "Geez... this lady robbed a man of his life savings while *in* prison."

"Big Bertha," Calvin murmured.

"Yeah—hold on, have you read this entire book? It's, like, four hundred pages."

"Cop," he reminded me absently, pointing at himself, still scrolling on my phone.

"It should be the last picture. What're you looking for?"

Calvin turned the phone around. "When'd you take this?"

It was at his old studio, of him and Dillon asleep on the bed together.

"When you were sleeping."

"No shit."

I laughed and shrugged a shoulder. "Stop being cute and I'll stop taking photographic evidence."

Calvin gave me a mixed expression—part questioning, part amusement. He pulled up the photo of Muttonchops and set it on the tabletop between us. "This is him?"

"Yeah. He's memorable-looking. Might help," I said before returning to the mugshots.

Calvin got out of his chair and moved around the table. He leaned over my shoulder and studied the photos with me. "He's going to be at least ten years younger—I'd suspect midtwenties—if he's in this collection. And keep in mind, he might have put on the weight and grown the facial hair after the fact."

"I know."

"Look at some of these aliases. Aleck the Milkman, Big Dick, Three-Fingered Jack...." Calvin pointed at one photo. "Ah. This man rented an apartment fewer than ten blocks from here and made counterfeit silver coins on the third floor."

"They don't make criminals like they used... look at this guy!" I quickly enlarged the page for easier reading. "John McCormack. Alias, Kid John. Burglar, sneak, second-story man."

Calvin reached over me, picked up the phone, and held it up against the tablet to compare photos.

"What do you think?" I asked, looking up at him.

"Same nose and deep-set eyes. No muttonchops, but he's got impressive sideburns. Says he was twenty-nine in 1886. Was considered a first-class burglar in what sounds like the tristate area today. Arrested in 1884 after being caught on a second-story job and—he murdered a servant while trying to escape the house. Sentenced to ten years at Sing Sing, escaped in April of 1885."

"Holy shit. Was he caught?" I studied the block of small, dense text.

Calvin shook his head after a moment. "No, doesn't sound like it."

"Work on the Kinetoscope didn't even begin until six years after his escape. By then, if he hadn't been recaught, I doubt anyone would even remember him," I said.

"It's possible," Calvin murmured. "Add thirty pounds and the muttonchops, and he's never going to be mistaken for *Kid* John...."

"So help a guy with shitty eyesight out," I said, leaning back to stare up at Calvin again. "Are John

McCormack and Muttonchops one and the same?"

Calvin's cell phone rang. He reached into his pocket. "The probability is high enough that I wouldn't bet against you."

"This isn't Vegas."

"Hey, Quinn," Calvin answered.

I watched Calvin's stance stiffen as he listened to his partner on the other end of the call. Out was my boyfriend; in was the police officer.

"When was the body found?" he asked.

Shit.

"I'm on my way," Calvin confirmed. He ended the call and glanced at me.

"What happened?"

"James Robert was found dead in his home by his housekeeper."

"Oh my God. Was he—I mean, he was ninety and smoked, Calvin. Maybe—"

"He was murdered," Calvin interrupted. He took his wallet from his back pocket, removed several bills, and put them on the table. "I have to go. I can drive you to your father's first," he offered.

I shook my head. "I'm going to hit up NYU."

"All right." Calvin leaned down and kissed me. "Be safe."

"You too." I touched his hand and gave it a final squeeze before Calvin left the table.

I sighed and set the tablet on the stack of books. I grabbed my phone, held it close, and began the arduous process of sifting through New York University's 101 webpages in search of a phone number that would at least get me through to the correct school. This would have been a lot easier if I hadn't put Dr. Freidman's business card in my so very cursed messenger bag.

I was lost in art history undergraduate courses when the waiter returned to collect the dishes from the table.

"Is your partner finished as well, sir?"

I looked up. "You can take his. Duty called."

He picked up the plates. "I understand the feeling. Mine's finishing his fellowship in pediatric surgery." He flashed a smile. "Duty calls at the least opportune times."

"Yeah, I guess so." I met his smile with one of my own. Once he'd left, I continued poking through university pages before finding a listing of graduate faculty members.

Lo and behold! Dr. Bill Freidman.

I tapped the phone number provided on his bio page and put the cell to my ear. I was expecting voicemail this early in the morning, so color me surprised when Freidman—a man as gritty as gravel but with a voice as smooth as whiskey—answered.

"Bill Freidman."

"Er—hi, Dr. Freidman. My name's Sebastian Snow. I used to be one of your students. Uhm… about twelve or thirteen years ago…."

He didn't say anything in return.

"Anyway," I said, continuing onward. "I run an antique business now, and I'm really in need of expert advice on some footage I've acquired—"

"Mr. Snow," Freidman interrupted. "I am not an authenticator, appraiser, nor do I make evaluations for businesses. Thank you for taking my course. If you'd like to learn more about cinema, I'd suggest a visit to the Museum of the Moving Image. Have a pleasant day."

"No, wait! This is about W. K. L. Dickson. Please don't hang up."

Silence.

"Dr. Freidman?" I squeezed my eyes shut. I couldn't believe he hung up on me. "Goddamn—"

"How *exactly* does your footage pertain to Dickson?" Freidman asked suddenly.

I opened my eyes. "I've reason to believe someone threatened Dickson's life while he was employed by Edison. I've… ah, sort of come into ownership of footage shot by a Kinetograph camera that has left me with more questions than answers." I paused before adding an ego stroke for good measure. "I've already visited the museum. They suggested I contact you."

Freidman didn't say anything.

"If you could spare me *any* time today," I prodded. "Ten minutes, even."

"I have class at 9:30."

"Okay."

"Be here in thirty minutes. I'll call the front desk and put your name on the visitor's log. Snow, you said?" As if he cared so little he'd already forgotten.

"Yes, sir."

"All right." He hung up.

I ended the call and noticed the waiter had dropped the bill off. I picked it up, gawked at the cost of waffles I hadn't even finished, and double counted the cash Calvin had left before my phone starting ringing. The number was a mild surprise.

"To what do I owe the pleasure?"

"What do you know about the Colt Walker revolver?" Neil asked in return.

I held the phone between ear and shoulder, gathered my books, and stood. "Good morning to you too. Are you in the Cash Cab or something?"

"This is a serious question."

"No doubt." I made my way toward the open door.

Neil sighed, long and hard. "Good morning."

"Good morning, Neil."

"Can you answer a question for me?"

"Sure."

"Are you familiar with the Colt Walker revolver?"

"A bit."

"I need your... *professional* opinion."

I stopped just outside the restaurant. "Why not ask a firearms specialist?"

"Because this is a weapon of American origin from 1846, and that's *your* area of expertise."

"1847," I corrected in a polite tone.

"Fine, 1847. I need a qualified individual to confirm the value of such an item," Neil continued.

"Over the phone? Without seeing it? That's not how it works," I answered.

"Sebastian, please—just—" He struggled to sound civil. "*Guess.*"

I walked to the curb, juggled my books, and managed to flag a taxi down without looking like a complete moron. I climbed into the back seat, gave the driver the street address for one of NYU's East Side buildings, and sat back as he merged into traffic.

"Did you find the gun that shot up the Emporium?" I asked. "You wouldn't be calling about an antique lead-ball-shooting, black-powder-using, single-action revolver otherwise."

"I did some checking of my own," Neil replied. "To see if any weapons old enough to shoot lead balls had been reported as missing or stolen this year."

"James Robert?" I guessed.

"No. An antique dealer reported one as stolen late last week."

"What? Really? Who?"

"That guy you don't get along with," Neil answered.

"Wow. You're going to have to be more specific," I replied. "Wait—are you talking about Marshall's Oddities? Gregory Thompson?"

"You said it, not me."

"Huh."

"So again. Can you confirm the value of this item? He's looking to have the theft registered with the FBI's NSAF."

I caught the driver taking a few too many glances at me in his rearview mirror. "Well, it had a very limited production run. Just over a thousand revolvers were made, mostly to fulfill a military contract. There was one that sold at auction a while back… if I remember correctly, it went for nearly a million dollars. But, Neil, you have to take into consideration the history of the item, *as well as* its current state. That particular revolver, I believe, had seen action in the Mexican-American War."

"Regardless, it's still worth a shit-ton of money," Neil replied.

"Shit-ton isn't a unit of measurement I use in my professional life, but yes."

Lee had been to Marshall's Oddities.

"Neil," I said with a sort of dazed realization. That last clue suddenly fell into place and it was as if Lee was Colonel Mustard in the library with the wrench. "It's Lee Straus."

"Who?"

"Calvin's ex-military-boyfriend-person," I said. I lifted my hips up to dig my wallet from my back pocket. I hurriedly took out a few bills as the driver parked outside of a tall building waving the NYU flag from the second story. I passed the cash through the window between us, grabbed my books, and climbed out of the taxi.

"What do you mean, *it's him*?" Neil asked.

"I think he's behind all this," I whispered as a few students walked by me. "He's a teacher at the academy Casey Robert attended. He was at the Emporium when the grandfather called me. He admitted to going to Marshall's Oddities just last week—the same time Greg's revolver goes missing—and then my place gets shot up with lead balls?"

"Seb...."

"And he's retired Army," I finished.

"*Winter* is retired Army," Neil countered. "Does that mean he's also mentally and emotionally capable of killing a teenager?"

"Do you not see how all these clues connect? Neil, come on. Calvin won't look any further into it, not until he gets Casey's school transcript."

"He's right to do that," Neil said.

"For fuck's sake!"

"I have to go," Neil said. "I'm on my way to a crime scene."

"Is it a brownstone on the Upper East Side with a red door?"

"Do you have a police scanner?"

"Yeah. About six foot three, dark suit, lots of freckles—"

"I get it."

"How long are you going to be?" I asked.

"Why's it matter?"

I moved to the front door of the building. "It doesn't matter. Call me when you're out of there, will you?"

Neil let out a breath. "Don't do anything illegal until then, okay?"

"I'll try my best." I ended the call and stepped inside.

Being in a college atmosphere after nearly a decade was... odd. Especially being surrounded by a lot of young-somethings, who were far more hip-looking and put-together than I was now, let alone when I'd been their age. Memories resurfaced as I peered around the lobby. I'd met my second boyfriend—Brian—in this building. On the stairs, actually. I'd tripped and done the classic flail-and-fall, dropping all my books and a take-out container of chicken fingers. He'd helped me collect everything and bought me a new lunch. It was one of the only nice acts he'd done for me in the year and a half we dated. But that was neither here nor there.

I went to the security desk and set my stack of books on the counter. "Sebastian Snow for Dr. Bill Freidman."

The guard, sitting in front of a few security monitors and a computer screen, began clicking as he searched the daily visitor log. "May I see your ID, please?"

"Sure." I took out my nondriver's license from my wallet and handed it over.

He did the look at me, look at the bad-hair-day photo, back to me, then the photo one last time for good measure before returning it. "Sign in here," he said, passing me a clipboard.

I did as instructed, stuck a visitor sticker to my shirt, and collected my books.

"Do you need directions?" he asked.

"He's still on the fourth floor, right?"

"419B, that's right."

"Thanks," I answered, then went to the elevator. There was a sleepy-looking, summer-classes crowd waiting outside the doors—earphones in, coffees in hand, and some texting one-handed quicker than I could while utilizing *both* thumbs.

Not worth the wait. I could do with the walk anyway.

I turned around, went across the lobby, and hoofed it up the stairs. At the second floor, I remembered how steep the steps were and why I'd always had a tendency to trip. By the third, I was out of breath. Upon reaching the landing of the fourth floor, I just hated myself entirely. I walked through a small sitting area, went down a tight hallway, passed the office in question, then walked backward a few steps. The books felt like boat anchors in my arms. I shifted them and knocked on the door.

"Come in" was the muffled response.

I turned the knob and poked my head inside. "Dr. Freidman?"

I took a few steps into the tiny office. It was stacked to the gills with movies. The walls from floor to ceiling housed a collection of films on both DVD and VHS that was more impressive than the school's own film library. And in precarious piles here, there, and nearly everywhere were canisters of footage on 16- and 35mm, media players, and projector parts. Near the window was a desk cluttered with stacks of paperwork and a hunched-over professor who didn't appear to have aged a single day since my last encounter with him. And behind his chair were shelves so heavily loaded with books, they were leaning *ever so slightly* to the right.

Dr. Bill Freidman glanced up from his computer. He still wore the little rounded spectacles I remembered from school, and had the same salt-and-pepper beard. "Mr. Snow." He smiled a little and leaned back in his chair. "Film History. Theory and Criticism. First row, sunglasses, magnifying glass, and a know-it-all attitude."

I sat down across from him.

"Now I remember you," Freidman concluded.

"Thank you for seeing me on such short notice," I answered. "How're your summer courses?"

"The same as every year. Fresh young minds eager

to learn, argue, and sleep during lectures. You said you had footage in connection to William Dickson?"

Straight to the point, as always.

"I—did, yeah."

Freidman picked up a pen and rolled it between his fingers. "Past tense?"

"It's a long story that involves a break-in, murder, and being robbed on the subway."

He narrowed his eyes. "Are you writing a crime thriller or something?"

"No, just trying to get through life one day at a time."

Freidman never did find me very funny.

I retrieved my phone, brought up the photo of who might possibly be John McCormack, and offered it. "Does this man look familiar to you?"

Freidman took the phone, held it at a distance, and studied the screen. "Yes."

My pulse leaped to my throat. "Is he John McCormack?"

Freidman set the cell down and eyed my books. "You brought *From Edison to Hollywood* with you?"

"Oh, yes, sir." I held it out.

He took the book and flipped through the pages. "If you'd done a bit of research first, you wouldn't have needed to come here at all." He stopped and turned the hefty textbook around. "The original Kinetoscope crew, 1892."

I leaned over the desktop and squinted, studying the small photo and the faces of men who I'd have probably never recognized on my own. "Which is him?"

"Second to the right."

Where, where—ah-ha! Okay, he definitely wasn't

pencil-thin like Kid John from the mugshot, but he didn't appear to have those glorious muttonchops yet either. This photo would have been seven years after his escape from Sing Sing, and three years before murdering the man on film—

"His name is Johnathan Cormack," Freidman said. "The first written account of him working for Edison is in November of 1891."

"When did he quit?"

"1896."

"Why?" I asked.

"Edison's general manager ousted him."

I tapped my chin absently. "Johnathan Cormack is awfully similar to John McCormack."

Freidman shrugged.

I opened Calvin's tablet and showed him the mugshot. "I think this is him. I think he changed his name before working for Edison."

Freidman stared at the photo for a long moment. He eventually sighed. "I suppose that could be him. By 1896, there were some unsavory rumors about *Cormack's* past— that he'd done time for thievery and such. That's why he was given the boot."

"Bad for Edison's reputation," I concluded.

"That's right."

I shut the tablet case. "I need help identifying two more men on the team. One who may have been named Tom. And another who was killed—murdered—in 1894."

"There was a Tom," Freidman agreed. "No known photos, though. He was only on the crew for about a year and a half."

"Are you sure?"

He gave me a long, hard stare, then raised the textbook. "I wrote this book, Mr. Snow. What do you think?"

"Sorry."

Freidman slowly leaned back in his chair once more. "Tom Howard quit in late 1894 to open a Kinetoscope parlor here in the city. But after buying the machine and collecting various films, he went bankrupt and never saw his business to fruition."

That... explained why an "assistant named Tom" had a Kinetoscope and all these rare films in his possession, before they were eventually sold to the now-murdered collector, James Robert. So perhaps, when Tom quit to cash in on the latest entertainment craze sweeping the nation, he took the compromising movie footage with him. He *was* the one who passed on the story that it had to stay hidden to protect Dickson....

But if that were the case, Tom would have to have known about the murder too. Because that's what this all had to be about. The man who'd been murdered was somehow a threat to Dickson. Perhaps John McCormack here, already guilty of killing the servant in the case that sent him to prison, murdered not because he and the other man had a beef with each other, but because doing so was meant to... protect Dickson? And in an attempt to help cover up the death, Assistant Tom took the test reels with compromising footage on them, and left Edison's company permanently.

"Is that *A Study in Silence* you have?" Freidman asked. He leaned over the desk a bit to stare at my pile.

"Yes, sir."

"Which edition?"

I opened the book and held it close to my face as I scanned the copyright and publisher information. "Second edition."

Freidman tutted under his breath. His chair creaked

as he spun around in order to study his bookshelf. "We use the third edition in class now."

"Have there been significant additions to the content?"

"Enough that I don't want students missing out." He plucked the massive book from a lower shelf, then set it on his desk and sifted through the pages. "There *was* a death on the crew," he said after a long bout of silence. "Unfortunately so many details were swept under the rug that I fear we might never know the truth of the matter."

I leaned forward in my chair.

"Ah, here." Freidman tapped a page. "It's suspected the man was one Albert Martin."

I patted my pockets, swore, and grabbed a sticky note and spare pen from Freidman's desk without asking permission. I jotted the name down as he ignored me and kept speaking.

"I suspect the identity is correct, but scholars have never been able to confirm his name beyond a shadow of a doubt. As for murder—yes, that might have been his unfortunate fate. Personal documents from a few of the original Kinetoscope crew members suggest this man—Albert—was highly suspicious of Dickson. There was attempted sabotage at one point in the inventing process as well. By the accounts we've unearthed, this fellow, if it is indeed Albert Martin, did not get along well with his teammates."

I stopped writing. The story Greta had told me over beers and pretzels came to mind. About something—or *someone*—putting Edison's general manager on the scent of Dickson. He'd been removed by 1895 because he'd been moonlighting for other companies. Could the rat have been Albert, and he'd gotten evidence of Dickson's betrayal to the company before being silenced in the most horrific way possible? If so, the wheels would have been put into motion, and even his death couldn't have kept Dickson's job safe.

I looked at Freidman. "I had a piece of test footage that shows John McCormack killing another man in 1894."

Freidman's eyes grew a little.

"Could Albert Martin be that man?"

"P-perhaps so," he stuttered in a sort of astonished tone.

"Could Albert have snitched to the general manager about Dickson's moonlighting, just before his death?"

"It's highly probable snitching is what got Albert killed. But moonlighting wasn't the only factor in Dickson's removal from the company," Freidman replied.

"Then, what? Did Albert ever make a threat against Dickson's life? Something that would have provoked the other teammates into protecting him?"

Freidman's expression grew more serious as he shook his head. "No, no. It wasn't Dickson's life that'd been threatened. There are personal accounts that indicate a dispute over the ownership of now long-lost prototype drafts. Dickson designed a number of inventions that would have put Edison's fledging film company out of business. He drafted these new machines while employed for Edison. So Gilmore, the general manager, threatened Dickson to hand them over under the claim that the inventions belonged to the company."

"But he didn't?" I asked.

"No," Freidman answered. "And Dickson left in 1895." He shut the book with enough force to make me jump. "Had Dickson built those inventions and sold them, there's little doubt Edison would have gone after him legally in order to protect his own interests."

"It would have destroyed Dickson," I said, piecing my thoughts together out loud. "He wouldn't have stood a chance against someone like Thomas Edison. His finances and reputation would have been ruined."

Freidman nodded. "Dickson left America. The drafts never resurfaced in Europe."

As long as the Kinetoscope and footage were kept hidden, Dickson would be okay.

"One of the teammates hid the documents, then," I concluded. "Dickson would never be celebrated for the genius that he was while alive—"

Freidman smiled a little. "But Edison would never get the credit for those inventions."

CHAPTER FIFTEEN

Lee was after the drafts.

Obsolete now they might be, but early schematics of countless inventions that would have otherwise altered the course of the entertainment industry as we know it today would be worth an unprecedented amount at auction. *Especially* when presented in front of the right audience... like the elite of Hollywood.

And Lee taught at a film academy. While he certainly was no doctor of cinema history, who could say he hadn't learned of the Dickson stories on his own? And if the murdered Casey Robert had been one of Lee's students, Casey could have easily told his teacher that his grandfather owned a mysterious Kinetoscope and footage.

The relentless attempts at procuring the three reels made me believe Lee felt they were necessary clues that would lead him to the location of the lost drafts. And *maybe* he would have figured out where they were hidden after watching the test movies.

But while Lee Straus might have been more

handsome than me and stronger than me… he was not *smarter than me*.

The Emporium was still shuttered after having lost the front window for the second time in the same year. I bent down, set my books carefully on the sidewalk, then unlocked the metal gate. I hoisted it up and eyed the exceptionally classy plywood that my new landlord had put up while the police had been investigating yesterday.

He'd thought to spray paint "Snow's" across it in big blocky letters.

Real charming, but I'd have to deal with it later.

One crisis at a time.

"Yoo-hoo!"

I turned to my left. Beth was waving from where she stood at the rear of an open delivery truck.

"Morning," I called, waving in return.

"What're you doing here?" Beth asked before signing the electronic scanner our mutual delivery woman, Jamie, held out to her.

"I work here," I answered.

"Smart-ass. Isn't it Calvin's birthday?"

"He's working too," I called.

"It's your fault, isn't it?" she asked.

"Not technically."

Jamie jumped off the back of her Citywide Delivery truck and walked down the sidewalk toward me. "Are you open?"

"No."

"I've got a package for you. Want me to scan it as recipient not available—come back tomorrow?"

"Who's it from?" I countered.

"You think I've got that entire truck memorized?" she asked in a falsely annoyed tone, jutting a thumb over her shoulder.

"I know you do," I replied. "This entire block would go to hell in a handbasket if they put you on a different route."

Jamie smiled at that. "You're such a sweetheart, Sebastian. Last name on the package is Robert."

I dropped my keys. "James Robert?"

"Yeah, I think that was it."

"I'll sign for it," I quickly answered. I bent down and retrieved my keys as Jamie returned to the truck.

What could he have sent me? Mr. Robert would have had to get the package prepared and dropped off sometime between 2:00 p.m., when I left his house, and 6:00 p.m., when Citywide's overnight delivery cutoff was. I supposed he'd given up on Barnes Brothers Shipping after the Kinetoscope snafu. Anyway, now I knew there had been a window of roughly fifteen hours in which to kill him. Good thing he'd mailed this package *after* I left, and I had multiple alibis to account for my whereabouts the rest of the afternoon and into the night. Otherwise the NYPD would be breathing down my neck about now.

I unlocked the front door and punched in the security code. I grabbed the books and tablet from the sidewalk and stepped into the dim shop. The place was a mess. Forget going to the fair before it ended that afternoon—I was going to be busy sprucing up after the shooting and police investigation. I set my things down on the nearest display table and returned to the doorway to meet Jamie.

I signed for the package, then exchanged her scanner for the box. "Thanks a lot."

"No problem. Tell your boyfriend I said happy birthday."

"Oh. Thanks, I will."

Jamie clipped the scanner to her belt and left the

threshold.

I shut and locked the door, walked across the shop, and put the box on the counter. I stood there for a good minute eyeing it, before I got up the nerve to grab a pair of scissors. Halfway through slicing the packing tape, my cell rang and I jumped.

I grabbed it from my pocket and answered. "I almost stabbed myself with scissors."

"I'll try harder next time," Neil said with a serious tone.

"You know," I began, finishing with the tape before putting the deadly weapon to one side, "I almost like this new 'fuck it' relationship we seem to be nurturing."

"Yeah. Me too. Clearly I need to make some friends."

"Have you finished at Mr. Robert's house already?" I pushed the flaps of the box back and hesitantly dug into the packing peanuts. I pulled out— "An egg beater?"

"What?" Neil asked.

I stared at the rotary kitchen tool before setting it aside. "Huh? No, nothing."

"I left early."

"Why?"

"Because something in my gut told me you were up to no good."

"It was probably indigestion," I replied. "I'm at the Emporium." I reached into the box again and this time retrieved a flour sifter, then cookie cutters…. The package was full of all the vintage kitchen supplies I'd been admiring at Mr. Robert's house just the day before.

"But where did you plan to go after that?"

"Sunrise Film Academy."

"This is why I left," Neil stated.

"I *know* it's Lee Straus," I told him.

"What the hell are you going to do, Seb? Confront him?"

"I've done dumber things."

"Don't leave before I get there."

"Bye, Dad." I ended the call and stared at the baking tools for a moment. A small pang went through my chest. Mr. Robert had given these to me, no doubt with the intention that "my boyfriend who likes to cook" should use them. I suddenly wished I could call and thank him for the thoughtful surprise.

Here I'd been too distracted all week to seriously focus on gift-getting for Calvin, and a murdered old man ended up saving my ass. I carefully put the items back into the box, resealed it, and spent a few minutes wrapping it. Maybe Calvin wouldn't notice the paper was from the Emporium....

My phone rang again as I knotted the ribbon into a bow. I picked it up and glanced at the caller ID. "Morning, Pop."

"Hey, kiddo. Where'd you two hop off to so early?"

"Sorry about that," I answered, adjusting the bow a bit. I was a master at gift presentation—my one award-winning domestic skill that came in useful about twice a year until Max and I had started offering gift wrapping to customers at the Emporium. "We went out for breakfast before Calvin had to get back to work. Sorry I left you with the dog again."

"Not to worry. There are far worse fates in life than babysitting a good boy like Dillon."

"I'll come by in a few hours," I said, walking toward the Kinetoscope, which was still behind the counter. "There's something I have to do first."

"Just give me a ring," Pop answered. "I might bring the kids to the dog run again. It's going to be a beautiful day."

"Gotta make the best of it before the inside of your mouth is cooler than the air outside," I said.

"There's my positive thinker," Pop said with a chuckle.

I crouched down in front of the Kinetoscope and ran my fingertips along the base. Just like the man in the footage had done. Like *Tom Howard* in the footage, hiding the Dickson documents. The frame around the base of the Kinetoscope moved—ever so slightly. I took a breath, grabbed on to it more firmly, and gave a tug.

"By the way," Pop continued. "Is this your hoodie you left here?"

"Hoodie?" I asked, practically on autopilot. I set the corner piece of wood aside and got down on my hands and knees to inspect a bit of curled, aged paper seemingly stuffed into the very frame of the machine.

"This black one here... says Sunrise Film Academy on the breast."

"It does?" I asked suddenly. I'd never bothered to inspect the clothing I'd torn from my subway assailant.

"Hm-hm. There's some candy in the pocket... oops...." It sounded like Pop was bending down to retrieve something dropped. "I thought you didn't like licorice?"

Licorice....

That gross candy put the little punk outside my apartment. I had to hand it to him, he was fast *and* strong. So Lee was off the hook for the assault—*son of a bitch*— but that didn't mean he hadn't orchestrated all this. I'd bet my next paycheck this kid and Casey Robert were classmates. *And* that Lee was their instructor. He might have even persuaded my subway pal to kill Casey—so his own hands were clean of the entire mess. Lee would get off scot-free, while one kid was dead and another would inevitably end up in prison.

But at least he wouldn't have the Dickson inventions.

The front of the cabinet easily popped free after the base had been removed, and inside a tiny cubbyhole were rolled-up documents from a previous century.

"Pop, I have to go," I whispered.

"All right. I'll talk to you later."

"Love you," I said.

"Love you too, kiddo."

I hung up, grabbed some gloves, and while holding my breath, eased the drafts from their 120-year-old hiding place. It was true that just before the shop got shot up, I'd accidentally noticed something awry with the cabinet— but I'm not sure I would have made the connection without the last movie. In the test reel shot inside Black Maria, all I could assume was that Assistant Tom must have known Albert and Gilmore were already suspicious of Dickson, and he took it upon himself to protect the inventions of his beloved boss.

I laughed suddenly. It was overwhelming. I was holding a man's legacy in my hands.

This was his passion, his creation, his *genius*.

I was holding *everything* that would have put Dickson's name in textbooks instead of Edison's.

I shifted on my knees and reached under the counter for a stack of plastic sleeves kept beside shopping bags and gift boxes. In the dim, silent shop, I carefully unfurled the lost camera inventions of W. K. L. Dickson and slid the documents in between the protective covers. I'd barely gotten to my feet and set the drafts beside the brass register when there was a knock at the front door. I leaned over the counter to peer past the column to the left and saw Neil cup his hands around his face and look through the door's glass front.

I walked down the steps, through the maze of clutter, and unlocked the door. "You won't believe what I found."

"The code to the Voynich manuscript?" Neil asked, stepping inside.

"It's heartening to know that the men in my life have *in fact* been listening when I talk," I said, putting a hand to my chest.

"We tune you in and out," Neil corrected.

"Asshole."

"What did you find?"

I walked to the register and lifted the pile of now-protected documents. "The lost inventions of William Dickson."

"Who's that?"

"To make a long-winded story short?" I held out the papers. "*This* is motive."

"Are you sure those documents are going to be safe at the Emporium?" Neil asked as he drove us to the Sunrise Film Academy in Midtown.

"Inside a hatbox on the top of a display shelf beside the bathroom is a hell of a lot safer than me holding on to them. Especially if we're going to see Lee."

"You honestly think it's him?" Neil spared me a glance.

"He teaches at the same school the first victim and the unknown assailant attend."

"And why couldn't those teenagers be working this together without the influence of a third party?"

"It's not possible," I said firmly.

"Are you sure you aren't merely *hoping* it's not possible?"

I turned my head and glared at Neil. "*Really?*"

"You were led to believe unsavory narratives about me."

"That was different."

"Not really."

"I know those two kids aren't doing this alone," I said again with a tone of finality. "I know *someone* is pulling the strings. And Lee visited Marshall's Oddities just before the revolver went missing, and he was with me when I learned of Mr. Robert's home address. Just wait until Calvin gets Casey Robert's transcript. That'll prove it."

Neil turned west on Twenty-Fifth Street and made his way through uptown traffic on Third Avenue. "Just remember that this case belongs to Winter and Lancaster." He parked on the corner of East Twenty-Eighth Street. "I'm not here as an officer of the law. I'm here as your friend."

"How sweet," I said dryly.

Neil gave me that charming, annoyed expression I'd never once missed since we broke up. "And unless Lee Straus looks me dead in the eye and says, 'I murdered the Roberts, please arrest me,' I can't do anything."

I gave him a mock salute. "Understood, Detective Millett." I climbed out of the car.

Sunrise Film Academy was directly across the street from a Starbucks and a bar, which I thought was pretty excellent planning on the school's behalf. We walked to the sidewalk and toward the heavy glass doors, where a handful of summer-course students stood smoking. Neil grabbed the handle first and pulled it open, letting me walk in.

"Afraid I'm going to hit you again?" I asked over my shoulder.

"I can never predict what you'll do next, Sebastian."

I approached the guard's desk and set my arms on the counter. "Good morning. I'm here to see Lee Straus. He's an instructor."

The guard picked up a sheet of paper with a few lines on it. "Name?"

"Ah, it might not be on the guest list. I was... called... last-minute."

The guard raised an eyebrow. "Called for what?"

"Seb," Neil murmured from behind me.

I ignored him. "Acting. We're actors. For his... *acting class.*" The guard didn't appear entirely convinced of *my* acting, but she set the paper down and picked up the phone. "What was the name, again?"

"Lee Straus."

She dialed a number and put the receiver to her ear.

"You're looking for Mr. Straus?"

I turned to my right. A girl with a wicked Mohawk, those gauged ears my friend Aubrey had, and a backpack sagging off her shoulders had stopped about two feet away from me. "Um, that's right."

"Class was canceled today."

"He's your teacher?" I asked.

"Yeah." She reached into a pocket of her—I think—purposefully tattered jeans and removed a compact mirror. Mohawk flipped it open and checked her eyeliner. "He rescheduled for tomorrow."

"Where is Mr. Straus now?"

She was taken aback by my forwardness. "He had some event to go to. Our teachers *are* working professionals, you know." She said that with a hint of pride, as if no other colleges hired teachers with actual experience in their field. "It's at the Javits Center, I think. Some of my classmates are working there too."

"The antique fair?" I asked.

"That's it," she answered, snapping the compact shut. "I guess there are supposed to be some collectors there with film exhibits? But I don't know. The ticket was too expensive for me."

I thumped my fist against the counter in annoyance, nearly turned away, then paused. "What class do you have with Mr. Straus?"

"I thought you just said you were here for his acting class?" the guard interrupted.

Mohawk looked confused. "We only have one teacher for the summer intensive classes."

"Of course," I answered quickly. "Do you have a classmate named Casey Robert?"

She raised a lip. "Casey, yeah. He's in my group. He's supposed to be working at the show, which I guess is why he's flaked out of class for the last few days."

"You don't like him?"

She pulled out some kind of gloss from another pocket and wiped the wand over her bottom lip in a distracted manner. "He's kind of weird," she finally said, then smacked her lips together. "Him and this other guy in class were talking once about how they were going to make a million dollars."

"Next Hollywood blockbuster?" I asked.

"*No*," Mohawk said with a disbelieving laugh. "Like, robbing someone. Or—I mean, it could have been that. I know trouble when I see it, so I stay clear of them. I'm here to seriously learn. I want to direct movies when I get older." She finally tilted her head a bit and took in Neil's appearance. "Are you guys cops or something?"

"Seb, let's go," Neil murmured.

"Hold on," I protested when he took me by the shoulder. I turned to Mohawk one more time. "This other kid Casey hangs out with—does he like licorice candy?"

"How'd you know that?"

"My sponsorship lanyard was in my bag," I told the ticket guy in the lobby of the Javits Center. "My bag was stolen yesterday by a punk-ass kid who might be responsible for a murder or two."

Ticket guy startled and looked at me as if I were insane. Couldn't blame him. I was starting to feel that way.

"For Christ's sake." Neil joined me at the counter and showed his badge. "Detective Neil Millett, CSU. Can you tell us if there's a Lee Straus registered and attending the event today?"

The guy swallowed convulsively at the sight of Neil's badge. "I don't—I think I need a warrant to show you that information," he stammered. "It's just—because it has people's addresses and credit card numbers, you know? I can't afford to get fired, I'm late with my rent."

"Then we need to go downstairs into the exhibit hall," Neil concluded, tucking his ID away.

Ticket guy nodded quickly. "Sure. Whatever you want, man." He cupped a hand around his mouth and shouted to the security personnel at the escalators to let us pass without lanyards.

Neil led the way, pausing briefly and looking over his shoulder when I accidentally stepped on the heel of his expensive shoe. "You okay?"

"Fine."

I caught the motion of Neil raising his head upward, and then he wrapped his hand firmly around my wrist. Not romantically. It was all business. But it was nice that he'd put two and two together pretty quickly about the lighting of the Javits Center.

We bypassed Bruno the Security Officer and got on the escalator, making a slow descent. The noise level rose exponentially as the huge crowd came into view. The layout seemed pretty organized despite the teeming masses—uniform rows of dealer booths in the middle of the showroom, with sponsors lining the ends. I had to admit, while dealing with Pete White might have been a disaster, this was an awesome turnout and I was sort of glad I'd sponsored.

"This is crazy," Neil stated. He stepped off the escalator and pulled me to the side.

"Yup."

"I mean, us being here."

"I know what you meant."

"Winter is going to have my ass for this."

"I just want to talk to Lee," I replied. "I have a knack for getting the guilty party to spill their most intimate secrets."

"You just harass them until they'd rather be in jail."

"How did we manage not to kill each other for four years?" I asked, motioning back and forth between us.

Neil finally smiled. "So what do you want to do—walk around and hope for the best?"

"Actually, I want to talk to Greg first."

"Who?"

"That guy I don't get along with," I teased. "Marshall's Oddities has a booth over on this side." I pointed to the left of the exhibit hall.

Neil took my wrist again, and we walked through the crowds to the far wall. We kept close to the rope barriers, where there weren't quite as many attendees as the middle of the aisle. We'd walked about halfway through the exhibit hall before I could make out the general shape of who I knew was Gregory Thompson. Blurry though he might have been, it was hard to mistake the tall, lanky build and ponytail for anyone else.

"Just up ahead," Neil said, confirming my poor eyesight.

I bumped into his back when he stopped abruptly. "What gives?"

"Traffic jam."

I peered around Neil's shoulder as a group of people untangled themselves and headed in different directions. One came straight our way, made eye contact with me, and froze dead in his tracks.

Mr. Licorice, aka my assailant and thief, aka JD Malory, according to the girl from the academy. He had a lanyard around his neck with a vertical badge—which I'd realized indicated staff, versus the horizontal passes of attendees and dealers—and a fucking *Twizzler* hanging out of his mouth. I was pretty sure Calvin was still waiting on convention staff to return his inquiries about Casey Robert's involvement with the event, but after speaking with his classmate and seeing JD here, it was confirmed for me. They had been working together, and JD was here with Lee.

JD did a quick about-face and walked the way he'd come.

"Neil," I said, pointing at JD's quickly disappearing figure. "That's the kid—JD Malory."

Neil, with his extra half a foot of height, was able to follow JD through the crowd. "Are you sure?"

"I'm a *thousand percent* sure. I told the responding officer the night I was attacked that the guy smelled like licorice. He's eating some now!"

"Sebastian—"

"I saw his face twice before. I'm *positive*."

"Okay, okay." Neil turned and held his hands up in

front of himself. "Don't move. I'll go talk to him."

I nodded and watched Neil ease into the foot traffic, but I quickly lost sight of him in the blurry sea of gray faces. I went ahead and finished walking toward Greg, dragging my fingertips along the rope so as not to lose my sense of direction. Greg's table was still close enough to where I'd been told not to move from that Neil would easily find me upon his return.

"Greg," I called.

"Sebastian," he said coolly, leaving his setup and moving to stand in front of me.

"Look, let's just pretend for one minute that we like each other, okay?"

Greg's eyebrows rose, but he crossed his arms and leaned his weight to one side. "All right."

"I heard you had a Colt Walker revolver stolen."

"Yes, last Thursday. Should I also pretend you aren't using your police contacts to your advantage?"

"Actually, I was contacted as a professional, to verify the value of the weapon. Don't worry," I continued, waving a hand. "I said it was worth *a lot*, even without having seen it for myself."

"Warms my heart to hear you agree with my appraisal."

"Do you know who took it? What I mean is, I've had a break-in this week too and lost something."

"A pistol?" Greg asked, now curious.

"No, a movie from the 1890s."

"Apples and oranges."

"True, but I think it may be the same person. Or people. Have you had any teenagers hanging around your place the last week or two? Their names are Casey Robert and JD Malory."

"Teenagers? No, not that I remember."

"What about a guy named Lee Straus?"

"I'm not on a first-name basis with lookie-loos," Greg retorted.

I rolled my eyes behind my sunglasses, removed my phone, and did a quick and hopeful search of Sunrise Film Academy's website. Sure enough, there was Lee on the faculty page. He'd begun teaching at the Academy this year, had a diploma from NYU's continuing education school, and a few production crew credits on some indie-as-fuck-sounding projects.

"Well?" Greg asked, a touch of impatience in his tone.

I turned the phone around. "This guy. Do you remember him?" I squinted and studied Greg's face.

He reached back and ran his fingers through his ponytail while staring at the screen. "Actually... yes. He was in my store last week. He bought a Bolex camera and told me something about teaching his students to load film rolls in the dark."

"Did you realize the revolver was missing by the weekend?"

"I realized the next day—Friday," Greg corrected. "I guess I was too busy prepping for the fair to notice it'd been missing the same day." He looked embarrassed to have admitted such a fault and cast his eyes downward.

I furrowed my brow and tucked the phone into my back pocket again. "What day did Pete come by Oddities to pick up your things for the fair?"

"Thursday," Greg confirmed.

We were both quiet. After a moment of thought, if I didn't know better, I'd have said the color had drained from Greg's face. He opened his mouth the same time my phone jingled, which I was barely able to hear over the noise of the hall.

"Sebastian… you don't think…?" Greg murmured.

"I'm getting whiplash from how quickly this is all changing," I said, retrieving my phone. I answered the call, put the cell to my ear, and covered my other to block out the commotion. "Cal? Hang on a minute. I can't hear you." I looked at Greg. "Do you know where the bathrooms are?"

He turned to the left and pointed. "All the way at the end. They're not hardly as busy as the ones near the escalator."

"Thanks," I replied. "I'll be back in a few minutes."

I grabbed on to the rope barrier once again and jogged down the length of the hall. The west side was significantly less crowded, which was unfortunate for those dealers and sponsors, but it was still relatively early in the day. The attendees would eventually branch off and realize there was untouched real estate on this end.

"Calvin?" I said into the phone as I rushed into the men's room, a bit out of breath.

"Where are you?" he asked, sounding as if he was on speaker phone.

"I'm at the Javits Center. I have a name for the second teenager," I said quickly, pushing open each stall door to assure I was alone. I reached the last one, took a deep breath, and said, "JD Malory. He was Casey's classmate. He's here working at the fair."

"Are you alone?" Calvin demanded.

"I came with Neil. He went after JD."

"Where are you?"

"In the bathroom so I can hear you. It's a madhouse here."

"I'm on my way there."

"Calvin, what's wrong?"

"James Robert had his throat cut, just like his grandson. CSU found a knife under a chair in the parlor with a bloody fingerprint on the handle," he explained.

My heart skipped a beat and then slugged hard against my chest.

"I got Casey Robert's transcript from the academy," Calvin continued.

"Lee?" I whispered, but... *I knew*.

"Lee took over his class last week when the original teacher was fired for misconduct and unapproved absences."

I swallowed, and it sounded thunderous in my ears.

"It's Pete White," Calvin said. "His fingerprints are on record from when he was hired at the school. I had forensics do a preliminary comparison to what was on the weapon—you need to find Millett. Don't leave his side until I get there."

I felt like the blood had left my body. I shivered convulsively.

Pete White?

Creepy, awkward, flip-flop-wearing Pete White, who I'd concluded early on was simply too dumb or lazy to manage anything even close to robbery—let alone a double homicide—was behind it all?

Neil was right.

I had *wanted* it to be Lee. And the clues had worked in his favor, which made it even easier to accept.

But there was no denying how bizarre it had been on Tuesday when Pete wouldn't stop pestering me about the Kinetoscope footage. He must have been trying to obtain it without having to resort to dangerous measures....

"Baby," Calvin said in his cop voice.

"Wh-what? Yes, find Neil."

"Quinn and I are almost there," he answered. "Are you downstairs?"

"Yes."

"Two minutes. Maybe less."

"I know what he was after," I said as the bathroom door opened and the racket of the fair followed someone inside. "Original documents. Inventions by Dickson. They'd be worth millions—"

Pete White came around the corner. He smiled that huge, stupid smile, waved, and went to the sink. He held his hand under the soap dispenser and started lathering them together under a strong stream of water. He had those damn flip-flops on, cargo shorts, and a zipped-up hoodie.

He looked harmless.

Dorky and so unassuming.

And yet Calvin had tangible, physical, *forensic* proof that this man had literal blood on his hands.

"Sebastian?" Calvin said to my silence.

"Ah… yup. Okay. I'll let you go, then," I answered, keeping one eye on Pete. I was at the opposite end from the door. I'd have to pass the row of sinks to reach it.

"What? No, don't hang up," he ordered.

"Oh, my boyfriend is waiting for me," I answered, making up a conversation that I hoped would keep Pete at bay.

I heard Quinn murmur something in the following silence.

"Is he there with you?" Calvin finally asked.

"Uh-huh," I answered, trying to not sound nervous.

I took a step forward as Pete flicked his hands dry and reached for a paper towel from the motion-sensor machine. I felt so strange inside. Afraid, because I'd seen what had been done to Casey, but that emotion felt misplaced when I assigned it to fucking *Pete*.

I took a few more steps.

Four stalls.

Three.

Two.

"Hey, Snow," Pete called.

I halted midstep and turned my head.

Pete made eye contact in the mirror. "Got a second?"

"Sebastian," Calvin said into my ear. There was a sound like wind—he was out of the car and moving. "*Where* downstairs are you?"

Pete kept staring at me.

I felt my underarms begin to sweat.

"All right, buddy," I said to Calvin. "I really do have to go. I'm at the ass-end of the hall and it'll take me forever to get back to the front." I gave Pete a smile.

He returned it.

"I'll see you later," I finished. I lowered the phone and stuffed it into my pocket without ending the call. "Hey, Pete."

"I thought you weren't coming until this afternoon?" Pete asked, tossing his paper towel and turning around.

"Oh. Yeah, I guess I kind of wanted to see the place in action after all. It's an incredible turnout."

"About ten thousand total," Pete said with a bit of a chest puff.

"Who'd have thought this many folks liked old junk?" I joked, taking one step closer to the door.

"I told you, it's all about enticing the younger generation. I used to teach—did I mention that?"

I scratched my arm nervously. "Yeah, vaguely."

Pete nodded. "Sometimes you're lucky to get through to one or two out of a class of thirty."

Would that have been Casey and JD?

"I better get going," I answered, moving past the last stall.

"Snow, come on," he drawled.

I glanced over my shoulder and Pete pulled what I figured was the stolen Colt Walker revolver out of his sweatshirt.

I froze.

Pete scratched his beard with his free hand. "I've only got two rounds left. Don't make me use them, okay?"

"Okay," I whispered. I slowly put my hands up.

"You found the Dickson drafts?" he asked.

I nodded.

"How? Was there a fourth film?"

I frowned. "No. What do you mean?"

"All the research I've been doing... it all pointed at needing the *films* to uncover where Dickson hid his inventions. I got those films from you—"

"JD did," I corrected.

"Well, if you dangle a million dollars in front of an eighteen-year-old from a low-income family, you can get them to agree to the craziest things."

"That's cruel, Pete," I said quietly. "Come on. Put the gun down."

"So if I have all the films," he continued without missing a beat, "and none of them show the hiding spot, how did you find the documents?"

I didn't respond.

Pete cocked the hammer back on the revolver.

"It was dumb luck," I said quickly.

"Bullshit."

"The clue that was most important was that the assistant, Tom Howard, said the films *and* Kinetoscope had to be kept safe. The movies simply put to rest the tragedy of Albert Martin."

"Who gives a shit about some 120-year-old dead guy?"

"B-but the movies also laid out the facts of Dickson's final months at Black Maria. One film shows a man in the background, crouched in front of a Kinetoscope."

Pete used his free hand to make a motion, like, *speed it up*.

"Dickson's paperwork was stashed inside the frame of the cabinet," I said in haste. "Pete—"

"Oh man!" He laughed and shook his head in disbelief. "That's... wow. Okay, I gotta hand it to you, Snow." Pete pointed at me. "Smart. *This* is why I like you."

"Lucky me," I whispered.

"I've been searching for those inventions my entire adult life," Pete said with an almost sweet expression. "Even joined this waste-of-time convention committee in the hopes of expanding my reach. Then I come to find one of my film students, his fucking grandpa owned the Kinetoscope with the Tom Howard story. Casey and I tried to get the guy to let us put the Kinetoscope in the show. That way we could access the films, find where the documents were, and return them with him none the wiser."

"But he thought his grandson was going to steal it," I finished.

"Well, the old guy refused to put it in the show. After it went MIA, Casey checked his grandpa's computer history and found your shop in the search engine. I honestly could have cared less about the bizarre and morbid shit you sell, it was obvious in the beginning that you weren't relevant to my search—but when Casey confirmed the Kinetoscope ended up in *your store*...." Pete smiled in an odd manner, his lips pulled thin over his teeth, and shrugged, like, *there was no alternative.*

"And there you were," I said.

How much longer would it take Calvin to reach the west-end bathrooms?

Could I keep Pete's finger off the trigger for one more minute?

"Why'd you kill Casey?"

Pete lowered the revolver a bit. "Look. No one was supposed to die."

"But they did. Pete, he was a kid!"

"After the second time he broke into the Emporium to get the film reel back, Casey wanted out. He was going to tell his grandpa and—those documents are worth millions to the right buyer, Snow. *Millions.*"

"And James? He was ninety. Did you have to kill him too?"

"I couldn't figure out the documents' location. I thought he had a fourth reel kept stashed in that museum he lived in."

My heart was pounding hard and fast.

Adrenaline sped through my veins.

If he would lower the revolver a bit more, it could allow me just enough time to hurl myself through the door….

"You stole Greg's gun," I stated.

Pete glanced at the Colt Walker, then nodded. "Yup. Sure scared the shit out of you yesterday, didn't it? I wasn't trying to kill you, if it makes you feel better. But you needed to understand how serious I was about the Kinetoscope—that we weren't going to stop until you gave up the film."

"O-okay, but why *that* gun? Because ballistics would have a harder time with a lead ball and black powder?"

He smiled wryly and scratched his beard again. "*No*. I stole it because it's a million-dollar weapon. And you call yourself a dealer."

"You can't sell it," I protested. "Greg knows you stole it. It's being reported to the FBI."

"I can't sell it through *legal* channels," Pete corrected. "For the record, I stole that knife too."

"You left it at the crime scene. With your fingerprints in James's blood! The cops are going to prove you killed Casey with it too."

"And *you* know all that because you're fucking the redhead. Who's a cop, I've learned." Pete raised the revolver to be even with my head.

Fuck. Fuckfuckfuck.

"Give me the documents. Then I won't have to shoot you. I'll take off for an exotic foreign country, and we'll never have to see each other again. Sound good?"

"You have a buyer in that country?" I asked.

"There's always a buyer," Pete agreed.

"I don't have the documents," I said, voice catching.

Pete shook his head. "Don't yank my chain."

"I don't!" I protested, looking down at myself briefly. "Th-they're at the Emporium." I swallowed, and it hurt. "Someone is going to hear the gun go off."

He gave me that *oh well* sort of expression again. "Bet you wished you'd given me a shot now, huh? Maybe then I wouldn't have to give you one."

There was a burst of smoke from the revolver as the powder was ignited, a delay—then the last stall door I'd managed to walk past seemed to explode.

"*Goddamn it*!" Pete swore.

He'd missed.

Holy fuck—!

Thank God for mechanical inaccuracies.

I leaped toward the door, slamming hard into it before realizing Pete had thrown the dead bolt upon first entering. My hands were shaking as I grabbed the lock, turned it, and fell through the doorway.

The *flip-flop, flip-flop, flip-flop* of Pete charged after me.

I bumped into an attendee as I ran onto the showroom floor, stumbled forward, and as I tried to right myself and ended up falling sideways, a second crack fired.

It echoed through the event hall.

People cried out in fear and confusion.

I spun and crashed to the hard floor. A searing, white-hot pain like nothing I'd ever experienced in my entire life blossomed from my right side. A wet warmth pooled underneath me.

Everything was out of focus.

It was too loud.

But the madness eventually settled.

And sound grew distorted, as if the world were encased in a fishbowl.

I felt adrift in a cloud of gray.

Somewhere far away.

And no one I loved was with me.

"Sebastian!"

Calvin....

CHAPTER SIXTEEN

I wasn't certain if it was a dream.

Or if I was awake.

There was an out-of-body feel to it all, really. A sense of not quite belonging. Like… this trauma wasn't mine. This deep, soul-reaching ache dulled by a nauseating cocktail of chemicals wasn't mine. This *dying* wasn't mine.

Although—if not mine, then whose?

The beep of a tired heart lit up the darkness. A beacon just past the horizon promising safe passage in uncharted territory.

I let the sluggish but constant sound lull me back to nothing for just a bit longer.

I was aware of my own consciousness for a while. I'm not sure how long. I just sort of… realized I was awake. With that sense of self came pain that nearly overwhelmed me—nearly sent me into a tailspin. I was ready to cry. Ready to scream for someone, *anyone*, to help me.

But it occurred to me, in a very drug-induced state of mind, that this pain was my anchor to the present. I couldn't be dead if everything hurt.

Right?

I tried to get my bearings by what senses were available.

Cataloging.

One by one.

It was silent and still.

It smelled clean, but in the way that chemicals do.

It felt... warm. Scratchy.

It felt like *life*, and that if I could only bear opening my eyes....

Dark.

Gray.

Blurry.

But I instinctively knew *that* was my dad asleep in the chair to my left. And I knew *this* was Calvin holding my hand, on my right. He was nearly falling out of his own seat, head resting against my arm on the bed.

I didn't do anything, but Calvin woke with a start. He turned his head, like stretching out a kink in his neck. He rubbed at the overgrown stubble on his jaw. He looked at me, and I could feel his shock at seeing I was awake.

"Sebastian," he whispered. Calvin was out of the chair. He leaned over me, still holding my hand tightly in his own. He pressed our foreheads together.

I realized I couldn't speak. Something in my mouth was prohibiting it. But it was okay. I reached up with my free hand and shakily touched Calvin's face. He kissed the inside of my wrist.

"Welcome back," he said.

Everything was going to be okay now.

CHAPTER SEVENTEEN

Being shot sucked.

Being shot with a lead ball that flattened upon impact, lodged into my side, and transferred its kinetic energy to my body for absorption sucked even more.

I'd almost died in May. No two ways around it.

Doctors had told me if the revolver had been just half an inch more accurate, I would have probably bled out before reaching the hospital.

I didn't know what happened after death. Maybe nothing. Maybe your consciousness just... ceased to be, your body gently rotted back into the earth, and... that was all she wrote.

But I liked to think there was *something* waiting.

Not much. Perhaps an empty hallway. Or an office with no windows. Just enough that I could be cognizant that I was *me* and this was *that* place and I could spend eternity never forgiving myself for abandoning Calvin.

Anyway....

We were both okay.

Now, I meant.

Neil had run toward the bathrooms after hearing the first shot. He'd been too late for the second, but had body-slammed Pete to the floor and handcuffed him. That son of a bitch was now awaiting trial with a laundry list of charges against him, including two accounts of second-degree murder, attempted murder, multiple accounts of robbery, and a slew of lesser offenses I wasn't even interested in.

Calvin had almost reached me that day.

Almost.

He'd witnessed me being shot instead.

And Pop told me that he hadn't been doing so well by the time I went in for surgery. But Calvin had had support, and for that I was grateful. It was a small comfort knowing that if I ended up cashing in my curiosity lives too soon, at least there were people in my absence who would love and care for Calvin. Maybe not his biological family, but the misfits we'd surrounded ourselves with were far better anyway.

Family was what you made of it, right?

The first four months, as I was in and out of the hospital, recovery, and physical therapy, our little band looked after the Emporium, our dog—

us. I'm not the most eloquent guy, but I hoped they all understood. Without Pop, Max, Beth, Quinn, *Neil*—it could have been very different.

"Central Park is two and half miles long," I stated. "Pretty sure we've walked its entire length at this point."

Calvin asked, in a rather preoccupied sounding manner, "What does your StepTrack say?"

I raised my wrist close to my face. "That I've already

walked two miles."

"You didn't restart it when we entered the park."

Busted.

I shrugged and changed the subject. "I hope you've actually been looking for this elusive maroon tree, because we both know *I* won't pick it out with any degree of success."

It was peak foliage season in the city. Central Park was brimming with locals and tourists enjoying the colored canopy I'd heard a passerby describe as "as stunning as an oil painting." I supposed I could agree with that comparison. Even my world wasn't simply *black and white*. There were always enough shades of gray to make it interesting.

I held Dillon's leash in one hand and Calvin's hand in the other. The sky was a pleasant overcast, the air crisp and cool, and the mismatching leaf litter crunched underfoot.

The day was just shy of perfect.

"Central Park has been a National Historic Landmark since 1962," I stated.

I glanced up at Calvin. He'd been acting... weird today. For the last few days, really. Not that his silence was necessarily strange. I was the one who couldn't shut up, and Calvin was the one who nodded and encouraged my obsessive sharing of little-known facts. But I was pretty sure he hadn't heard a word I'd said all morning. In fact, I feared he'd have let go of my hand a half mile back and wandered off in another direction if I hadn't been holding on to him with a viselike grip.

"Have you seen the Alice sculpture in the park?" I prodded.

Calvin didn't answer, just stared ahead along the path.

"There's a quote from 'Jabberwocky' on it," I

continued.

Nothing.

"It seems very pretty. But it's rather hard to understand!"

"What?"

I looked up again. "Alice. In reference to 'Jabberwocky.' Never mind. Are you okay?"

Calvin let out a little sigh and stopped us under the shade of a dark-leafed tree. He tugged his hand free and moved to stand in front of me.

"Is this maroon?" I asked playfully, pointing upward.

Why isn't he smiling?

"Calvin, you're starting to freak me out," I stated. My heart was actually beginning to pound. "Have I done something wrong?"

"No," he answered, shaking his head. "Of course not."

"Then what's going on? Why have you been a hundred thousand miles away today?"

Calvin stared at me. He reached into his coat pocket and removed a small box. He gripped it hard, working it in his palm before seeming to steel himself, and snapped the lid open.

I glanced from his stony expression to the contents. My heart went from racing to a full, dead stop.

Calvin got down on one knee. "Sorry, sweetheart. I've racked my brain trying to come up with a romantic lead-in to this...."

I made a weird sound. I think it was a cross between a laugh and a sob. It was really loud, and a few folks walking by glanced back at us in curiosity.

Inside the little box was a ring. Nothing fancy, because God knows fancy wasn't an adjective associated with me. It was dark-colored. Subtle. Pretty.

Dillon was busy looping his leash around my legs as he paced.

"Are you serious?" I blurted out. I realized belatedly… that was probably not the response Calvin was hoping for.

But he didn't falter. "I know you've got a soft spot, but nothing I came up with seemed all that original."

"No. I mean, not *no*! I—the romantic—oh my God. It's fine," I said, stumbling over every word like English was suddenly a foreign language to me.

Calvin hesitantly smiled.

"You can just…." I took a deep breath and waved at him. "Ask me."

His smile grew, lighting his entire face up brighter than I'd *ever* seen. "Sebastian, will you marry me?"

No quotes.

No bullshit.

No wisecracks.

For once, I only had one thing to say.

"*Yes.*"

Sebastian Snow and Calvin Winter return in:

The Mystery of the Bones
(Snow & Winter: Book Four)

C.S. Poe is a Lambda Literary and two-time EPIC award finalist, and a FAPA award-winning author of gay mystery, romance, and speculative fiction.

She resides in New York City, but has also called Key West and Ibaraki, Japan home in the past. She has an affinity for all things cute and colorful and a major weakness for toys. C.S. is an avid fan of coffee, reading, and cats. She's rescued two cats—Milo and Kasper do their best on a daily basis to distract her from work.

C.S. is an alumna of the School of Visual Arts.

Her debut novel, *The Mystery of Nevermore*, was published 2016.

cspoe.com

ALSO BY C.S. POE

SERIES:
Snow & Winter
The Mystery of Nevermore
The Mystery of the Curiosities
The Mystery of the Moving Image
The Mystery of the Bones

A Lancaster Story
Joy
Kneading You
Color of You

The Silver Screen
Lights. Camera. Murder.

NOVELS:
Southernmost Murder

NOVELLAS:
11:59

SHORT STORIES:
Love in 24 Frames
That Turtle Story
New Game, Start
Love, Marriage, and a Baby Carriage
Love Has No Expiration

Visit cspoe.com for free slice-of-life codas, titles in audio, and available foreign translations.

Join C.S. Poe's mailing list to stay updated on upcoming releases, sales, conventions, and more!
bit.ly/CSPoeNewsletter

Made in the USA
Monee, IL
31 January 2022

90354809R00156